This Time For Us

A FABLE NOTCH NOVEL

BOOK THREE

ELENA MARKEM

Books by Elena Markem

Fable Notch Series

Once More With You
Meant To Be His
This Time For Us
Can't Let You Go
Bring Back Her Heart
What You Wish For
Just Right For Him

Dedication

♥

With love to Florrie Cohen, my honorary aunt.
Not every writer has fans within her family.
I'm so grateful to have you as both.

Chapter One

♥

A nother night, another city. Cole Hanson hardly knew where he was, and it didn't matter. He was fairly certain it was late October, but he could be wrong. Ever since this tour started, places and dates had blurred together. That wasn't uncommon while they were on the road, but it was worse this time.

The roar of the crowd at the end of the song brought him back to the present and the concert he was performing with Emporium, the band he'd started in high school. It was the third time in as many days he'd zoned out during a show. If he didn't know the words and the music so well, his mental disappearing act might have been noticed, but so far, no one had mentioned it.

Screams continued from the fans. "I love you, Cole," he heard from someone in the front row, where a girl was reaching for him, tears streaming down her face. There had been a time he'd found that exciting. Now, it was... boring. He'd seen that look on the face of thousands of girls over the course of eight tours in twelve years. He used to let himself get lost in the adoration and attention, in their willingness to do whatever he wanted for a night. He never dreamed he'd tire of it.

He caught the eye of Paxton Jones, their lead singer, and she gave a nod, signaling him to start their last song. On this tour, they closed with the final track from their newest album, a rock ballad that had topped the charts and was likely to earn them their next Grammy nominations in a few weeks.

The song opened with his short solo on lead guitar and as soon as the crowd heard it, the cheers erupted again, making it nearly impossible for Cole to hear what he was playing, even with the earpiece he wore. As she had at the last few concerts, Paxton put a finger to her lips. He stopped playing, and she waited for there to be near silence. He'd been amazed the first night she'd done it. The room went almost still, and Paxton held everyone in the palm of her hand. And he'd come to love those beats of quiet. Finally, as the fans seemed to hold their collective breath, Paxton sang the first words of the song, and he and the band resumed playing. This time, the crowd remained quiet until she finished with a flourish.

The ear-splitting cacophony returned moments later. Cole kept from wincing at the sound as they joined Paxton at the lip of the stage, took their bows together, waved to the crowd, and left.

Within an hour, he'd showered, changed, and gotten on the tour bus to wait for the others. It would be a while before they joined him. They would meet and greet fans, maybe talk to some local press, but he was fine being alone and having the space to himself. In fact, it was probably better if he was alone.

When had he started to hate his life?

That was the question plaguing him since this tour started three months ago. Even writing the songs for this album, usually his favorite part, had been a struggle.

He made himself some tea with honey to soothe his throat — wouldn't fans be shocked to know this is what most rock stars did after a concert — and sat at the table of the bus's kitchen area. As he sipped the warm drink, he pulled out his phone to check his email and see what he might have missed in the hours since he'd arrived at the stadium. Two new texts, one from each of his brothers.

He opened the one from Nick, his younger brother, first. *Finally got a puppy!* The text included a picture of Nick and two dogs, one big enough to be a pony and the other not much bigger than his forearm. Cole had to smile at the ridiculous grin on Nick's face. Nick had turned thirty a few months before, but looking at the image, Cole saw the boy who had begged for a dog when he was nine.

It thrilled him to see Nick so ecstatic, but the image brought with it a wave of longing he didn't want to think about. He sent a smiley face and thumbs up before reading the next one, wondering how this one would make him feel.

Theo, his middle brother, sent a video. When Cole hit play, he saw Theo with Eden, the woman who'd stolen his heart back in high school. Theo held up her hand to show him a ring and exclaimed, "She said yes!" Cole watched as they kissed. He couldn't be happier for them. They deserved this joy and so much more. Theo went on to say he was flying out to California for a company meeting in a few weeks and noticed he'd be in the same city as Cole's band. "I hope you can find some time for us to get together." Cole typed his congratulations and said he'd make the time. It had been too long since he'd seen either of them. Work kept all three of them busy and in different parts of the country.

Or it used to. In the last few months, Cole's brothers had done something they'd never expected—moved back to their hometown of Fable Notch, New Hampshire, where among other things they'd both reconnected with the women they loved when they were young. Had he ever seen his brothers so happy? If so, it had been a long time. All he'd wanted since the day their father had left was to make sure his brothers were safe and taken care of. It had been his priority in one way or another for over twenty years. He was glad all he'd done for them through the years had paid off.

"What the hell is wrong with you?" Cole almost jumped when Paxton took the seat across from him. He'd been so lost in his thoughts he hadn't heard her get on the bus. "Don't think I haven't noticed you've been phoning it in for the last few weeks. Tonight, I thought I was going to have to shake you to bring you back."

Guess his phasing out hadn't gone unnoticed. He was about to deny it, but Paxton knew him too well. "I've got a lot on my mind." She gave him a look that said she wasn't buying it and was waiting for the rest of the story. They'd come so far from when she joined the group and replaced their original lead. He'd hated her then, but over time they'd grown close, and she was like the sister he never had. He scrubbed his hand over his face and said, "I don't know."

"Does this have something to do with what you said in New York?" He'd been waiting for someone to ask him about that slip-up.

During a group interview they'd done when Emporium played at Madison Square Garden, the disc jockey had asked their bassist about what it was like to be on the road with his wife and new daughter at home. Cole had winced at the question. It had been Hugh's first tour without his wife since they'd met, and being away from her and the baby had been hard. Hugh, who had joined the band after their original bassist left to go to college on the west coast, responded he was glad the fans still wanted to see them, and he'd have a break to be with his family during the end-of-year holidays. When a follow-up question was asked about how he planned to handle it in the future, Cole had interrupted, saying, "We don't even know if there will be another tour. No group lasts forever." The comment was so unexpected there was total silence from everyone in the room.

Cole surprised himself when the words slipped out. Wondering about how much longer he wanted to do this work had been there for a while, teasing at the back of his brain, but he hadn't let himself think about what it meant because the benefits were too good to walk away from. Usually, he kept his feelings to himself, especially in public forums, but that day he'd forgotten to install his internal filter.

But worse than what he said were the surprised looks he'd gotten from the other members of Emporium, which gave the reporters even more ammunition. Paxton had shifted the conversation, but the damage had been done. It must have been a slow entertainment news cycle because the next day word of his "dissatisfaction" spread and was fodder for social media across the globe. To fix the damage, the label's press people put out pictures of them having fun backstage and images of Hugh talking to his wife and daughter via Zoom. The gossip moved on, but Cole's bandmates had looked at him a little differently ever since.

"Do you want to talk about it?" He'd forgotten Paxton was waiting for an answer.

Their fans would never recognize the woman sitting with him, wearing a loose shirt and leggings, her face without makeup, and her red hair in a single braid down her back. Stage Paxton was put away until the next concert. His friend was asking him a question. He trusted her, but once he said what he was thinking, things would change. As the silence continued, Cole let his feelings speak for him. "I want to go home."

"The tour only has a few more weeks before the holiday break. You'll be back in Colorado before you know it." She thought he was referring to his place outside of Colorado Springs, which had been his base for years. The house was nothing special, but the studio he'd built on the land was where he wrote and composed most of Emporium's songs, and he loved being there. Most of the time.

But it was Fable Notch he was thinking of now. He'd made a promise to someone to stay away, but that was twelve years ago. She wouldn't hold him to it after all this time, would she? Theo was engaged, and Nick was expanding his family. Okay, it was a dog, but someday it would probably be a baby. And where would Cole be when he got the video of Nick holding his child?

No, he was not missing any more milestones.

"New Hampshire. I want to go home to New Hampshire."

Paxton must have heard something in his voice because instead of replying, she took his hand and gave it a squeeze. After a minute, she got up, kissed the top of his head, reminding him of Millie Sinclair, the woman who'd practically raised him, and said, "Then that's what you should do. We're behind you, whatever you choose."

Cole wondered if that was true. Once his brothers were on the right track, his concern about taking care of them had morphed into doing the same for the members of the band. Over the years he'd held Paxton through a series of broken hearts and public break-ups, gotten Brian off the pain pills he'd become hooked on after a backstage accident, and, most recently, helped Hugh set up his finances so that no matter if their next album did well or not, he'd never have to worry about his family. Cole had been glad to do it and loved seeing each of them be successful in and out of the group.

But what about him? Sure, he was set financially, but he didn't have much else. And he'd been so damn numb for the last year or so. He was already dreading having to write the songs for the next album after the struggle he'd had on this last one. His creative well was drying up. Could being with his family refill it?

When Hugh and Brian got on the bus, their driver soon followed and announced they'd be leaving in a few minutes. Once they hit the road, Cole said good night to his friends and made his way to the bunks where everyone slept. Maybe he'd dream his way into an answer.

He woke disoriented and groggy. After years on the road, Cole was used to waking up and not knowing where he was, but when he opened his eyes, he expected to see an unfamiliar hotel room with the afternoon light trying to get through the curtains not a stranger hovering over him shining a light in his face.

What the fuck was going on?

He tried to move, but the man holding the light put a hand on his shoulder and kept him pinned. "He's coming around. Sir, do you know who you are?" That was an odd question. Of course he did. And why was this person calling him sir? He tried to answer, but only croaked out his first name. "Yes, that's right. Cole Hanson. Do you remember what happened?"

That was a much better question, and one he couldn't answer. He remembered the concert, the messages from his brothers, and talking to Paxton. As he tried to recall anything after that, his eyes darted around. He saw red and blue flashing lights, heard and saw people moving around him, and re-alized he was cold. He was outside. Where was the bus?

He must have mumbled something because the man said, "Right. The bus was in an accident. From what we can tell, some idiot jumped the median. Your driver tried to swerve out of the way but ended up going off the side of the road. Don't try to move. We've got a collar on you until we're certain about your neck, and we don't know where else you're hurt."

He must have been asleep when it happened. "Where is everyone?" And why couldn't he take a full breath?

"I don't know. I think they pulled everyone out alive." Think? Someone could be dead? He tried to get up, but the paramedic put a hand on his shoulder and kept him in place. "Sorry, sir, but you can't get up. We need to take you to a hospital. You've lost consciousness, which may mean a concussion, and I can see some serious cuts, probably from broken glass and things flying as the bus went over. Your blood pressure oxygen levels are low."

"And hard to breathe," Cole said, or at least thought he did because a second later, the world went dark again. He woke next as they pulled the stretcher from the back of the ambulance. He felt the air go from the warmth of the ambulance to the cool of October for a few seconds before they wheeled him into what he assumed was a hospital emergency room.

Now instead of a small light in his eyes, the room was painfully bright, and instead of two attendants, there was a crowd of doctors around him trying to figure out what had happened and what needed to be taken care of first. They asked him more questions about his blood type, medical history, any medication he was on, and he did his best to answer. They brought in two different machines, and a nurse explained they were going to do an ultrasound of his abdomen and an x-ray of his chest.

He appreciated the nurse's calm voice. She had a kind face, warm eyes. She reminded him of someone else who was a nurse. He wished she were here. No, couldn't think about that. What about the band? "Do. You know. About. The others?" Talking hurt. Staying awake was hard.

"No, I'm sorry, Mr. Hanson." He almost shuddered at the name. Mr. Hanson made him think of his father. He never let anyone call him that. "I can find out, but you need to focus on yourself and let us help you."

If he had the strength, he would have laughed. Focus on himself. Let someone help him. When was the last time he'd done that?

The beeping of the machines around him was maddening. They were out of tune and keeping different beats. He tried to take a breath deep enough to calm his racing heart. It wasn't working. He was about to ask a question when the nurse came into his field of vision. She hesitated before speaking. That couldn't be good. "Mr. Hanson, you have a broken rib, and it's punctured your lung." She used several big words to explain what was wrong with him, but he couldn't concentrate. The increased beeping told him his heart rate had jumped. "We're worried that there may be other complications. Is there anyone we should call?"

He thought of Martin and Millie Sinclair, but he didn't want to worry them. Images of Theo and Nick came into his head. God, he loved them so damn much. When was the last time he'd told them? Was he ever going to see them again? As the darkness threatened to come back, his deepest regret surfaced. There was so much he wanted to say to... "Mia."

Chapter Two

♥

Even on her days off, Mia Durant was out of bed by seven. When she started working in the emergency room of White Mountain Regional Hospital, she imagined sleeping late on the mornings she didn't have to go in. It wasn't long before she discovered that the later she slept on her days off, the harder it was to get going again when her shifts began. And an extra hour was all she needed.

At least Bowie, her Saint Berhusky mix, appreciated her being up early. As soon as he heard the coffee being made, he bolted downstairs and joined her in the kitchen. He waited until she filled her travel mug, then headed to the door.

By the time she got back from their walk, she heard the shower running upstairs. Good, she thought as she poured herself a second cup of coffee. Since the beginning of the school year, Dean, her fifteen-year-old son, was up in the mornings without her help. When he'd first come to live with her a little over a year ago, after losing his mother and Mia's best friend, Ashley, the change in his life and living arrangements had made for a difficult child who didn't want to talk to anyone. Mia supposed he wasn't that different from most teens, except that Dean's attitude came from grief and loss. She'd taken a three-month leave of absence and gotten them both into therapy. After a rocky year in eighth grade, things were much smoother.

"Good morning," she said when he stumbled into the kitchen a few minutes later. He was wearing his usual uniform of a hoodie and jeans, his blond hair still wet, the blue streaks he'd put in it recently even more vivid. She gave a quick check to make certain his jeans weren't getting too short. He'd grown three inches in the last year, and she was sure he wasn't done.

He acknowledged her greeting with a grunt and headed for food. While he didn't drink coffee, he was pretty much non-communicative before his orange juice and cereal. She smiled when he grabbed a hard-boiled egg and ate it in two bites. She told him she'd buy the sugary breakfasts he preferred as long as he paired it with a little protein, at least on school days.

Mia left him in the kitchen with Bowie, who was looking forward to cleaning the bowl, and went into the living room. As she sipped her coffee and ate a protein bar, she thought about her schedule for the day. First, she'd spend some time visiting her father, Joe. He was enjoying his move to Crawford Senior Living Center, but she saw him at least twice a week. Then she'd work on her article for the *Journal of Emergency Nursing* and look through what material she needed for the quilt she was making for Dean for Christmas before laying it out. The holiday was almost two months away, but she could only work on it when he wasn't around, so that limited her time.

Oh, and she'd find a family lawyer because yesterday she'd come home to a certified letter from Ashley's sister, Heather Buckley, who had decided to sue her for custody of Dean. Things were going well—her father was settled and so was Dean. She should have known normal and steady wouldn't last.

She'd been in such shock when she opened the letter and read the contents that Dean had to say her name three times to get her attention. When she finally looked at him, her expression must have been horrible because he asked, "Is someone sick?"

She took in the fear on his face and was sorry that her reaction had scared him. "No, nothing like that." She'd given his shoulder a reassuring squeeze. "It appears your aunt has learned of your mother's death."

"I have an aunt? I didn't know I had any family."

That had been interesting to learn. Not only did Ashley not have contact with her family, but she never spoke of them to him. He thought he was alone in the world. *Ashley, this is not fair. I shouldn't be the one explaining this.* "Your mother has a younger sister. She lives in Andover, Massachusetts with her husband and two kids."

"So, I have cousins, too. Does she want to see me?"

"She wants custody of you." Maybe she shouldn't have blurted it out like that, but Mia was still too stunned to put in filters.

Dean's brows lowered. "Why?"

It was a good question, and one that hadn't occurred to Mia. She loved Dean and loved having him in her life. Naturally his aunt would, right? "I suppose because she misses her sister and wants to do the right thing." At least that's what Mia hoped.

"Are you going to give me up?"

This time she knew the answer. "Not without a fight." She had no question in her mind that she would do whatever it took to keep Dean with her and honor what Ashley wanted. He was not going through another transition, another loss.

Today, she'd take the first steps to start that "fight" and hope that it would resolve easily. Trying to clear her thoughts, she took her hair out of the twist she wore it in and gave her head a shake before pinning it back up.

She went to the closet for a folder to put the letter in, along with whatever future paperwork was coming. She would treat this the way she did emergencies at work—one step at a time, biggest concerns first. She was reading the letter again, which she'd practically memorized in the last day, when Dean called from the kitchen. "Mama Mia?" She smiled at his name for her. She loved it.

On his first night, he asked if he should still call her Aunt Mia, which is how Ashley referred to her. She had no idea what a teen should call a new parental figure. The only decision she'd made was to do her best and make sure he knew she was happy to have him in her life. She told him to use whatever he was comfortable with. Aunt Mia became Mia, then four months later he'd called her 'Mama Mia.' It made them both smile — and a little weepy — and the name stuck.

"Could you come here?" He sounded concerned, so she closed the folder, took her coffee, and went to him. He pointed at his phone. "Cole Hanson from Emporium is the guy you knew when you were younger, right?"

'Knew' was an understatement. He'd been her whole world until decisions and priorities pulled them apart and took them in different directions. That had been an unexpected downside to Dean's coming to live with her. Her past with Cole was long ago enough that people rarely mentioned how she'd once been involved with Cole, as well as the original lead singer of the band. However, when the kids at Dean's school found out who he was living with, they were quick to pass on information from their parents about her connection to the popular rock group. Small towns had long memories. "Yes, that's him. Why?"

"There was an accident with their tour bus last night." He handed her the phone so she could see the news report he was reading. "It says some of them sustained serious injuries, but there's nothing more specific, other than the bus driver died."

With shaking hands, she scrolled through the article and tried to make sense of what was there. Three hours outside of Chicago. Drunk driver. Bus forced off the road. Flipped. Extensive damage. Band members rushed to area hospitals. Tour on indefinite hold. Mia's heart raced and her thoughts jumbled together. Memories of the last time they spoke. The last time they sang together. The last time she saw him. Kissed him.

"He could be okay," Dean said, breaking into her thoughts. It wasn't until she turned to him and his face was blurry that Mia knew her eyes were watering. Dean took her hand in his. "Mom's rule was no panicking until you know for sure what's wrong."

Mia almost laughed. That had been her rule to Ashley. It had been fine when it came to tests and boys who didn't call back. It hadn't been much help after the double line appeared on the pregnancy test. "Let's see if we can find out any more information."

They went to the living room, turned on the television and scrolled through the news stations, finding nothing. She finally found it being discussed on an entertainment channel, but there were no more details than what she'd already read. Unfortunately, however, there were pictures of the crash site and the wrecked vehicle. Seeing that was too real. Mia covered her mouth with her hand and tried to keep calm as the reporter stood outside the hospital in St. Louis where they'd been taken.

No panicking. Not yet.

At the commercial break, Mia noticed the time and shooed Dean out the door for school. He offered to stay with her, which she appreciated, but there was nothing he could do. She promised to text him if she heard anything. Once she was alone, she tried to take her own advice on keeping calm, but it wasn't easy. She opened the internet on her phone but every site had the same information. She didn't know how long she sat there searching for answers when the phone rang. In a daze, Mia walked to the kitchen and looked at the caller id.

The number was unfamiliar, and there was no name.

It couldn't be work asking her to come in. They used her cell phone. As the phone rang again, she considered not picking it up, but that would only delay what was on the other side. She tried twice before her hello came out clearly.

"Is this Mia Durant?"

There was something familiar about the woman's voice, but she couldn't place it. "It is. Who's this?"

"This is Paxton Jones." *Cole's dead.* There was no other reason for Emporium's lead singer and the woman Cole chose over her to be calling. Her logical brain wondered why Paxton was calling her and not one of Cole's brothers to give them the news. Her emotional brain huddled in a corner, rocking back and forth, and wanting to run from what was coming. Mia found a chair at the kitchen table and sat down heavily. "Are you still there?"

Yes and no. "I'm here. I heard about the accident."

"I'm sorry no one's reached out sooner, but I was just told about Cole a few minutes ago. He asked for you to be contacted."

Cole asked for her? That was a surprise, but not one she could think about now. "Is he...." She couldn't say it.

"No, he's not dead," Paxton said immediately. "Oh, my goodness, I'm sorry if that's what you assumed. He had a procedure to repair a tense pneumonia lung or something like that. He broke a rib in the accident. He also needed stitches in a few spots."

Tension pneumothorax. Mia's medical training provided the information that was confusing Paxton. A serious issue but treatable if attended quickly. "Do you know his prognosis?"

"He was in surgery for nearly two hours, then taken to recovery. I believe they've moved him to a room, but he's still pretty out of it. I haven't seen him. I haven't seen any of them." Paxton's voice broke with worry for her friends. "Once I learned the news of the accident had become public, I thought I should call as soon as possible."

"Has anyone gotten in touch with his family?" Theo and Nick would be in a frenzy when they heard, as would the Sinclairs. Her heart ached for them.

"No, not as far as I know." Paxton paused, and Mia wondered what was coming next. "Would you be able to do that?

Mia closed her eyes and sighed softly. The bearer of difficult news. That was her role all too often. Yes, she sometimes got to tell ER patients when things were good, but it was more common for her to have to explain that the positive was tied to the difficult-to-hear as well. She squared her shoulders and said, "Do you have any more details I can give them?"

Mia heard Paxton's shuddering sigh. How odd to finally be talking to this woman who she'd hated for years. The woman who'd proved that Mia was re-placeable both in the band and in Cole's life. Okay, that wasn't entirely fair. It was Mia who had decided she needed to leave the band when she did. What happened next couldn't have been predicted.

Trying to focus on the present, Mia jotted notes down as Paxton explained what happened in the accident, and how Cole's brothers could get in touch with people at the hospital. "I'm sorry I don't have more details, but that's all I know. Every time I try to find out, they tell me I need to relax and concentrate on myself. As if that's an option when I don't know how the rest of them are doing."

Mia had seen enough incidents with multiple people injured to understand what Paxton was go-ing through. "Do as they say. If they see you listening, they'll be more likely to tell you what you want when you ask. And thanks for letting me know. I'll call Cole's brothers and pass along what you've told me."

"I'm sorry." Mia wondered what Paxton was referring to. Was she sorry about Cole being injured? Sorry about having to be the one to tell Mia? Sorry for taking Mia's life? *Yeah, gotta let that go*. It was a waste of time. "We're setting up a private namings system so only family can get information from doctors. It's a way to keep the press out."

Clever. She imagined the hospital operators were being inundated with calls from reporters and fans alike trying to get news or, even better, be put through to the band member's room. "Do you have the name?"

"Yes, for Cole they're supposed to ask for Danny Torrance." Mia would have laughed if the reference didn't bring back so many painful memories. Cole had been a Stephen King fan for as long as she'd known him. Apparently, that hadn't changed.

After awkwardly ending the call with Paxton, Mia sat staring at the phone, wondering what to do next. She hadn't spoken with Cole's brothers since they'd moved back to Fable Notch. Calling for this reason seemed particularly awful. She did, however, have contact with the women in their lives. She'd referred patients to Eden Barrett, who was a physical therapist involved with Theo, and Bowie was a patient of Dani Novak, who was back together with Nick. Mia decided reaching out to Dani was the best choice.

She called over to the veterinary clinic only to be told that Dani wasn't in. Mia wondered if she'd heard the news. Flipping through her phone contacts, she found Dani's cell phone number, which the other woman had given her when Bowie had to stay at the clinic after having a tooth pulled. Dani picked up on the first ring. "Hi Mia, I'm not in the office today. If you need help, Doc Wheeler can take care of Bowie."

Like Mia, Dani was good at remaining calm, but she could hear the worry in the other woman's voice. "I'm assuming you heard about Cole's accident." As soon as Dani said yes, Mia went on. "I got a call from Paxton Jones, and I have some news."

"Is he okay?" When Mia told her he was, she heard Dani's sigh of relief. "We're all at the Sinclairs. Could you come over and talk to everyone? I don't trust myself to remember." Mia could picture them together, worried. It wouldn't look much different from the hospital waiting room.

"I'll be there in fifteen minutes. Maybe less." Small towns had good points and bad. Today, being able to get where she needed quickly was a good one.

Mia motioned to Bowie, who followed her out of the house, then jumped in through the driver's side door of her Subaru Forester. She was not looking forward to talking with Cole's family. She could already imagine the expression on their faces, the fear and uncertainty, but she also knew that not knowing what was going on was probably driving them all crazy, and she was glad she had a way to help them.

As she drove, she mentally re-planned her day. If she was late getting to her dad, it wouldn't be a problem. And she still had time before the article deadline. Finding a lawyer, however, couldn't wait. It had been over twelve years since she'd seen Cole.

How was it he could still find ways to throw her life into chaos.

Chapter Three

♥

Waking up in an unfamiliar room wasn't unusual for Cole. Not after more than a decade of tours. Waking up in a hospital, however, was different. The clock on the wall told him it was almost eleven, but he had no real concept of how much time had passed since the accident. He vaguely remembered being brought here after surgery and the nurses coming in throughout the night to take his vitals.

He tried sitting up, but pain shot through his chest. He pressed the call button and someone came in to help him raise the bed a little, then take another round of blood pressure and oxygen levels. While she worked, he asked about the others.

The first thing he learned was that their bus driver, who had been with them for the last two tours, had died. Cole made a mental note to reach out to the man's family to see what they needed and how he could help. He was relieved to hear everyone else was doing well. He'd been hurt the worst. Paxton was the least injured, having been in an area of the bus where nothing loosened or fell on her. Hugh had a broken leg and a shoulder injury. Brian had a concussion and a broken nose. Everyone was being held for treatment or observation.

The nurse also told him they had contacted his family. He needed to talk to his brothers. Let them know he was okay. His cell phone was with everything else at the accident site, so he made the call from his room phone.

Fortunately, they were together at the Sinclairs' house. Cole could picture the six of them in the living room. Martin and Millie in their recliners, Theo with Eden, Nick with Dani. Theo would be standing up every few minutes to pace, and Nick would be fidgeting. Millie would ask if anyone needed anything, then disappear into the kitchen to get people food or something to drink. How long would it be before the Sinclairs' friends stopped by the house to check on them? The whole town would be talking about him, one of his least favorite things. At least this time it wasn't about their alcoholic mother or the trouble one of them got into.

Soreness from his injuries notwithstanding, Cole took his first easy breath while speaking with Theo and Nick. He was glad to reassure them, make sure they didn't worry. They had their own lives and although they didn't need him to take care of them anymore, it was hard to let go of the big brother/protector role. He told them he was getting good care, and it wasn't necessary for them to come.

They were at the hospital before the end of the day.

His heart constricted when they walked in the room. He was damn glad to see them. Hugs were out of the question because of his injuries, which he hated, but having them close brought him a much greater relief than he expected. He was surprised to learn Mia had given them the details of the accident and more surprised to learn that Paxton called her because he'd asked for her. He had no memory of that. Paxton had stopped by his hospital room after they discharged her and before she left for her home base in North Carolina, and he tried to remember their conversation. She'd asked if he'd spoken to his family, but he didn't think she'd said anything about talking to Mia. That must have been an interesting conversation.

He listened to his brothers as they talked about their lives and the Sinclairs. It was so good to have them close. They were allowed to stay well past the time visiting hours ended — perks of being famous—and Cole rested easily for the first time after they left.

The next morning, he was pretty sure it was Friday, his first visitor was someone he'd hoped not to have to see for a while. Brett Searle, Emporium's agent and manager, showed up wearing a suit that probably cost more than most people paid for their mortgages in three months. No surprise he showed up to check on his investment. He'd been with them since the start, always pushing them to do more and earn more. "Don't you look like shit," he said, taking a seat and making himself at home.

"Good to see you too, Brett," he said insincerely as he raised the bed to a sitting position and tried not to wince. Cole had never liked the man. He pretended to be there to support his artists, but Cole knew where his priorities lay. At the bank. It was Brett who forced their lead singer change over a decade ago and cost Cole the woman he loved. "I hate to break it to you, but I don't think we're going to make it to tonight's concert."

The man barely cracked a smile. "Yes, we assumed that. I've already spoken to the others and let them know that we've postponed the tour until after the new year. You didn't have a lot of upcoming dates because of the holidays, so it's not a big deal, but come January I'm going to need you to be ready to go again."

Had Brett heard that Cole had been... less than focused for the last several concerts? He couldn't be sure, so he said, "You can count on me."

"I knew I could." Brett leaned forward, hands on his knees. "Gotta tell you, the fan support since the accident has been incredible. You should see the gifts and things arriving here. I've never seen so many stuffed animals in one place. If you guys are up for it, I want to put you in front of the press before the end of the day. You can tell everyone you're okay. Thank them for their love."

"Maybe tell them we're donating all the gifts to the pediatric ward." Cole didn't know if this hospital had a pediatric ward, but it didn't matter. He knew what Brett wanted.

Sure enough, the man's face lit up, and he clapped his hands once. "That's a great idea. People will eat that up, be less disappointed about the concert delays. It's been a while since you've had some good publicity."

That damn interview. "Are you suggesting this accident was a good thing?"

"Of course not," Brett said, and almost sounded as though he meant it. "But I can't change what's happened, only use it to support you going forward."

Cole didn't want to think about going forward. "I'm really tired, man. Is there anything else you wanted?"

Brett paused, and Cole wondered at the things he was considering. Finally, he said, "You guys are bigger than ever. If you play your cards right, get a few Grammy noms, and finish this tour strong, you'll have a lot of leverage for your next contract. Paxton may be the face people recognize, but I know you're the one who keeps this group together. There's a lot at stake here. Don't let them down."

"I won't," Cole said. He was always aware of his responsibilities. He'd signed his first contract to take care of his brothers and kept signing them because the band needed him. What did it matter that he'd come to dread almost every part of this work?

Later that day, Brett got his wish. All four members of Emporium spoke to a packed room of waiting press to tell them about the great care they were getting, thank the fans for the outpouring of love, and send their condolences to the driver's family. The gifts were donated and, unsurprisingly, social media blew up, or so he heard from Nick when his brothers came back to visit. Cole was glad he got to see Paxton, Brian, and Hugh before they were discharged. Like him, they looked tired but on the mend.

When Cole left the hospital two days later, Theo and Nick offered to follow behind the private ambulance the label had hired to take him from St.

Louis to Colorado Springs, or fly ahead to meet him there, but Cole told them it wasn't necessary. Seeing them was one thing, having them hover was another. Instead, they agreed to leave once he said everyone could come and spend Thanksgiving with him in a little over two weeks. Millie said she'd send him a list of everything he needed to buy so she could cook for them.

It was weird arriving home by ambulance, but it made it easier to get through the small crowd of press who were waiting for pictures in front of his property. He needed to warn his family about those images and tell them the wheelchair was protocol, not a requirement. He didn't want anyone worrying about him. He was fine.

The home health aide arrived a few hours later while he was still getting his bearings. Her help was great for the first day, but soon he was uncomfortable with all her attention. How could he relax when a stranger kept popping into whatever room he was in, making sure he was okay, handing him medication, and checking his blood pressure? He tossed her out before the end of the second day. He couldn't wait for her to go to the press and tell them what a terrible patient he was. He considered warning Brett, then decided fuck it.

Not that it would matter. A little "bad boy" was good for his reputation. An ironic twist for a man who worked hard to set a good example for his brothers, even if he did get suspended once for fighting and made extra money by hustling pool at the local bar and burger joint.

As glad as he was to have the aide gone, he was soon tired of streaming services and reading. The newest Stephen King book was long and engrossing, but it wasn't enough to distract him from the noise in his head. Maybe he'd been too hasty in sending his brothers away. By his third full day home, all the thoughts he'd been trying to avoid during the tour had made themselves clear.

He'd spent a lifetime making sure the people he loved were cared for. The one time he hadn't been able to do that, two hearts had been shattered, and a promise had been hastily made.

"Don't ever come back," Mia had said. "If this is what you decide, I don't want to see you in Fable Notch again. My life is here. Make yours somewhere else."

He was so upset about hurting her and not being able to do anything to help, he'd agreed. And for the last twelve years, he'd kept his word, only coming for Christmas once and Nick's college graduation. But things had changed. Theo and Nick lived in Fable Notch, and Cole wanted to be with his family.

The time had come to break his promise.

The injury to his lung meant flying wasn't an option for the next few months, so he checked Google to learn what it would take to drive. Over thirty hours of driving was long, but doable if he took his time. By the end of the day, Cole had packed two weeks of clothes, chosen where he was going to take his breaks and stay overnight, and couldn't wait to leave first thing in the morning.

That night he lay in bed thinking about what it was going to be like to arrive in Fable Notch. Because he didn't want to be talked out of it, he hadn't told anyone he was coming. He imagined their surprise at his arrival, how happy they would be to see him. He imagined Millie making Thanksgiving in her own kitchen. The house would smell incredible, there would be people everywhere, and for the first time since they were kids, he'd share this holiday with his entire family. It was going to be amazing.

Maybe not all of it. He'd need to talk to Mia, tell her he was there, and planning to move back. It wasn't going to be an easy reunion, but since learning that he'd asked for her after the accident, and that she'd brought the news to his family, he hadn't been able to stop thinking about her. Truthfully, that had been happening more frequently over the last year, and especially since both of his brothers had reconnected with their first loves. He didn't think that was possible for him and Mia—he'd blown things completely with her—but he wanted to see her.

The first two days of driving weren't bad. More exhausting than he expected, but somewhere in Ohio, Cole realized he might have underestimated his post-accident strength. The trip looked easy on the GPS. Practically a straight line. But he was sore. Every bump he hit, he felt in his ribs and even turning the steering wheel was unexpectedly uncomfortable. He'd ditched the prescription painkillers and managed on the over-the-counter stuff, but he was regretting not hiring someone to do the driving. Or taking a train.

It wasn't just the driving that was draining. He hadn't been sleeping well and had taken to using drive-thrus and eating in his car after a crowd recognized him when he'd stopped for dinner the first night. He wasn't ready for any serious level of people-ing.

On the fourth day—and he'd originally hoped to make it in three—he looked at the clock and the directions for the day. New Hampshire was less than six hours away, which meant he could get a few more hours of sleep and still be at the Sinclairs before dinner.

Shortly before five, he drove up to the Sinclairs white Dutch colonial. He couldn't remember the last time he was there, but years of memories flooded back at the sight. Holidays spent with Martin and Millie and their son, Ryan. Doing homework at the dining room table, watching Boston sports teams. Millie teaching him to play piano and helping him learn guitar, the skill that changed his life and helped him leave this town.

He got out of his car and breathed in the familiar scent of New England fall. The air in Colorado was clear and crisp, but it was different here. Maybe it was because they had different trees, oak and maple. Maybe it was because this had once been home. He walked to the door, hoping his exhaustion didn't show, and automatically wiped his feet on the mat before going into the house. The door wasn't locked. He knew it wouldn't be.

He'd barely taken a step inside before the familiar smell of meatloaf hit him, making his mouth water. Millie saw him and squealed, "Cole? Is that really you?"

She called for Martin as she ran for Cole. He braced himself for the hug he knew was coming. He would welcome it even though it was going to hurt like hell. Millie must have noticed the change in his posture because she stopped inches from him and instead of wrapping her arms around him, she reached up, put her hands on the sides of his face, and brought him down for a kiss on the forehead. "I can't believe you're standing here."

Martin came in and gave Cole's upper arm a squeeze. He was grateful they understood his injuries because there was no way he could or would turn down hugs from two of his favorite people. They both looked older, grayer than the last time he saw them. Noticing the passage of time was hard, but he was so glad to be here he couldn't dwell on it.

"Why didn't you tell us you were coming?" Martin asked as they walked into the kitchen, always the site of any important conversations.

"I didn't know how long it would take me to get here. I had to drive." Cole explained how flying wasn't an option. "One of the many downsides to puncturing a lung. Zero stars. Do not recommend."

"What can I get you?" Millie asked, opening the refrigerator. "Dinner won't be ready for another half hour, but there's plenty of fruit, some left-over spaghetti from last night, or maybe orange juice?"

"The juice sounds good." Surprisingly, he wasn't very hungry. He hadn't been all day. Mostly he wanted to see everyone, sleep for twelve hours, then see them some more.

Millie put the filled glass in front of him and included cookies as well, shortbread from the looks of it. Another thing he couldn't remember when he'd had last. "I'm so glad you're here. Talking to you on the phone isn't the same. I've been so worried ever since Mia came over to tell us the details of your accident."

He wanted to ask them about Mia, wanted to know how she was doing, how she looked. But there would be time for that later. "Guess I'll have to thank her. That couldn't have been easy."

"Good idea," Martin said. "She was trying to hide it, but I think she was pretty shaken up when she came over. Where are you staying while you're here?"

Cole looked at him quizzically. Clearly, his injuries affected his brains. His focus had been on getting here, and he hadn't thought passed that. "I have no idea. I could call over to the Stewarts to see if they have open rooms in the hotel or maybe one of the cabins." It could be fun to stay there as a guest after years of hanging out with Gabriel and Lucas, the two oldest of the eight Stewart children, when they were kids. The cabins had kitchenettes, and he wouldn't need much more than that. "Or I could look into a short—term apartment rental. It's not quite ski season. There should be availability." Finding a place that was open through Thanksgiving could be a challenge, but he'd figure something out.

"I supposed that's an option." Millie said, although something in her voice suggested that wasn't what she wanted.

Martin said, "You could also see if your old house is available."

Nick had renovated the house they grew up in and rented it out to tourists. Even though he'd heard it looked nothing like what it did when they were kids, he couldn't stomach the thought of going there. He had more bad memories of the place than his brothers did. He shook his head. "I understand why Theo stayed there when he came to help, but I'd rather not."

"Theo's apartment with Eden is probably too small, but you could ask Nick about staying with him. The place he built is plenty big enough."

"And has Dani and his puppy. No, things are still pretty new for them. I don't want to intrude." But it was more than that. He was the family caretaker. He would not invade or disrupt his brothers' lives because he didn't know what to do with his.

"Then that settles it," Millie said, bringing him back to the moment. "You'll stay with us. We've got more than enough room."

Cole almost laughed. He was the only one of his brothers who didn't have a chance to live here since Theo and Nick moved in after Cole graduated from high school and attempted college. "No, Ma, that's not...."

"Don't say it. It *is* necessary. I'll even buy Moxie for you."

Was there a more fitting taste of home than Moxie soda? His brothers used to make gagging noises when he drank it, saying it tasted like molasses, but it was Cole's favorite. His splurge of choice as a kid when he had a little extra money and something Millie kept on hand for him once they started coming over. "You're making it very tempting."

"Good. Then I won't hear anything more about it. In the meantime, we need to let your brothers know you're here. They're both in town, right, Martin?"

Martin put out the salad dressings he'd taken from the refrigerator, thought for a second, then said, "Theo is. Nick was in New York last week for a few days, but I'm pretty sure he's back. I'll call them. You go relax. You're looking tired, my boy."

"Sounds good to me." Martin was right. He was feeling tired. He didn't know why driving was so draining. All he'd done was sit on his ass, but it was. He made his way into the living room, put a pillow on a couch arm rest and stretched out with a sigh. He was glad to be home.

He must have fallen asleep because it seemed only seconds later Theo and Nick were bursting into the house with the same energy they had when they were kids. Greetings were exchanged, backs slapped, fists bumped. Hugs would wait.

"What the hell are you doing here?" Theo said. "We weren't expecting to see you for two weeks."

Cole found himself unexpectedly emotional and hoped his brothers didn't notice. He didn't think he'd ever cried in front of them, not when his father hit him, not when their mother died. He wasn't going to start now. "Thought I'd surprise you all by coming here instead. You didn't have your hearts set on traveling over Thanksgiving, did you?"

"Well, I was looking forward to a little time on that west coast powder," Nick said, referring to skiing in the Rockies, "but this means we have extra time with you, so no argument."

If Cole got his wish, it would be more than extra time. Fable Notch would soon be his home base again. As long as a certain someone was okay with him living here. The thought of seeing Mia again had his stomach tightening and his ears ringing.

Wait, why were his ears ringing?

Theo said something that Cole didn't hear, but before he could ask him to repeat it, Theo put a hand on Cole's shoulder and gave him an unreadable look. "Dude, are you okay?"

"Just a little tired from the trip. Why?" This was the second time someone asked how he was feeling, although now that he thought about it, the room seemed too warm. He sat down heavily.

Nick sat next to him and said, "You're not looking good, bro. No color in your face."

Cole couldn't believe what he was about to say, but if he didn't say it quick, he wasn't sure he'd be able to say it at all. "I think I need help."

Chapter Four

♥

Mia was near the triage area when she heard a familiar voice calling for help. If she hadn't seen Theo a few days before, she wouldn't have recognized it. She ran out to see Theo and Nick on either side of Cole, holding him up under his arms. Cole looked waxy and pale. His eyes were closed, his head bowed forward. What the hell was he doing here? He should have been at home recovering. He looked worse than he did at the hospital press conference that she hadn't been able to avoid watching. He couldn't have flown here, which meant a cross-country train trip or drive.

Idiot.

Of all the reunion scenarios Mia imagined with Cole, having him carried into her ER at the end of her shift was not one of them. A thousand thoughts and memories hit her, but they were interrupted as Nick said, "He collapsed. He got here less than two hours ago. We were hanging out at the Sinclairs. Theo noticed he wasn't looking good. A second later, Cole said he needed help, then he went down."

Cole asked for help. It must be bad. She turned back to get a gurney and call for a doctor. "Did he lose consciousness?"

"Maybe," Theo said. He didn't have much more color than Cole did, but Mia recognized it as worry, not a medical condition. "It was more like he was phasing in and out. He kept mumbling about contracts and Moxie."

She gave Theo a questioning look, then decided she didn't need to know. They'd figure out what was wrong soon enough. Seconds later, they left his brothers in the waiting room and had Cole in a treatment area, where they started the necessary diagnostic work. With the help of another nurse, who couldn't stop the gasp and exclamation of "That's Cole Hanson," they took his jacket and shirt off so that she could take his vitals.

She first noticed the stitches and bruises from the accident, then stupidly noted how muscular his arms were. Years of guitar playing definitely kept his upper body in shape. His skin was also covered in tattoos that hadn't been there the last time she'd seen him undressed. She found herself lost in the image of a hawk in flight on his broad chest and a staff with music on it encircling his arm.

Focus, Mia. Do your job. He was a patient, nothing more. "Cole, can you tell me what's wrong?" Mia asked as she wrapped his arm in a blood pressure cuff and put a pulse oximeter on his finger. "Does anything hurt?"

His reposes were slow and broken. "I'm tired. So damn tired. Need rest. Then I can take care of things." As the machine inflated the cuff on his arm, Cole opened his eyes and stared at her. For some reason, Mia found herself surprised they were as blue as she remembered. Did she think time would change that? Dull their morning sky color? She could tell the moment he recognized her. "Little bird," he said on a whisper, then gave her a smile before closing them again.

The muscles in her legs went weak, and she put her hands on the bed rail to steady herself. How could two words affect her so much? "Little bird" had been his nickname for her from the first day they met. He'd heard her singing a song he'd played in the cafeteria at lunch. She'd thought she was alone, walking through the woods behind the school. "A little bird is singing my song," he'd said, coming up next to her. She'd apologized, and he'd told her his music had never sounded better.

The beeping of the blood pressure machine brought her attention back to the present. Shit, the numbers were really low. The doctor came in and she said, "His BP is 84 over 52, and he was recently treated for a punctured lung. He also sustained a broken rib and has stitches from a car accident less than two weeks ago."

With that news, the doctor cursed and said, "This is our local rock star?" Everyone had heard what happened. Big news in a small town. "Didn't anyone tell him he shouldn't travel? We need to make sure he hasn't reinjured himself somehow." He checked the incision left by the chest tube and the other injuries. Mia's stomach clenched at the proof of Cole's brush with death. It was one thing to know, another to see.

As the other nurse put an oxygen tube in Cole's nose, crooked as ever from when his father broke it over twenty years before, Mia started an IV and took some blood samples. She drew two vials so they could get a complete chem panel, then she hung a bag of fluids. Not finding anything obvious to treat, the doctor asked, "What was he doing before he arrived?"

"I don't know." She'd been so shocked to see Cole, she hadn't asked Theo or Nick any questions. A mistake. "His brothers brought him in after he collapsed, and they didn't mention anything in particular setting it off, only that he arrived a few hours ago and that he didn't look good." It was an understatement. Cole's skin was gray.

The doctor checked his lungs. Cole moaned. Yeah, punctured lungs and broken ribs left a person sore. The doctor took off the stethoscope and said, "Breath sounds are good, so I think the lungs are still fine, but I don't like the lethargy. I'm ordering a chest CT to see what that tells us."

"What's happening? What's wrong?" The fluids and oxygen were having an immediate effect, but now Cole was agitated. He took in his surroundings, and Mia heard the monitor report the jump in his heart rate. "What am I doing here? Thought I was done with hospitals."

Mia put a hand on his shoulder and gently eased him back on the mattress. Using her best nurse's voice, she said, "You lost consciousness at the Sinclairs. Your brothers brought you in. We don't know what's wrong, so we need to run some tests, but your blood pressure is low. Are you taking any medications? Any opiates?" After the surgery he would have been given painkillers, and she wondered if they could be contributing to his current condition.

"Hate those. Made my head fuzzy. I junked them when I got home from the hospital." Mia did the math. That meant he stopped taking them only a few days after his injury. While the pain had probably mitigated, there was no way it was gone. Stubborn man. Some things never changed. "I'm on blood thinners. Can't remember the name. In my bag."

Another common post-surgery protocol. "We'll find it." She'd ask his brothers to check. It would give them something to do. "Anything else I should know?"

"I'm sorry," he said and took her hand. The zing that traveled through her body was more intense than she expected or had experienced in years. The last time he'd touched her, he was putting her on a plane to come back to Fable Notch. A few months later, 'I'm sorry' were the last words he'd spoken to her.

Looking at him brought her back to that awful final phone call. Everything had been going their way. Emporium had signed their first recording contract when she and Cole were in college. They all dropped out and flew to California to record an album. After its release, they spent the next seven months on tour, opening for bigger name acts and trying to get their name out there. Everything was going their way until Mia received a call from her mother saying she'd been diagnosed with pancreatic cancer, and Mia needed to come home to help care for her since her father had to keep working.

Mia didn't want to leave. Emporium was getting better known, and the label was talking about a second album. In another few years, they might have a tour of their own. She was doing what she loved with the man she loved. She sent home as much money as she could to help her parents. Wasn't that enough?

But she knew the answer.

As her parents' late-in-life and unexpected child, her mother told her frequently how different things would have been if she hadn't come along — early retirements, vacations, moving to a warmer part of the country — so Mia needed to pull her weight. By the time she was eight, her brother and sister, each more than ten years older than she was, had left. Over the years, more and more of the household duties had fallen to Mia. She had accepted her role and didn't usually mind it. She knew her parents hadn't wanted her, but she enjoyed being needed. This, however, would ruin everything.

When she told Cole about her mother, he said he understood. He was the one who took care of his family, too, although he did it without parents around. It was one of the things that had drawn them together — understanding the responsibility that came with family. He went with her to their agent to see what could be done.

Mia should have suspected something when Brett Searle was quick to agree to her time away, but she was so relieved she didn't stop to think. Paxton joined the group the day after Mia left, and two days later made her debut as the band's new lead singer. As her mother's cancer treatments progressed, so did Emporium's popularity. Paxton with her deeper voice, full lips, doe eyes, and long red hair made an impression on fans and reviewers alike.

Within three months, the record company made it clear they didn't want Mia back. They offered her a quarter of a million dollars to remove her from the contract. Cole, who had been increasingly distant on their rare phone calls, claimed he tried to get the label to change their mind, but they'd left him no choice. He couldn't leave — the band's income was keeping his family going — and she wasn't welcome back.

Their relationship ended at that moment. There was no way she could be with him as long as the band didn't include her. With the costs of her mother's treatments piling up, she took the money and left music and Cole behind.

After over a year of grueling treatments, successes and setbacks, Mia's mother was deemed cancer free. Mia wasn't sure what to do with her life, but taking care of her mother had given her a new appreciation for medical professionals. She'd returned to school and gone into nursing, grateful to find work she liked and which made a difference.

At the moment, however, she'd rather be on bedpan duty at the senior center than at Cole's bedside.

Before she could think of a way to respond to his unrequested apology, he said, "Wanted to see you. We need to talk."

They did, but now was not the time, and she wasn't ready for a heart to heart. In fact, if she were smart, she'd keep her heart as far away from Cole as possible. She put on her best 'Listen to me' voice, the one she used to calm and direct patients, and hoped it would offer her the emotional distance she needed. "I understand, but that's going to have to wait until we can figure out what's wrong and get you better. Priorities."

He gave her a small smile, and she wanted to smack herself. Minutes in his presence and she'd fallen back into their shorthand. There had been many occasions throughout high school where plans had to be changed or were ditched all together because one of them got an unexpected phone call. All they had to say was 'priorities,' and the other knew what was up. They made a commitment early in their relationship to always support one another through these moments, no matter if it meant time apart.

That time apart had become twelve years. A lifetime of changes and separate lives.

"Priorities," he repeated. "But we're going to talk since I'm going to be here through the holidays. I want to move home. I've missed you so much."

Mia's heart stopped. As if she didn't have enough going on in her life, Cole was going to be close by again? This was not something she wanted to think about. Especially not the part of her that melted at his words. That part needed to be squashed. Quickly.

He'd done what she'd asked all those years ago — stayed away. It had been the only thing she could think of doing to move on with her life. The last thing she'd said to him was, "I don't want to see you in Fable Notch again. My life is here. Make yours somewhere else." His response was, "If that's what you want, I'll do it. I'm sorry."

She didn't know what she wanted. All she knew was that her heart was breaking, and she wanted a complete separation from him. She didn't mind if he came to visit the Sinclairs occasionally, but she couldn't stand the idea of him being around. Even with him gone, it had taken years before the talk about her being replaced and them breaking up had died down.

Yes, she'd thought of leaving Fable Notch, but this was the only place that felt like home. After graduating from nursing school, she got her own apartment until her mother died two years ago and she moved back into her old house because her father needed her around more. Ultimately, the living arrangement had turned out to be a good thing, because when Dean arrived last year there was plenty of room for him. Sometimes she marveled at how situations that were thrust upon her led to ones that worked out.

And now Cole was going to be here for at least the next several weeks and then move back? How was she going to manage that when she was already fighting with herself not to stroke his beautiful, black hair and tell him everything was going to be okay?

She gave herself a mental shake, determined not to let this throw her. She was an ER nurse. She would handle this like triage and keep her focus on the things that mattered most and where she could make a difference. At thirty-three her life might not be what she'd once imagined, but there was a lot in it that made her happy. Dean, her friends, her work. Cole's moving back didn't change anything. There was no reason she couldn't keep him out of her life and her heart.

Chapter Five

♥

I want to move home. I've missed you so much. He couldn't believe he'd said those words out loud. When he'd decided to drive east, his thought was to be with his family as he recovered, stay through the holidays, and figure out what it would take to move back. But once he saw Mia, he knew that he'd been kidding himself. She was the one he really wanted to see.

And here she was, standing next to him, looking more beautiful than any of his memories or the picture he kept in his wallet. Hugh saw the photo once and teased him about having an actual print, but he hadn't been willing to chance the possibility of the images on his phone getting deleted. Yes, she looked older — didn't they all — but her eyes were still a warm, inviting brown, the same color as her hair, which was pulled into a low ponytail at the nape of her neck. He imagined the waves in it when she wore it loose. He imagined what it would be like to kiss the exposed skin under her ear.

Maybe he was feeling better.

If only she would smile, then he'd know he had reason to hope that she might forgive him for the way he left. But instead, she said, "One step at a time, Cole," and removed her hand from his. He didn't like the detached tone in her voice. He wasn't another patient, damn it. Yes, it had been a long time, but he'd held her heart for years, just as she held his. He'd rather she be upset than neutral. Upset meant his being here mattered.

She walked over to the laptop another nurse had left to add something to his chart. He wanted to call her back and tell her he needed her close. He'd always needed her. She'd been the first person to understand the burden he was under—how he had to hold things together for his family and then do the same thing for their new band. But it was those responsibilities and commitment that had him agreeing to Paxton becoming lead singer.

After Mia was replaced, he'd been off balance for months. Brett had noticed and told him to shape up or the band was through. Knowing each of them needed the band to succeed — and not wanting Mia's firing to have been for nothing — he got it together. A little over a year later, they were celebrating their Grammy nomination for Best New Artist.

His biggest regret over the choices he made—not that they felt like choices at the time — was how he'd hurt Mia. He ached to show her how sorry he was and find some small way of making it up to her. She wouldn't want money, but maybe there was something the hospital needed that he could provide. There had to be a way he could show her he'd never stopped caring.

When she came back to his bed, she was carrying a pitcher of water, a cup and something wrapped in plastic. "In a few minutes, they're going to take you for a head CT and an x-ray. There's no telling how long this will take, but it will be at least an hour, most likely two, before they have the results for you. In the meantime, I'm going to give Nick and Theo an update and let you rest."

"Will you be back?" Did she hear the urgency in his voice? Did he want her to?

"Probably not. It's the end of my shift, and I need to get home." He wondered if there might be someone waiting for her. He didn't like the thought. Something must have shown in his face because Mia took a step closer and said, "Are you okay?"

"Yes. Fine." What could he say? She looked as though she was going to press him for a more truthful answer. The fact that she didn't was a reminder of the distance between them. *Give me time*, he thought. The thought made him look at her hand. No ring. "You're not married." *Subtle Cole*, he thought to himself.

"No," she said, then paused before going on, "but there's someone in my life. I'm going to get your brothers. They can keep you company."

He didn't know how to react to that bombshell, and she left before he could ask anything about this man. A few minutes later, Nick and Theo came into the curtained-off area to stay with him. The look of apprehension on their faces was painful to see. It reminded him of how they looked when their mom came home hours after dinner, knowing she'd been drinking, but not knowing if she'd be in a yelling or a silent mood.

"Relax, guys, it's probably just exhaustion." He used the remote control on the bed to sit up more so he didn't feel as helpless, but winced as the motion pulled at a muscle in his chest. So much for 'just' exhaustion. "When was the last time one of you drove three quarters of the way across the country?"

Cole was trying to lighten the mood, but neither of his brothers were willing to hear it. Theo said, "I've logged plenty of long driving trips since I can't fly to sites with Harlow, but never less than two weeks after being in the hospital." Harlow was Theo's arson dog. "Why did you do it?"

It seemed like a good idea at the time was not going to cut it. "Do you want the long answer or the short answer?"

"If this hospital is like the one I was in, we're going to be here for a while," Nick said, sounding as annoyed as Theo. "Give us the long answer."

Cole stared at his brothers and thought about what to say. "By the time I'd been home three days, I was climbing the walls. The place was too quiet. I mean, how many television shows can one man watch? How many naps can you take?"

Theo stood and paced in the small space. Cole couldn't help but smile. It was what Theo always did when he was on edge. "Then you should have called us. We could have found a way for at least one of us to come out sooner."

Cole shrugged and managed not to grimace. Coming here had seemed like a smart thing when he thought of it. Driving gave him something to focus on other than how miserable he was, and gave him the chance to see everyone sooner. No, it was more than that. He could have asked them to come out, but if his brothers came to Colorado, eventually they'd leave, and he'd be there. Alone. "I didn't want to wait."

"I'm not buying it," Nick said. "I realize we have a family tradition of not talking to one another when things are rough." Nick hadn't told anyone when he had a severe panic attack that looked enough like a heart attack that he'd been admitted to the hospital. Theo hadn't let anyone come and see him when an accident at a fire site left him with a broken femur. "But we all agree that's not necessary and a bad habit."

Yeah, sometimes the three of them were too independent for their own good. Nick was right, and Cole was ready to change that. He needed his family. "You're both here. The Sinclairs are here. Being out west seemed ridiculous."

Theo must have heard something in his voice because he said, "Does that mean this is more than a visit? Are you moving back? That would be terrific."

It was exactly the response he was hoping for. "You don't think I'm crazy?"

Theo shook his head. Nick laughed and said, "If you had told me a year ago that I'd leave New York and start a home design business, I would have asked you what you were snorting. I thought nothing could make me change my plans, and I certainly had no interest in going into a field as erratic as construction."

"And look at me," Theo said. "No one was happier to put Fable Notch in my rearview mirror. I swore never to set foot in this town again. Didn't visit for a single holiday or even come back when Martin had his heart attack."

"You came when he needed you," Cole said. Martin had reached out to Theo when he'd been hurt after an arsonist attacked several properties back in April. Since that was Theo's area of expertise, Martin had asked Theo to come home and help.

"Reluctantly. *Very* reluctantly. And even after seeing Eden again, I had no intention of staying. Didn't think it was an option." He paused and took a breath. "Didn't think I'd be welcome."

Of the three of them, Theo had the most challenges in their small town. Cole was seen as the brave one holding his family together. Nick was the baby people wanted to help. And Theo had been the troublemaker, involved with the rich girl who was "too good" for him. Cole was glad Theo had gotten past that.

Nick continued, "What we're trying to tell you is you're not the first Hanson brother to realize that this town may be home after all." He paused before asking, "Does this have anything to do with Mia?"

"Because you wouldn't be the first Hanson brother to realize they weren't over their first love, either," Theo added.

Nick nodded in agreement. "Nope, you're the last on that one."

Cole smiled at them. "Yes, she's part of this, but I'm moving back even if she's involved with someone else." He didn't like the way his gut tightened at the thought, but he'd worry about that later. "I was already feeling antsy before the accident. And then after, I had a lot of time to think."

Theo gave a snort and said, "That can be dangerous."

"No kidding," Cole said, rolling his eyes. His thoughts had been a dangerous place for quite a while. Maybe talking about them with his brothers would help. "Nick, when you sent me the pictures of you and the dog, and, Theo, your video the night you proposed to Eden, it made me realize how much I want to be with you for all of your news, good and bad."

"We'd love that too. Time to sell the place in Colorado and move," Nick said, and Cole loved the enthusiasm in his voice. So different from the disinterest in Mia's tone. "I'll start looking for houses for you to buy. Maybe one I can redesign for you."

"It's not quite that simple. I made Mia one promise after they replaced her." All these years later, he still hated saying those words. He never should have let her go. He should have said if they released her, he'd walk too, but he was told Emporium would never get another contract if he didn't agree, and the money they were promising for a three-album contract was too good. It would cover Nick's college and would make sure that Theo had what he needed when — Cole never let himself think 'if' — he came back from Afghanistan. Emporium was his way of taking care of his family and do everything his parents couldn't. And Brian and Hugh needed the band to be a success as much as Cole did. "I promised I'd never come for more than a visit as long as she was here."

"Then you need to change her mind," Theo said.

"I need to change her mind." But he wanted to do more than that. If it was possible, he wanted to change her heart.

Chapter Six

❤

M ia left the hospital without knowing the results of Cole's blood work or what the doctors were going to do with him. She'd considered staying past the end of her shift to find out what was wrong, then reminded herself she wasn't supposed to care. Besides, she had a teen waiting for her and someone coming over to join them for dinner.

She'd texted her friend, Casey Shaw, as soon as she left Cole's bedside. *Need to talk. Come for dinner?* The "sure" and thumbs up emoji arrived almost instantly. When Mia pulled into her driveway, Casey was sitting on the porch swing, Bowie at her feet.

Mia and Casey had become friends while they were in nursing school together and after graduation, they'd rented neighboring apartments in the area. Coping with her mother's ongoing needs through her cancer, Mia learned she preferred situations where she could make an immediate difference before moving on, so emergency medicine was a good fit for her. Casey, who loved working with patients on an ongoing basis, got a job at Crawford Senior Living Facility. Casey was all heart, and Mia was grateful for their friendship.

Bowie ran off the porch to greet Mia, and she gave him some attention as she made her way to the door. She'd adopted the lumbering Saint Berhusky mix after another brief relationship ended. She wanted someone around who was happy to see her every day, and there was the added benefit of him being a good companion for her father when she was at work. With his dark brown fur and ice-blue eyes, he looked like an alien, making her think of Ziggy Stardust. Her father said he wasn't calling a dog Ziggy, so the name was chosen. She walked to the house and said, "I'm glad you were free to come over."

"I'm glad you texted me," Casey said, giving Mia a hug, which lasted longer than a quick greeting. Mia tended not to share her problems until they'd gotten to a breaking point. She was good at taking care of everyone around her, but not always taking care of herself. In the nearly ten years they'd known each other, Mia found Casey to be endlessly patient and willing to wait until Mia was ready to talk. She was glad Casey understood her process. "Rough day?"

"On top of an already rough week. Not what I needed."

Casey held up a box and Mia saw the sticker from Pie in the Sky Bakery. "I brought reinforcements, and Dean said something about heating a casserole." Mia always did a lot of cooking in advance, a habit she'd gotten into when taking care of her mother. This way, if there was a bad day, meal prep wasn't an issue. It worked well for getting food on the table at a reasonable time on her workdays.

Mia and Casey walked into the house, Bowie racing for his favorite spot on the couch. Mia breathed in the welcoming scent of chicken and broccoli alfredo. Good, she needed comfort food tonight. Her stomach clenched as she went through the mail Dean had left on the table until she saw there were no new bills, no certified letters. Good. At least something was going right, if only temporarily. As they went into the kitchen, Mia said, "Please let there be chocolate in that," pointing at the pie box.

"Will a deep-dish peanut butter chocolate chip cookie pie do?" Casey opened the box and flashed the tantalizing dessert.

Mia would have thought it was the sexiest thing she'd seen all day if it weren't for the fact that she'd seen Cole a few hours before. Fortunately, the pie was here, and Cole wasn't. "Those are some of my favorite adjectives. Sounds wonderful. Could we start with that?"

"Wouldn't we be setting a bad example? You do have an impressionable teen in the house, after all."

"Oh, I'm not that impressionable," said the teen in question, coming into the room and giving her a quick squeeze as she took dinner out of the oven. Mia's heart melted a little every time he did that. He'd been so stiff and sad when he arrived. She'd repeatedly asked permission before she offered any sort of physical affection, and he'd turned it down for the first few months. Now he gave and accepted it freely. "But the chicken smells really good, so I'm happy to dive into that first. Hi, Casey."

She looked at Dean and saw Ashley in his eyes and smile. His blond hair and strong nose came from the summer resident who got Ashley pregnant, but the rest was her friend. Mia would always miss Ashley, but always be grateful to have this part of her. Ashley trusted Mia with her son, and Mia wouldn't let her down. She would win this custody battle no matter what it took. "Are you taller than you were this morning? Maybe I should stop feeding you?"

"Ya think?" Dean stood a little straighter at her words. He was three inches shorter than her 5'7" when he arrived. A year later, he was almost an inch taller. If his big feet were any indication, he wouldn't stop there. "Guess I'll need more of this then." He moved the spatula and helped himself to a heaping portion of dinner. "If Casey's here, I'm guessing you two need to talk. Okay if I eat in the living room?"

He may be a teen boy with most of the classic teen boy issues, but he was also an understanding person, and she appreciated it. "Go for it. Take a napkin." He ripped off two paper towel sheets, grabbed a can of ginger ale, and headed off to watch television.

Mia poured two glasses of wine. She and Casey helped themselves to more reasonably sized meal portions — she was saving room for pie — then sat at the kitchen table. Mia took a long drink of her wine, then slouched in her chair.

"Talk to me," Casey said. Mia wished there were some sci-fi way to transfer the day's memory into Casey's head so she wouldn't have to go through it moment by moment. It had been tough enough the first time. As if she knew what Mia was thinking, Casey added, "Whatever you want to share is fine."

"Cole Hanson is in town." Casey blinked twice and refilled Mia's wine glass. She took a small sip before continuing. Getting drunk wasn't going to change anything. "He arrived today after driving across the country, but the trip was too much too soon. First time I see the man in twelve years, and he's in my emergency room."

"What happened?" Mia explained the basics of what she knew about Cole's condition. "That's not what I meant. What was it like seeing him again?"

"Confusing," Mia admitted. "Seeing him looking so awful and then seeing the bruises and stitches from his accident. It made it much more real that he could have died."

"You could have lost him."

"I lost him a long time ago," she said, and hated the misery in her voice. Casey didn't say anything. Mia had told Casey her history with Cole one night in their old apartment. She'd come in after class, heard an Emporium song playing on the radio, and angrily turned it off. Since then, Mia had barely spoken about Cole, but her silence probably said as much — or more — as her words. That, combined with the fact that she never dated anyone seriously made some truths painfully obvious, even if she didn't want to admit them.

Casey drank some of her wine and said, "You said you were the one he wanted to reach after the accident."

She could still hear Paxton saying, *He asked for you*. "It's probably because I'm a nurse used to giving bad news."

Leaning back in her chair, Casey gave Mia a pointed stare. "Oh, yeah, I'm sure that's how logically he was thinking after his tour bus flipped over."

"I can't let that mean anything," Mia said, and hated the truth in her words. When Cole didn't fight for her to remain as Emporium's lead singer, when he agreed to stay away from Fable Notch, Mia saw it as proof that she'd never meant as much to him as he did to her. She'd always thought it would have been easier to accept being replaced if she'd known Cole had argued against Paxton joining the band. But when she got the call from Brett and asked if this was what the group wanted, he'd told her they all agreed that Paxton was the right choice. All, which included Cole. "He told me he wants to move back."

"Given everything that happened, along with his brothers living here again, that can't be a complete surprise."

It wasn't, but she didn't have to like it. And she could wish that it wasn't happening now. "When I left Emporium, I made him promise that as long as I was here, he wouldn't be."

"Are you going to hold him to that?"

Mia took a bite of her Alfredo rather than answer. Part of her wanted to make him go away again. Her life was complicated enough with Dean and the custody petition, but she already knew the truth. She swallowed and said, "I can't. As you said, Nick and Theo are here. How could I tell him to stay away from his family? Besides, those were the words of an angry twenty-one-year-old who wanted her boyfriend to fight for her rather than agree to her foolish demands. I've grown up since then." Or at least she hoped so.

"Will you be okay with him living so close? With the possibility of running into him? And people talking, because you know they will."

"I'll manage. I always do." It was true. Through every loss, she'd found a way to handle it. It was what she was clinging to every time she thought of the custody issue. She had no time to worry about what having Cole around might mean. Making sure Dean stayed with her was her priority. Dean had found an instant place in her life and her heart, and she would give him the home and love he deserved. They may both have been the results of unplanned pregnancies, but unlike what she was told, she was determined to make sure Dean knew he was wanted. "Besides, it's not like he'd be around all that much. Touring takes months out of the year. And if it's really terrible, I can move after Dean graduates from high school."

Casey gave a nod and asked, "How can I help?" That was something she and Casey had in common. Whenever there was a situation, they looked for ways they could fix it. Unfortunately, there was no easy fix for this.

"I appreciate the offer, but I don't think there's anything to do. Not unless you can convince Cole to leave and Heather to drop her custody suit." Casey was the first call she made after getting the letter.

Casey leaned forward and said, "Do you realize you always turn down offers of help?"

That couldn't be right. "I accept help," she said.

"When?" Casey crossed her arms across her chest as she settled back in her chair. And waited.

As Mia tried to think of an answer, she remembered overhearing a per diem nurse say, "I love working when Mia's on. There's almost nothing for anyone else to do." When she thought about the years of caring for her parents, first through her mother's cancer, then her dad's decline, she remembered. "I hired someone to come take care of my dad for a month when I went to Florida."

"You didn't go to Florida for a vacation, Mia. You went because your best friend was dying. You only asked for help so you could help someone else. There's a big difference," Casey said. Mia hated that Casey was right. She stared at the wine, decided that more wasn't going to help, and ate another bite of her dinner as Casey continued. "When we were in school, I was always the one who suggested we study together because I could see when you were struggling. Would you have asked if I hadn't said anything?"

It was rhetorical, so Mia said nothing. More often than not, people were too busy with their own lives to have time for her. She was good at doing things herself, even if she was often tired. "What's wrong with relying on yourself?" Mia could hear the defensiveness in her voice, but she didn't care.

"Nothing is wrong with it, unless help would make things better. Easier." Casey reached out and gave Mia's hand a squeeze. "You've got a lot going on with Dean. You're a single parent, and Cole being here is going to be an emotional challenge, whether or not you admit it. I want you to know that you don't have to keep it all together. I'm here."

"Thank you. Really." She appreciated the offer. Even if she didn't know what her friend could do, it was nice to know she wasn't alone. "I need help finishing that pie. Does that count?"

Casey laughed. "It'll do for now."

Mia went and took the pie out of the box. For a second, she considered not cutting a slice, just digging in directly, but thought better of it and got out utensils and plates. She didn't want to deal with the sugar headache she'd have later if she overindulged. There were enough things in her life making her head hurt. And now she had one more thought pinging through her mind.

What kind of help was she going to need to keep her heart safe now that Cole was back?

Chapter Seven

♥

Cole was released after a few hours. He was glad they didn't admit him. His last hospital stay was more than enough. The diagnosis was he'd let himself get drastically dehydrated, which led to low blood pressure, and he was slightly anemic, so he had a prescription for iron. He refused painkillers.

Millie made a huge fuss over Cole when he came back. He would have told her she was overdoing it, except she'd saved him a plate of her meatloaf and mashed potatoes and, as promised, she had bought Moxie in the few hours he was away.

Eden and Dani were waiting for them, and he'd enjoyed not only seeing the women his brothers loved again but seeing the four of them together. There was so much love and connection. It solidified his desire to come back home. Whatever it took for Mia to accept his presence, he'd do it.

Watching his brothers, he could only hope that Mia would do more than accept him. She said there was someone in her life. Was it serious? Because if it wasn't, he was going to do whatever it took to replace that man.

And if it was? If she was in love with someone else?

Then he'd have to accept that as a consequence of his decisions. But he was still going to be moving back, no matter how painful it would be to see her happy with someone else.

Soon after he finished eating, Cole said goodnight to everyone and went to bed. He wished he could stay awake longer, but he was beyond exhausted.

Staying with the Sinclairs brought back memories of when Cole was fourteen and he and his brothers met the couple who would, for all intents and purposes, save them. Cole couldn't imagine what would have happened if Martin and Millie hadn't come into their lives. Foster care probably, because no matter how much Cole worked to bring in extra money, there was never enough. He was a kid playing a grown-up role.

That was why getting signed had been so important. Sure, they were all dazzled by the promises the label made about fame and fans, but it was the first check and the promise of more to come that had gotten rid of a huge set of worries for Cole. Before they left to record their first album, he'd given more than half of his signing bonus to the Sinclairs to help them look after Theo and Nick, and for the next several years he'd lived as frugally as possible so he could continue to support his family. Not until Nick graduated from college did he use more of the money for himself. That's when he bought the house and built the studio in Colorado — which he now hoped to sell. He was all in on moving back.

And now that he'd seen Mia? It was probably going to take a miracle for her to forgive him, but it would be worth it to try.

Thinking of her, for the first night in months, he fell asleep easily.

When he woke, he was surprised to see it was after eight. True, that was six Colorado time, but he'd slept longer than he had in a long time. He threw on a t-shirt and sweatpants and headed down to the kitchen to make coffee and figure out what to do with his day.

And his life.

By 8:30, he was halfway through his first cup when Millie came in looking ready to go wearing a dark sweater and black pants. "Good morning, my sweet. You always were the only early bird in the family," she said, kissing the top of his head and helping herself to a mug of coffee. She took a sip and gave a happy sigh. "Thanks for making this. It's nice to have it ready." Cole made a mental note to buy her a programmable coffee pot so she could always have it waiting for her. "How did you sleep?"

"Pretty well," he said. "I suppose there's something to be said for total exhaustion."

"You gave us quite a scare yesterday. Please don't do that again." She said it with a smile, but he knew she meant it. *Take care of yourself,* she was telling him. That was his intention. Moving back was the first step.

"I'm sorry to have worried you, Ma. I won't do anything today. How does that sound?"

"Perfect. I'll be working in my greenhouse for part of the day, and then I have a few music students coming this afternoon." He liked that Millie still taught piano out of the house. She was a great teacher. He should know. She took another sip of her coffee, then went to the bread box — the only one he'd ever seen — and took out two English muffins. "How about I make you eggs over medi-um?"

The offer brought back more memories. When he and his brothers started coming to the Sinclairs, Cole had asked her to teach him to cook so he could do a better job at home. Eggs were one of the first things she taught him. "That's okay. Just some peanut butter on the muffin will be fine."

"Nonsense," she said, and took the necessary food out of the refrigerator. "You will have to suffer with turkey bacon. Gotta keep Martin healthy." Martin had had a mild heart attack two years before, so Cole wasn't surprised that there were a few dietary changes. Cole had been on tour in Europe at the time and couldn't get back. Both Millie and Martin assured him there wasn't anything to do. Even their son, Ryan, who had flown in, was sent back to California after a few days. "You'll have to go to the Kinsman for the real thing."

The Kinsman Diner, run by Millie's best friend Rosie, had the best breakfast in town. He'd have to visit there soon.

"I think I can manage," Cole said. "It's good to see some things haven't changed. I saw the Triangle General Store when I drove into town. I assume the Varnum is still around." Maybe he'd go to his old haunt and get in a few rounds of pool. He didn't need to play for money, but it could be fun.

"It is. And so are Demarco's and Cobblestones," she said naming two of the other area restaurants that had been there when he was a kid. "But there are lots of new places, too. A book store, a specialty pet store, some new food and coffee places and the Seven Brothers Brewery."

He had no doubt which family that was related to. "Which of the Stewart brothers opened that?"

Millie gave him a big smile he didn't understand before saying, "Laurel."

Cole let that sink in and then laughed. "Didn't see that coming." Laurel was the youngest of the Stewart kids and the only girl.

"I don't think anyone did, but she's made quite a go of it, even winning some important awards in the last year, according to Valerie." The Stewart family was always a wonder to Cole. Eight kids — three of whom were cousins adopted when Roger Stewart's brother and wife died — all loved and supported by Roger and Valerie. His folks couldn't manage three. And as someone who was forced into the parent role when he was too young, Cole admired anyone who could do the job well.

Thinking of the Stewarts reminded him of someone he should reach out to. "Do you know if Lucas is still in the area?" Lucas, the second oldest, and one of the cousins, had been one of Cole's only friends outside of his bandmates. They hadn't kept in touch after high school, but it would be nice to reconnect if he was around.

"As far as I know. He's a family lawyer, based in Concord."

Family law. An interesting but not totally surprising choice. Lucas had a thing about families and taking care of children, probably because he'd been eight when he came to live with his aunt and uncle. Cole remembered Lucas getting pissed that Cole had to do so much for his own family and couldn't rely on his mother. That grumpy passion probably served him well. "I'll see if I can reach him."

As she plated the food and put it in front of him, Millie asked, "I know you're going to rest today — and you better — but do you have any other plans for what you're going to do while you're here?"

Cole took a bite, buying himself a little time before answering. For years his days had been filled with the needs of the band, and before that, the needs of his brothers. And now? He didn't really know. There were songs that needed to be written even before the next contract was signed in order to keep to the eighteen-month schedule they'd been on for the last five albums. And he should look at real estate in the area to find a place to buy so he could move back. But his first priority was clear. "I need to talk to Mia."

He did as he promised and spent all of Tuesday on the couch. He napped more than he expected and enjoyed being taken care of by Millie, who insisted on picking up his prescription and reminding him to at least take Tylenol or Advil for the discomfort he still had. His brothers both stopped by, separately this time, and he knew he was going to love being able to see them regularly. Only the next contract's tours would take him away again.

By Wednesday, Cole was ready to move forward with his other plan — find a way to mend things with Mia. He went to the hospital only to be told she wasn't working. He called Millie to see if she knew where she lived, and Millie confirmed Mia lived in the house where she grew up. Cole could have driven there with his eyes closed. He'd spent almost as much time at her place as he did the Sinclair's. Anyplace was better than his own home.

He pulled up to the two-story colonial and marveled at how little it had changed. The house was still gray with slate blue shutters. It must have been painted since he saw it last, but it looked the same to him. He knew which window was hers, could picture where the bed was in her room. He looked to the garage, which wasn't used for the car but instead had been converted into an extra room. He remembered Mia telling him that when her mom unexpectedly became pregnant with her, the house didn't have enough bedrooms for three kids, so her brother moved into the extra space, her sister moved to the bigger bedroom, and Mia got the smallest one. "I suppose I'm lucky they didn't put me in a closet," she'd said. By the time Cole met her, both of Mia's siblings had moved out. The garage had gone from bedroom to television room. They'd lost their virginity to each other there.

He didn't realize how long he'd been sitting in his car until Mia came onto the porch along with a dog who came up nearly to her waist. Today she wasn't dressed for work, and he wasn't fighting to stay conscious so he could take in how lovely she was, although she appeared to be glaring at him. She wore black leggings topped with a loose gray sweater with black front pockets that looked as though it would be soft to the touch. Her wavy brown hair was loose around her shoulders, and he was surprised to see she was wearing lipstick. That didn't seem right.

He got out of the car and walked to the house. As he got closer, she said, "You look much better than when I saw you last."

"That wouldn't take much," he pointed out.

"True." She stood there, arms crossed in front of her, her eyes wary. He had his work cut out for him. "What are you doing here?"

Yikes, not even a hello. That wasn't a good sign. Maybe he should have stopped and bought her flowers. The type didn't matter — yellow was her favorite. He walked toward the porch and the dog came down to greet him. For a second Cole worried he was going to get growled at, but instead, the dog sniffed then licked his hand. Cole took that as an invitation and squatted down to offer scratches between the ears and under the jaw. When he stood, the dog returned to Mia's side. At least someone was okay with him being here. "I came to thank you for your help recently. Not only at the hospital the other day, but I heard you were the one to tell my family about my injuries after the accident. That couldn't have been easy."

She shrugged. "I wish I could say it was the first time I had to deliver difficult news, but it's a regular part of my job in the Emergency Room." She put her hands in the pockets of her sweater before continuing. "I was surprised when Paxton called. Never expected to speak to her, but she said you'd asked for me."

"I must have, but that night is a blur. I went to bed and the next thing I knew there were bright lights, a lot of noise, and I can't breathe. I was told I was in and out of consciousness before surgery, but I don't really remember." Since the accident, he'd had a few nightmares where he wasn't able to breathe.

They were awful. "Every time I think about what happened, it's as if more and more of the memory is gone."

"Trauma will do that. It's your brain trying to protect you." He appreciated the compassion in her voice, but it was gone when she continued. "You didn't answer my question. Why are you here?"

Because I still love you. Because my life almost ended, and I thought I'd never see you again. Because I want you back. That was probably too much to hit her with. Better to ease into things. "I've had a lot of time to think since the accident. Hell, I'd done a fair amount of thinking before the accident. Theo and Nick are living here now, and I've missed being near my family. I'm going to sell my place in Colorado and move back here. I know I promised I'd stay away, but that was a lifetime ago, and things have changed."

"More than you know," she said under her breath. She turned and went into the house. Since she didn't dismiss him, he followed.

Stepping into the house he saw there had, in fact, been changes. In the living room, the faux wood paneling was gone — the walls were painted a light sky blue — and the sectional was new, as was the flat screen television. The feel of the room was the same. A coffee table stacked with books and magazines. More books filled shelves along the wall, with scattered framed pictures covering the spines. He found Mia in the kitchen making a fresh pot of coffee. When it was running, she faced him and said, "I understand why you want to move back. I was young and hurting when I asked you to make that promise, so I'm not going to hold you to it." she said. "I appreciate that you stayed away as long as you did, but this really isn't a good time to discuss what this might mean. Someone is arriving in a few minutes. In fact, when I saw your car sitting in the driveway, that's who I thought it was."

"Is that who you put on lipstick for?"

Mia pressed her lips together. "It's not what you think."

Before she could say anything, an unfamiliar teenager came into the room, all long arms and legs, the hair in his eyes streaked with blue. Amazing what was acceptable at schools these days. "Need food," the boy said and went to the refrigerator, not noticing anyone else. He took out orange juice and poured a glass before opening a cabinet and pulling out a bag of pretzels. Clearly this was his home. Had Mia's brother or sister gotten married and had kids? Was this a nephew? "Is it okay if I head over to Logan's house? He's got a new game for his Xbox. And before you ask, yes, my homework is done."

"Sure. Text me if you're not coming home until after dinner."

"No problem." He turned to go and finally noticed Cole. "Hey, aren't you..."

"Dean, this is Cole Hanson, an old friend," Mia said before the boy could finish his sentence. Cole didn't like being called an 'old friend.' It was an upgrade from being her patient, but not by much. Of course, there probably wasn't a good way to describe who he was to a kid. And he hadn't been anything to Mia for a long time, so she could have called him worse.

Something about the boy was familiar, but Cole couldn't place it. Instead of standing there wondering, he held out a hand and said, "Nice to meet you."

"Yeah, I thought I recognized you. Mia told me about the history the two of you have," Dean said, shaking Cole's hand. Interesting that she'd told him. What else did he know? "I'm Dean, Mia's son."

Chapter Eight

♥

Well, that was one way for Cole to find out about her unusual living situation. Mia managed not to laugh at the look on Cole's face when Dean made his announcement, but it wasn't easy.

Once Dean left the house, Cole choked out, "You have a son?" Worrying about the visit from the lawyer and then Cole's appearance made her forget Dean was home after having only a half day at school.

She could see Cole doing the math and trying to figure out when she'd given birth. She let him stew for a few more seconds before she said, "Not biologically, but in every other way." He visibly relaxed, and she almost laughed. As if she'd keep information like that from him. "You remember my friend Ashley Stevens?"

"I do," he said. She saw the moment he remembered the details. "She got pregnant in your senior year and moved in with you."

Mia nodded. "Because her parents kicked her out. She moved to Florida after graduation, before Dean was born. She never did like our winters. Unfortunately, she was diagnosed with an aggressive case of breast cancer and died a little over a year ago. I was named Dean's guardian."

"Did you know that's what she had planned?"

"I did. I was his godmother." Of course, until the end, she believed Ashley was going to beat cancer, so becoming a parent still came as a surprise. So did how much she loved it.

"I'm sorry to hear she died. I remember how close you were. She came to a concert we did in Florida, right?"

Mia nodded. She almost hated that Cole remembered and definitely hated that his remembering touched her. She would have thought that not seeing him for so long would have given her some kind of immunity against him, but apparently that wasn't the case. Seeing him on the stretcher two days ago had been hard, but having him standing near her was harder. He wore a black turtleneck with his jeans, and it made his chest look huge, his eyes bluer. Her gaze kept going to the top of the tattoo visible from the opening of his shirt. She could imagine where the wings were, how they curved over his pecs.

No, she should not be picturing him without a shirt.

She tried to move away from him, give herself the benefit of distance, but the kitchen wasn't very big and there was nowhere to go without going into another room. The space had never seemed small to her, but at 6'1"— seven inches taller than her — his presence made it so. She'd always liked their height difference. When they met, his size made him seem like a protector, someone she could trust and rely on. Of course, that hadn't been the case in the end.

"And how old is he?"

"He turned fifteen at the beginning of July. He's a freshman." How he managed not to lose a year of school given the pain of losing his mother, she'd never know.

"Same age Theo was when our mom died. He's lucky he has you." As Cole had been lucky to have the Sinclairs. Mia had met him less than a year before Susan Hanson died. To say that Cole had mixed feelings about her passing would be an understatement. "Guess it's a good thing you weren't still with the band."

Did he think she was right to leave the group? Back then she didn't feel as though she had a much of a choice in the matter. Her mother needed her. The group — according to management — didn't. Few people knew she regretted the loss of Cole in her life much more than not being the lead singer of a rock and roll band, even one which became as successful as Emporium. "There are tradeoffs," she said. Nothing like stating the obvious.

"I can tell you from watching Hugh, trying to be there for his wife and new baby, being a performer doesn't go well with family life. You're either there all the time or not at all. I've had a lot of time to think in the last two weeks," he said, absently running a hand across his shirt where she knew there were still stitches from where the doctor had inserted a tube to re-inflate his lung. "I've been considering this since August when Nick moved back, but after the accident and three days in the hospital with doctors telling me how lucky I was that it wasn't worse, I knew it was time to come home. I want to be near my brothers, the Sinclairs."

For a second, she thought he was going to say "you," but that was some residual vestige of her younger self wishing for what was, what could never be again. Still, if there was anything she understood, it was commitment to family. She wouldn't keep him from the people he loved, even if she wasn't one of them anymore. It wouldn't be easy knowing he was around, but if this was where he wanted to be, she would manage.

She always did.

She put a hand on his shoulder. "Theo and Nick will be thrilled to have you close. Martin and Millie, too. You can imagine how hard it was for all of them when they heard you were hurt."

He took her hand, and the warmth of the contact surprised her. She wanted to ignore the shiver that passed through her. No, she *needed* to ignore it. Especially if he was staying. "I really appreciate that you were the one to tell them. As awful as it was, I'm sure the way you handled it made it easier."

She'd been told that by others. It may have been one of the hardest parts of her job but being able to tell people difficult things in a way they could hear them was one of her gifts. She frequently trained other nurses on it. "I'm glad I could help."

Standing there in her kitchen, her hand still in his, Mia was suddenly all too aware that they were alone in the house, the same house she'd grown up in, and where, when they were in high school, they'd spent hours together, ostensibly studying but more often wrapped up in each other. They'd lost their virginity a few feet away from where they stood. She learned about sex with him, from him. Love as well. And loss.

Memories and desires long packed away threatened to open. Fortunately, an alarm on her phone reminded her that she had no time for the past. She took her hand back and stepped away from him. "Since you're going to be here for a while, we can talk about this another time. For now, I need you to go."

"I knew there was a reason for the lipstick." She thought she heard something in his tone which was confirmed when he said, "Someone you're dating?"

"I have a fifteen-year-old living with me, a father at the senior center who expects to see me regularly, and a job where I work three to four twelve-hour shifts a week. When am I supposed to date?" Was that a smirk she saw? Most people would have missed it, but she knew Cole's expressions too well. She had been seeing someone casually, but she'd ended things shortly after Dean moved in. She was pretty certain the guy was relieved. "It's the lawyer who's representing me and Dean in a custody case."

"Why is there a custody case? You said you're his legal guardian."

This didn't involve him. And Mia did not have time for this discussion. She quickly explained the situation and was about to ask him to leave when the doorbell rang, and Bowie gave a deep bark and ran to the front. Great. "Glad you're feeling better. Use the side door." She pointed to the kitchen door, so he'd know which way she wanted him to go and left the room. She went to the front, smoothed her hair before opening the door, then plastered a smile on her face that she hoped looked more composed than she felt. "Hi, Lucas," she said as she opened the door. "Long time, no see."

Although he was a year older than her, Mia knew Lucas when they were in high school through his friendship with Cole. She hadn't seen him since he graduated, but she'd heard about him going into family law from Laurel. As soon as she'd learned about the custody case, she'd gone to the brewery and gotten his contact information from her.

Mia was glad he was willing to drive up from Concord to have this meeting in person. "Good to see you, Mia," he said as she welcomed him inside. He was a little shorter than Cole and everything about him was professional, from his short haircut to his dark blue suit. He had piercing dark eyes which she imagined intimidated those who weren't on his side. She found them a little intimidating herself.

"I can't tell you how anxious I've been," she said as they walked to the living room.

"Most people in your position are. It's perfectly normal, but I'm going to help you through it. No one expects or plans for this. This is unfamiliar territory for all my clients."

"That it is, but I'm hoping you have some good news for me."

Lucas tipped his head from side to side, and Mia's stomach dropped. "I wouldn't jump right to good, but there are things we can..." Lucas' voice trailed off, and she followed his gaze to find Cole standing in the doorframe of the kitchen. Why hadn't he left? "Cole? What the actual fuck are you doing here?"

Mia wanted to say "leaving" but the two men were already hugging. They walked to the living room talking like they'd seen each other only yesterday, not over fifteen years ago. Mia went to the kitchen, placed the coffee pot and mugs on a tray. She considered only putting two mugs there, hoping Cole would finally get the hint, but decided not to be that petty. She added the cookies she'd picked up from the Just Right Café. As she put the tray on the coffee table, Lucas said, "I heard about the accident. That sounded awful."

"Can't say I recommend getting run off the road," Cole said. Mia heard the pain in his voice and couldn't help but wonder about the emotional trauma of the accident. She only cared for patients for a few hours before they moved on to other care or were discharged, but she understood experiences like Cole's required more healing than what was needed for the body.

"I'll take it off my to do list," Lucas said jokingly.

Before the two of them could get into another conversation, Mia decided it was time to turn the focus to the reason Lucas was here in the first place. "So, tell me what I need to do to keep custody of Dean."

Lucas put his briefcase next to the coffee table and helped himself to coffee. As Mia watched, Cole reached for the sugar as she knew he would. She didn't know what she hated more—that he was still here or that she remembered how he took his coffee. Lucas took the loveseat, which left Mia on the couch. Unfortunately, that gave Cole room to sit next to her. He was too close. The truth was, having him in the same state was too close, but there was nothing she could do about that.

Before the two men started talking again, Mia opened a folder and laid out her papers. "I've got all the information you asked for. Financial information going back several years, recommendations from staff at the hospital, and I have some personal ones coming as well." Casey was sending one over later today. "Ashley's wishes have to count for something. She wanted her son with me. She had no contact with her sister. Heather didn't even know Ashley had died until recently." Mia still wasn't sure how that happened, but it didn't matter.

"And that's the biggest thing we have going for our case. Also, Dean has been here for over a year and other than the rocky moments you mentioned at the beginning, he's been doing well." Mia had told Lucas about the fights and low grades Dean had in his first semester. It was to be expected, but she didn't want it to cause a problem. "It's on Heather to prove at the first hearing that a change in custody is warranted. If the judge thinks there is, then we move on to the next step, which is a plenary hearing. From what you told me, Dean's happy and settled. Those things will count with the judge."

"I'm hearing a 'but.'"

Lucas nodded. "There always are. Let me give you the bottom line. On paper, Heather appears to have a more traditional home. She's married with two kids of her own, so Dean would grow up with his younger cousins. She doesn't work outside the house, so she doesn't have the unusual schedule you have. Dean wouldn't be alone some days."

Mia couldn't stop the snort. "He's fifteen, not five. And now that he joined the school newspaper, he's not home for long before I'm here."

"I know, and frankly I agree, but right or wrong, depending on the judge we get, this could be seen as a point in her favor. She's also noted that her in-laws also live close to give added support."

"I have plenty of support here," Mia said automatically, but without a lot of conviction. It reminded her of Casey's comment about her never asking for help. There was one day when she got caught in a trauma at work and asked Casey to stop by to make sure Dean was okay. Ta-da, an occasion of her asking. Her heart fell into her stomach. It probably wasn't enough. "I don't understand why she wants custody. She was Dean's age when Ashley got pregnant and was kicked out. I doubt she ever saw her sister again. Heather and her family are total strangers to Dean. He didn't even know he had an aunt before this. That's how little Ashley thought of her family. At least he knew who I was." Mia didn't realize how loud her voice had gotten until she stopped talking and the silence felt huge. She also didn't realize how much her hands were shaking until Cole put his over hers and gave a gentle squeeze.

"Which is part of the reason I have a list of weekends when Heather would like to come up and take Dean for a visit." Lucas handed Mia a paper with a list of dates between now and the end of the year. The presumptuous bitch had even listed the weekend after Christmas. "She'd pick him up here on Friday night and then you'd go get him from her house on Sunday night."

"Do I have a choice?" Stupid question. When did she ever?

"You can refuse, but it wouldn't look good. Even if you retain custody, there's a chance Heather will remain part of Dean's life. And he may want to get to know her and his cousins as well." Especially after he saw where they lived, Mia worried. She didn't know much about Andover, but when she looked it up after learning about Heather, she'd discovered it was one of the more affluent towns in Massachusetts.

"Let me see if I understand the situation," Cole said, breaking into her thoughts. "Because Mia's single and works long shifts, she could lose custody of Dean?" Mia cringed. Hearing the situation put so bluntly was hard. "Is there anything she could do to strengthen her case?"

"Not that I can see. I assume that changing jobs to something with more traditional hours isn't an option, and it would also impact your job security."

"And my salary."

Lucas nodded. "Exactly, and that wouldn't help. So, unless you have a ready-made family like Heather does, we're going to go with what we have and hope for the best. If I thought it would help, I'd lend you mine. You were Ashley's choice, and that counts for a lot. I'm sure you're Dean's choice as well."

Mia hoped that was true and would continue to be after he saw how his rich relatives lived. They'd probably want to take him to Disney or something.

"What if she had a husband? Would that strengthen her case?" Mia turned to squint at Cole. Why would he ask that?

"It might, although it shouldn't." Lucas laughed and looked at Mia. "Do you have one hiding in a closet? I'm pretty certain you can't get one from Amazon, but who knows. Maybe you can."

Mia appreciated Lucas' lighthearted response, but something about Cole's question had her staring at him. And worrying. His fingers threaded through hers before he kissed the top of her knuckles. The zing was neither appreciated nor desired. "Then you're in luck. Mia and I recently got engaged."

Chapter Nine

Now he'd done it. He couldn't believe what he'd said, but once he did, there was no taking it back. If he'd announced he was pregnant, Mia couldn't look at him with more shock. As Cole listened to Lucas talk about the challenges Mia was facing and seeing the growing sadness in her expression, he ached to do something. It wasn't a problem money could solve, which was too bad because he had more of that than he knew what to do with. Then Lucas talked about Heather's traditional family being a point in her favor, and the idea of posing as Mia's fiancé came to him. It was perfect. He could help her while giving himself an excuse to be close to her.

And maybe it would give him the time he needed to work his way back into her heart.

First, though, they had to get through the rest of this meeting. Then he was going to have to convince Mia this was a good idea. Because at the moment, she was staring at him as though he'd grown another head, but Lucas hadn't noticed. "This is a huge surprise—and potentially a huge help. Why didn't you mention it sooner, Mia?"

She looked at him and then back at Lucas. "I... we...."

Because she didn't know. Yeah, she couldn't say that. Since Mia was still speechless, Cole said, "We weren't planning to make it public for a while. The loner rocker is part of my brand." He hated lying to his old friend, and if Lucas found out this was a ruse, the chance of being friends in the future was going to end fast. But there was no going back now. "You know Mia and I were a thing when we were younger. Well, I reached out to her not long ago and one thing led to another and things between us rekindled."

"Sounds like what happened to your brothers."

Cole was happy to jump on that assumption. "Exactly. There's nothing like a brush with death to make you realize what's important to you, so as soon as I could, I asked Mia if she'd be willing to spend the rest of her life with me." It wasn't all a lie. More a... braiding of the truth with some things he hoped would be true thrown in. "That's one reason I came out east. Had to make it official in person. And since she said yes, I'll be moving back in the next few months."

There was a pause as Lucas took in this new information, and for a second, Cole was certain he didn't believe him. If this gave Mia what she wanted, it would be worth it. Just when Cole thought Lucas was going to tell him he was full of shit, Lucas' face broke into a smile. "Best news I've had all day. This is better than any recommendation you could get."

Mia continued to stare at Cole, not saying a word. He hoped Lucas would think she was looking at him with love as opposed to the ice he saw. Yeah, he'd really done it this time. Finally, she turned back to

Lucas and said, "It's still pretty new." That was an understatement. "We're being very selective about who we tell."

Good, she was going along with the idea. She might be ready to kill him, but if she was agreeing, it meant she also saw the potential this had to help her. He'd been counting on that. "You understand, the label wants me — us — to keep this quiet. When the press learns about it, they're going to have a field day."

"Absolutely. I'm glad you told me, but I understand why you wouldn't want this coming out. I won't tell anyone who you're engaged to," he told Mia. "We'll consider it part of attorney-client privilege."

Cole forced a laugh. "Thank you for understanding."

"Not a problem. Make sure you update your social worker, Mia. You can tell her you're engaged without telling her who it is, although she may want to schedule a meeting with both of you at some point to see how Dean is getting along with Cole. Hopefully she can keep a secret, too."

If he needed to meet the social worker, they were going to have to tell Dean. Crap. He had a terrible feeling this would not be the easy fix he'd hoped for. Didn't matter. He'd make it work.

After that, there wasn't much more to say. Lucas collected his things and left, promising to be in touch about the next steps and to let Mia know when he heard about a date for Dean to see Heather. Before leaving, he turned to Cole. "Let's find some time to get together, maybe play a little pool at the Varnum."

"Have you gotten any better?" Cole had always been able to beat him.

"Not as far as I know. Definitely won't be putting money on our game." Lucas gave Cole his cell phone number, and Cole found himself looking forward to the possibility of connecting more with his old friend. Although music and work had taken up a lot of Cole's time in his senior year of high school, and Lucas was more focused on getting good grades for college, they'd managed to have fun together.

The moment Lucas' car was out of the driveway, Mia rounded on Cole. "What. Were. You. Thinking?"

For a moment, Cole wondered if this was the voice she used when Dean did something wrong. If she did, it was probably very effective. "I thought — I hoped — I was helping."

"Helping? How could this be helping? Do you realize what you've done?"

"I've strengthened your case."

"You lied to my lawyer. To your friend." She looked as though she wanted to stomp her foot.

"Fine, yes, I did. But did you see Lucas' expression? He was thrilled. For the first time since he started talking about this custody dispute, he sounded hopeful. This could be what you need to guarantee Dean stays with you. Isn't that worth us acting as though we're a couple?" It wasn't going to be acting for him, but she didn't need to know that yet.

Mia sputtered and started her response three times before finally saying, "I'm not sure."

Ouch. "You didn't have to go along with it. You could have told him it wasn't the truth."

"In case you didn't notice, I was too shocked to say much of anything." She sat down heavily on the couch and ran her hands through her hair. "Holy hell, Cole. What are we supposed to do now?"

It was a good question, and he didn't have an answer. He'd seen an opportunity to support her — the first time he'd had that in forever — and he'd gone for it. His past decisions had taken so much from her. He wanted to give. Not to mention the fact that he wanted to be a part of her life again. Of course, he expected to ease her into that idea with an occasional date and some traditional romance. Sending flowers to her work was very different from pretending to be her fiancé. He sat down next to her. "Do we have to do anything? Lucas isn't going to tell anyone. If it turns out a meeting with the social worker is necessary, then we'll tell Dean."

"What a great example I'm setting for my child. 'Honey, the courts are biased so we're going to lie to them. Please don't tell.' And what's going to happen when I have to go to court? Are you going to sit by my side through that?"

He hated she had to ask. Sure, he hadn't thought any of this out before making the announcement, but that didn't mean he'd leave her in the lurch when she needed him. And he didn't have much of a plan beyond coming back here and seeing her again, but now that he'd jumped in with both feet, he was going to make this work. "I'll be there with you. After you win—"

"If I win," she said, the sadness and fear back in her voice.

"*When* you win and everything is legal and safe, you can tell anyone you want that you ended things between us." His stomach clenched. He hadn't even started to do what it might take to win her back, but the thought of not succeeding was already painful. Could this brilliant idea backfire? He didn't know how long it took before they heard custody cases, but he had every intention of making their relationship, if not their engagement, real by the time it was necessary to go to court. If he had his way, they were never splitting up again.

She didn't say anything as she put the papers back in the file. At least she was considering his... proposal. When she ran out of things to fuss with, she paced, walking around the room, running her hands through her hair. He hated the waiting, wondering if she was going to agree to this, but he wasn't going to push her.

When she finally stopped moving, she gave him a nod. "Fine. As ridiculous as this is, you're right. I want Dean to stay with me. I told my friend, Casey, I'd do whatever it took to make that happen, and if agreeing to this charade helps, then that's what we'll do. It's temporary." She gave a short laugh. "Guess that's not new for me."

"What's that supposed to mean?" She knew why he made the decision he did back then, didn't she? He distinctly remembered her saying she understood. It had nothing to do with his feelings for her and everything to do with being able to take care of his brothers, who were still young and needed him to do whatever he could to support them, at least financially.

"I was *temporarily* your lead singer and now I'll *temporarily* be your fiancé." The resignation in her voice and body language was painful to witness. She wouldn't even look at him. "At least this time I know there isn't someone waiting in the wings to replace me. There isn't, right? You don't have a secret girlfriend who is going to come charging into town demanding you come back. Because if there is, we need to end this before it makes things worse."

She thought he'd replaced her. He walked over to her and put a hand on her waist. "My little bird, there's no one else. There's never been anyone else."

When her gaze met his, the years slipped away, leaving nothing but the yearning he'd always had for her. He leaned forward slowly to give her a chance to register what he was about to do and step away if it wasn't something she wanted. When her eyes dropped to his lips, he closed what little distance remained and, for the first time in over a decade, he put his hand on her cheek and kissed the woman he'd never stopped loving.

Chapter Ten

♥

S he was kissing Cole.

Cole was kissing her.

Mia's brain couldn't process anything much beyond that once his lips met hers. As soon as he touched her cheek, she knew where it would lead. She was almost sorry he'd given her a moment to think, to move away, because she couldn't say that he surprised her or that she didn't have a choice.

She did. And she chose to let him kiss her.

The feel of his mouth on hers was so familiar, it was as if they'd only kissed yesterday, not a lifetime ago. She would have sworn even the scruff of his beard was the same as it had been when he'd kissed her before letting her walk to her gate at the airport. Her heart fluttered as she relearned the touch of his lips and the scent of his skin. The same, but different. As his lips passed over hers, she knew something she didn't know all those years ago — no one's kisses made her feel like his did. And now that he kissed her again, none of those others mattered.

Before she could stop herself, she raised up on her tiptoes to get closer, putting her hands against his chest then sliding them up to clasp around his neck. She felt the bump of the stitches through the material. If it bothered him, it didn't stop him because he responded by wrapping his arms around her and pulling her closer. She stroked his mouth with her tongue, and he responded instantly, as though he were waiting for her to let him know she wanted more. His tongue teased hers and when she responded, he gave a low moan that had her tingling from head to toe.

Part of her wanted to wrap around his body, hold him so tightly he would never think of leaving her again. As he trailed a hand down her back, she kept hers locked behind his head, knowing that if she moved, she'd only be tempted to touch him more, to find the edge of his shirt and lift it so she could feel his skin. He tasted like every dream she'd lost. Damn him.

Before hope for those dreams could well up in her, she found a drop of sanity and grabbed on to it. She pushed against his chest and ended the kiss but remained in his arms. "I don't think that was such a good idea."

"You don't seem to like any of my ideas today," he said and put on a pretend pout. It looked ridiculous on him. And she wanted to kiss it away. Oh, this was *not* good.

"I also don't seem to be arguing with any of them, but in case you haven't noticed, things in my life are complicated." Anger warred with a combination of confusion and desire. It was emotionally exhausting. She pinched the bridge of her nose. "Sorry, it's been hard for me to think clearly."

"And I've made that worse."

"Possibly," she said, tipping her head to the side and looking at the man she'd once known so well. "But that wasn't your intention."

"Thanks for giving me the benefit of the doubt. I know I only saw you with Dean for a minute, but your face lit up and your voice changed when he walked into the room. It was easy to see how much he means to you."

She walked over to a picture on the bookshelf of Ashley holding baby Dean. Mia had taken it. She'd been with her friend every minute of the delivery. "He's the best thing in my life. When he was born, Ashley asked me to be his guardian. I never thought it would be necessary, and I have to admit I've spent most of the time since he came to live with me worried about whether or not I'm doing enough or whether Ashley made the right choice. But when my custody was questioned, something snapped. As soon as I got the certified letter from Heather's lawyer, I knew I would do whatever was necessary to keep him. Even taking the equity loan on the house was worth it."

"Why did you need a loan?" He figured it out before she could answer. "For Lucas."

"He's not cheap, but from what I hear, he's worth it. Nursing pays well, but there are always extra expenses. The roof needed repairs. The hot water heater needed replacing. All the things Dean needs. Hearing aids for my dad which aren't covered by insurance, and I swear cars always seem to know when it's the worst time is for something to go wrong. It adds up." She didn't care. Every penny used to make Dean happy and feel settled was worth it. She'd spend it all again and more. She'd tap into her 401k if necessary.

"Do you need help? Is there something I can do?"

She wasn't surprised he offered. Cole always looked for what needed to be fixed and how he could fix it. It was the same reason he'd jumped in and said he was her fiancé. God, she still couldn't believe he'd done that. She put the picture back and said, "I think you've done enough, don't you?" They stood there in the awkward silence. Part of her wished he'd kiss her again, but there was no need to complicate an already complicated situation. Even if the engagement was fake, the offer to help was sincere, and she appreciated it. "Do you... want to join us for dinner? I usually make enough, so there are leftovers, which means there's plenty if you want to stay."

He put his hands in the back pockets of his jeans, which made his chest stand out more. She needed to not notice these things. "Thanks. As much as I'd like to spend more time with you and get to know Dean, maybe we should wait. You've been hit with a lot today."

That was putting it mildly. "What are we going to do about our arrangement?"

"For now, nothing. Lucas will let you know if anything changes. Maybe Heather will drop her suit when she hears the news."

"I hope so. I'll let you know if I hear anything."

He rubbed the back of his neck and looked as though he wasn't certain about what he was about to say. Considering they were "engaged," that almost seemed funny. "If you want to reach me, you could call the Sinclairs, and my cell phone number hasn't changed."

"In twelve years?"

"I made sure they gave me my old number when I got my new phone after the crash," he said with a shrug. She'd taken his name out of her phone the day she heard Paxton singing one of his songs on the radio and never imagined it could be the same. It was a small thing, but as they exchanged numbers — hers had changed — she felt another thread connect them.

After that was done, he went to the coat rack and put on his jacket. She joined him at the door and for a second, he stared at her mouth, and she thought he'd kiss her goodbye. Instead, he gave her a quick hug before heading to his car. She was still watching when he waved and drove off.

She went back inside, sat down on the couch, and stared at nothing as her thoughts swirled. The worst part of agreeing to let Cole pretend to be her fiancé was knowing he was right. It *was* a good idea. Mia didn't know what made him think of it, but it was clear from Lucas' response, this could be the thing that made sure she got to keep custody of Dean.

She also hated herself for hating that it was a sham. When Cole said to Lucas, "we're engaged," part of her heart gave a leap. She could almost feel her twenty-year-old self squealing and saying yes. Old images of the life she wanted with Cole came flooding back, as if his words were the key to unlocking memories she hadn't let herself look at since the day they released her from her contract.

There was a time when there was no one she was closer to than Cole. Yes, Ashley was her best friend, but Cole shared both her love of music and singing, as well as her commitment to family. For the year she was with Emporium after they signed their first contract, she watched as Cole sent every penny he could to his brothers. Even though the Sinclairs had accepted guardianship of Theo and Nick, Cole felt responsible, as he always had, for taking care of them. Their security was everything to him. As much as she'd wanted him to tell the label he would leave if she couldn't return, she knew why he hadn't.

It was the same reason she couldn't have refused her mother's request to return home. Responsibilities came first. But until that point, she and Cole had made their commitments work together. That had been the first time it took them in separate directions. To separate lives.

Which had crashed together again.

Maybe crashed was a bad choice of words.

She'd known she would see him sooner rather than later. At the end of the summer, when she heard Nick was living in Fable Notch again, she suspected it was only a matter of time before Cole moved to be near his brothers. She'd already decided that if he did, she would find a way to stay away from him. So much for that. Their fake engagement meant he was a part of her life again, part of what was important to her, even if it was in name only and temporary.

Cole was right. Their pretend engagement could end this custody process before it got to court. Did this mean she was accepting his help? It was a weird thought. She was the one who did things for others, often noticing what they needed before they had to ask. She was strong, self-sufficient, good in a crisis. These were the words she'd used to define herself. But had Casey been right? Was she afraid of needing help?

She collected the mugs, put them back on the tray, and returned to the kitchen. As she put things into the dishwasher, Mia considered all that had happened in the last few hours. She couldn't stop her thoughts from returning to her kiss with Cole, to what it felt like to be in his arms.

There's no one else. There's never been anyone else. Could that really be true? Alone with her thoughts, she could admit she wanted it to be true. She hadn't been able to avoid every image of or article on him over the years, so she'd seen women with him at awards shows or events. For a while she thought there was something going on between him and Paxton, but she believed it when the press said they were only friends.

His kiss was definitely not one you give a friend. And after an afternoon of roller coaster-like dips and spins, he'd felt warm and strong. He'd always been so strong. For his family, for the band.

And that was when the realization hit her: *He did this for me.*

She bobbled the cup, almost dropping it onto the tile floor.

She wanted to ignore the thought, but she could feel it was true. It wasn't like there was any benefit to Cole for announcing they were engaged. How did he know so damn quickly how much Dean mattered to her, that this custody was everything to her? She hadn't said anything to Lucas that would have let Cole understand how committed she was to keeping Dean and making sure he knew he was wanted. But because Cole knew her, he'd known.

She closed the dishwasher, went to the living room, and flopped onto the couch. Bowie thought this looked like a good idea, so he sat next to her and put his head on her lap. She gave the dog the attention he wanted as she sat there watching the room grow dim in the rapidly setting sun.

Too bad she couldn't triage her thoughts and feelings the way they did patients in the ER. There, it was clear which situation was dire and important. You dealt with it first and let the others wait. But feelings couldn't be managed like that. Instead, they were jumbled together into one big mess, and there was no easy way to pull them apart and handle them.

She was still sitting there, staring at nothing, when Dean got home from his friend's house and asked how the meeting with the lawyer went. Mia considered telling him about what Cole had said and her decision to go along with it. But until she could wrap her head around how she felt and what this might change, she decided to skip it and instead said, "Fine. Lucas knows what he's doing, which is a good thing since I'm clueless." She gave a mirthless chuckle. She hated not knowing what to do. "There's a lot to do between now and whenever we go to court, but I'll sort it out. Also, your aunt wants to meet you and have you spend a weekend with her and her family."

"Why? Because I might have to live with her?"

Mia heard the concern in his voice and wished she had some magic words to make it go away. Instead, she got up and gave him a quick hug. "Not if I have anything to say about it. I'm going to do everything I can to make sure you stay with me." Including pretending to be engaged to a man who's kisses still made her jittery. Nope, she wasn't going to think about that now. "But no matter where you live, she's still your family. She'd like to get to know you."

Dean shrugged. The typical teenage reaction eased her heart. "Okay. It's not like I have any big plans coming up."

Wanting to get this done sooner rather than later, she looked at the list of suggested dates that Lucas had left with her. "How about a week from Friday? That way, you won't give up your Thanksgiving weekend, and it won't interfere with your end of the semester studying."

"Sure, why not. What time's dinner?"

She liked that he moved off the topic so quickly. "Tacos will be ready within the hour. Start your homework, and I'll let you know when it's ready." He called for Bowie, and the two of them went upstairs. Mia knew she shouldn't be happy that he didn't have much of an interest in meeting his aunt, but she couldn't help it. She'd told Cole that being temporary wasn't new to her, but she couldn't bear the thought that she would only temporarily be Dean's mother. Listening to the music coming from his room, she whispered to herself, "This had better work, Cole." Because this time she would not be replaced.

Chapter Eleven

♥

He probably shouldn't have kissed her. He probably shouldn't have said they were engaged. Hell, there was a lot of "probably shouldn't haves" when it came to Mia, top on the list being he shouldn't have let her go, but there was no going back. He needed to make the best of it.

Kissing her had been amazing. Memories exploded in his head the moment their lips met. Their first kiss — tentative and shy as they walked home from school a few weeks after meeting. Their last as he put her on the plane to go to New Hampshire, her face wet with tears, his own heart already aching, not knowing how long they would be separated. But the memories weren't close to the wonder of having her near once more. The feel of her lips against his had been so familiar, and all he'd wanted was more. He wished he knew what she was thinking. There was a time he would have. Would she let him close enough for him to know again?

He'd gone to her house to thank her and take the first steps to rebuild their connection. Once he knew she wasn't seeing anyone, he expected it to be a slow and careful process to get her to trust and accept him again. But instead of a step, he'd ended up taking a giant leap. Right into the middle of her biggest challenge.

And she'd agreed.

That stunned him almost as much as his own actions. Once the initial shock had worn off, she could have told him and his idea to go to hell, but she'd agreed to play along and let him help. He was going to take this as a sign that he might be able to win her back. And although they agreed there was no need to tell anyone their lie, he thought he should at least see his brothers, tell them his plans and what was going on. There was only one place to do that.

In the morning, he sent a group text to Theo and Nick. *Breakfast at the Kinsman?*

He hoped it wasn't too early — he still wasn't sleeping late — and was grateful to receive answers from them both. A few more texts and they agreed to meet at 8:30. He got dressed, had a quick cup of coffee with Millie, and headed out.

Driving around Fable Notch brought back memories both bitter and sweet for Cole. None of the Hanson brothers had an easy time when they were younger. All of them had mixed feelings about the place and had left as soon as they could. Funny that this was where they'd all ended up.

He noticed that the town still had its fair share of businesses with clever names, from the Just Right Café with its logo of a bear holding a mug of coffee to the Bright Spot ice cream store. As a George R. R. Martin fan, he appreciated the name of the Thousand Lives Bookstore, and he was glad that Prince's Jewelers was still there. It hadn't been a shop he'd ever needed, but it made him happy that some places could stand the test of time.

The Kinsman Diner was one of those places. He pulled into the parking lot, taking the last spot in front of the building. The diner always had at least a small crowd. He stepped into the refurbished train car, saw the aqua, black, and white decor, and breathed in the scent of bacon and pancakes from the griddle up front. His heart gave a happy sigh. Still the same.

"Took you long enough," said a familiar voice.

Cole broke into a grin at the sight of Rosie Kinsman coming toward him. Like with Martin and Millie, he noticed the passage of time in the gray hair and wrinkles that hadn't been there the last time he saw her, but her smile and sass were the same. "Had to wait until my appetite was back before coming over."

"You Hanson boys are all so smooth. Is it any wonder my niece fell for Nick?" That went both ways. Nick had fallen for Dani when they were kids and Dani spent her summers with Rosie. Cole could only hope he'd be as lucky. "You meeting either of your brothers here this morning?"

"Both of them. Guess I'm the first to arrive."

"Then pick a booth. How do you take your coffee?" she said as she filled the mug she'd placed in front of him as soon as he sat down.

"Black, lots of sugar."

She gestured with her chin. "Sugar's on the table. Menus are there, too, but there's nothing on it you haven't seen before, and your favorite is still there."

Cole wasn't surprised that the menu was the same, or that Rosie remembered what he liked. He and his brothers didn't come here often. Only when there was extra cash, like when Cole played a gig or had a particularly good night of pool. But when they did, Theo always ordered the French toast, Nick had pancakes and bacon, and Cole ordered the Special — scrambled eggs with diced ham and lots of cheese, hash browns on the side. His mouth watered at the thought. "I want extra cheese on mine."

"Absolutely," Rosie said, toasting him with the coffeepot.

He'd barely taken a sip of his coffee when Theo and Nick arrived. Hugs were exchanged, orders put in. As they waited for their food, Nick shared the newest pictures of his dog, Lola, and Cole asked, "How did she get that name?"

Nick laughed. "Dani knew how much I was missing Presley — well, Princess — since I had to give her back, so one weekend we drove down to the New Hampshire Humane Society to see if there were any dogs I connected with. The minute I saw her, she started dancing around me. Dani said, 'Are you putting on a show, girl?' and once I heard 'showgirl', I knew her name was Lola. Fortunately, the shelter had her name listed as Luna, and she's not even a year old, so it wasn't hard for her to get used to the new name. She and Otis get along great."

"I assume Otis is the giant fur ball I saw in the picture."

Nick put his phone away and said, "His size shocked the shit out of me when I first met him, but you get used to it after a while. And he's a great big brother. Just like you."

Cole appreciated the compliment, even if the comparison was to a dog. He couldn't get over how well both of his brothers were doing and how happy they were. This was everything he wanted for them when they were growing up, and everything he feared wasn't going to be possible. It made the sacrifices worth it. And it made him more confident that this was the right time to go for what he wanted. "I have something to tell you, but it's not for public knowledge."

"You're up for Record of the Year again?" Theo guessed. Cole had forgotten that the Grammy nominations were due. Being here meant the world and worries of the band seemed far away.

"Not as far as I know."

"You're adopting a dog, too?" Cole liked Nick's suggestion, but until his life didn't involve so much travel, that was out of the question.

"Not even close. Mia and I are sort of engaged." They stared at him, looking a lot like Mia did when he made the announcement.

Theo's eyebrows were still near his hairline when he said, "You went from needing her to change her mind about you living here to being engaged? Dude, you work fast. I thought I'd proposed soon because I couldn't wait six months. How did you manage that?"

"And what do you mean, sort of?" Nick asked. "Is it because you didn't have a ring? Or because you're not telling anyone yet?"

"It's complicated." Great, he was back to understatement. "Have you heard that Mia has a son?" His brothers shook their heads. "He's her friend Ashley's child." Cole explained the whole story, including the recent custody issue. "She loves that boy so much. Listening to Lucas Stewart tell her the challenges of her case and seeing her worry was too much."

"It's a little extreme, but this seemed like an ideal way to help her. After the way she was cut from Emporium ... I owe her that, but I can see how it might help," Theo said. He took a sip of his coffee and asked, "What was her reaction?"

Before or after I kissed her? Yeah, he kept that detail to himself. "A lot like yours. Silence followed by confusion, but she agrees it gives her leverage so she's going along with it."

"Guess that means she's okay with you moving back," Nick said with a smile.

"If anyone understands family, it's Mia. I don't think she was surprised when I told her." He hadn't told her the part about wanting to be a part of her life again, but the kiss may have given him away.

When their food arrived, they dug in. At the first bite, Cole gave a moan of appreciation that had both of his brothers grinning. "What?" he asked, his mouth full.

"Nothing," Theo said with a laugh. "We made the same sounds not too long ago."

After a few more bites, Nick said, "If you're staying, you need to buy a house. I was thinking you might want to look into buying the old Northcott place. You could build a studio next to it since it sits on a good-sized piece of developable land and that's hard to find around here."

That was the downside to living on the edges of the White Mountain National Forest. Cole loved that Nick was making plans for his return. It made it more real. He remembered the property Nick was talking about. It was a gorgeous Queen Anne Victorian. He and his brothers would bike there sometimes, wondering what it would be like to live in such a fancy place. Then he remembered, "Wasn't that one of the places the arsonist hit, Theo?"

"She only got the barn," Theo said, "which means there's less to do if you want to build something new. Nick's right. It's been on the market for years, so I'll bet you could get it at a great price."

It blew him away to think he could easily purchase what he'd seen as one of the most elegant homes in town when he was young. Talk about a change. "It's something to consider."

They talked more about what Cole needed to do to move as they finished up breakfast, then headed out into the cold November air. He waved to them both as Theo headed to Concord, where he managed the New England branch of the arson investigation firm he worked for, and Nick went home since his new business didn't have a separate office yet. He was proud of them and happy for them. Jobs they loved, women they loved, and who loved them in return. And their excitement about his move told him they wanted the same for him. He was a lucky man, something he kept noticing since the accident.

Unlike his brothers, unfortunately, Cole had nothing on his schedule. On his way back to the Sinclairs, he decided to kill time by going to the house, where he grew up to see the changes Nick had made. He drove there without thinking, but when he pulled up in front, he had to look around at the other houses to see if somehow he'd forgotten where they used to live. He got out of his car to make a closer inspection.

The place looked completely different, and it wasn't just the extension Nick had put on the side. Nothing sagged, no paint was peeling. The lawn looked cared for. All the shutters were up and hanging straight. Staring at the house, memories flooded back. His father's yelling and violence. His mother's drinking made worse after Russel abandoned them. How it felt to stand in the kitchen and wonder if there was anything to make for dinner. How grateful he was when the Sinclairs came into his life and took some of the worry off his shoulders. How embarrassed he was anytime Mia came over. A lifetime ago. He was glad there was almost nothing recognizable. Nothing good had ever happened there until Theo stayed a few months ago and ended up living with Eden.

Eventually, the cold had him retreating to his car, and he drove to another familiar spot. The Souvenir Emporium, which billed itself as the largest souvenir shop in the White Mountains, was within walking distance of his old home. When Cole was fourteen, Alan Harris had given him his first job. He didn't have to rely on transportation — or an adult — to get there, which meant he didn't miss work.

And, of course, the band had taken their name from the place. He, Mia, and Brian, along with their original drummer, hung around the store so often while they were in high school, Alan finally offered to move things around and let them practice in the back storage area. If Cole wasn't at Mia's or the Sinclairs', he was here. When they booked their first gig — a dance at the high school — they were asked for their name. Emporium seemed the obvious choice.

It was early enough in the day that he was the only car when he got to the place. He knew things would pick up later as tourists came off the mountain and dropped in before heading home. He sat for a minute and looked at the long building with the iconic red and white striped awning, thinking of the hours he'd spent here, doing his homework between ringing up sales and unboxing orders. The occasional meals shared with Alan and his family. Many of Cole's memories of his childhood were rough, but the good ones were really good, and he didn't mind remembering those. He finally got out of his car and headed in. The bell over the door sounded. Something else that remained.

"Be with you in a minute," came a voice from the back. "Enjoy looking around."

Cole stepped further into the store and further back in time. The first thing that greeted him were shelves of stuffed moose toys, some wearing flannel shirts, others with skis or, ridiculously, surfboards. He'd stocked those shelves more times than he could count in the years he'd worked here. The refrigerator case still held a combination of national and local brands of sodas and there was a stand with candies and snacks near the register to tempt customers to buy one more thing before they left. In the back corner, he could see a huge display with an Emporium poster he and the band had signed, along with t-shirts, copies of their CDs and other merchandise. Since when was there an Emporium key chain?

"Good morning. Can I... hey there, stranger. Long time, no see." Alan Harris, a tall man Cole always thought looked like the farmer from the movie *Babe*, greeted Cole with a smile and a hug that included a smack on the back. Cole only winced a little. "Heard through the grapevine that you were around. Also heard about the accident. Good to see you doing better."

"I had to come by the old place. Looks like nothing has changed. How's Janet?" Alan's wife managed the books and occasionally worked in the store. It was a family business. He'd been told their daughter, Samantha, who was a few years older than Cole, started working at the register when she was old enough to make change. "Is she at the house?" The Harris' lived in the Colonial next door. Made it easy for Janet to bring her husband — and Cole — dinner on nights when the store was open late.

"She's good, but not around at the moment. She's away on her 'a little more summer trek.' She'll be back next week." Cole must have looked confused, because Alan explained. "About ten years ago, she got a bad case of pneumonia and went to Florida to recuperate at her sister's house. They had such a good time, she declared from then on it would be an annual thing, so for two weeks after leaf season and before the skiers show up, she goes for a visit. Says she stores up the sun and heat and brings it back with her to tap into during the winter. I don't know if that's true, but it makes her happy and that's all that matters."

Cole enjoyed hearing that the two of them were happy. "Glad she's doing well. That you both are."

"Can't complain. Well, I suppose I could, but what good would that do? Business is good. I've got my health, my family, and my cars." Alan was an antique car aficionado and always had at least two he was tinkering with. On several nights in the summer, the parking lot hosted an antique car show that drew a crowd of locals and tourists. Emporium played some of their first gigs as background music. "What are you doing while you're staying in town?"

"At the moment, nothing. Mostly recuperating." It really was weird not to have anything planned each day. If the accident hadn't happened, he and the band would be somewhere in Texas. He'd probably still be zonked out in a hotel room after the concert the night before. "Maybe I should get a job."

"I'd offer to let you work here again, but if word got out, we'd have a swarm of press on our hands."

Cole made a face, and Alan laughed. The paparazzi were a necessary evil in his work. They were usually more interested in Paxton than anyone else in the band, but after the accident, they'd followed all of them for several days. Alan was right. If they found out he was here, they might come sniffing around. "I suppose it's better if I keep a low profile."

"Not that your fame isn't good for business. You know, we might have closed shop or sold the place years ago if it weren't for you."

Cole's gut tightened. "What do you mean?"

"Being the home of Emporium and the place that inspired the band name as well as where you had your first performances has brought in a lot of income over the years. Worth every hour I had to hear what's-his-name banging on those drums in the back," Alan said with an eye roll and a chuckle. "People come here all the time to take pictures of the place where you got your start. And once they're here, they buy. Every time you have a new album, I've got to stock more t-shirts. Makes for a healthy bottom line. We threw Samantha a gorgeous wedding a few years back. Even helped her with part of the down payment on her house. Don't get me wrong, we still sell our fair share of maple sugar candy and New Hampshire shot glasses, but you guys are a big seller. Maybe you could sign a few things while you're here?"

"You know I will." Cole was fairly certain he'd kept the smile on his face, even though every word from Alan made him ache a little more. As they continued to chat, Cole's thoughts raced. It hadn't occurred to him that there were other people who needed him to be successful. He was almost sorry to know.

When he got back to his car after autographing some merchandise for Alan, his phone rang. The caller ID said Brett. Cole considered ignoring it, but it wouldn't change anything. "Hey there," he said, answering.

"Congratulations, man! You did it."

"Did what?" Brett was obviously happy, but Cole had no recollection of what they might have done.

"Five new Grammy nominations, including Song of the Year and Album of the Year." Cole probably owed Theo a beer. He was right. "You guys are going to be bigger than ever! You can ask for the moon in your new contract."

Brett rambled on, but Cole wasn't listening. He was looking at the red and white striped awning and thinking of the man inside. Then he pictured Paxton interacting with the fans, her face glowing with joy. He imagined Hugh with his daughter and what she was going to need in the years to come. Cole reminded himself that no matter how well his brothers were doing, he had other responsibilities that he couldn't get away from, even if he moved home.

Chapter Twelve

♥

The next few days were workdays for Mia, which meant there was no chance for her to see Cole, something she was grateful for. Unfortunately, it didn't stop her from being distracted by thoughts of him. Or their kiss. On several occasions she'd find her hand at her mouth as she remembered the feeling of his lips on hers, his body pressed close. She'd even dreamed about him one night and had woken for her shift overheated and exhausted. It's not as though she had some illusion that she was completely over him. Her lack of any relationships in the years they'd been apart was proof of that, but she'd lived with the unresolved feelings for so long they were familiar, almost comforting. She didn't have to worry about risking her heart again because she'd never gotten it back after Cole.

But now he was in Fable Notch and planning to stay, and after only seeing him twice, her heart was feeling very at risk.

And even though she knew a part of her still cared about him, if someone had asked her a few weeks ago how she'd react to seeing Cole again, she would have said she could handle it. She thought the part of her that was still mad at him was strong enough to keep her emotions under control. She was wrong.

And if her thoughts weren't traitorous enough, his return meant that people were asking her about him. His visit to the ER may have been brief, but it had been the most excitement they'd seen in the hospital in a long time. Since her first shift back, she'd been fielding questions about him — why was he here, what was he like. At first, she thought she was being asked because she was the attending nurse on his case, but it soon became clear that people were talking about her past association with him. She'd noticed several occasions where conversations got quieter or stopped when she walked by. She did her best to ignore it the same way she did when the news hit that Paxton had taken her place in the band and it was clear that her relationship with Cole was over.

But it wasn't easy.

Back then, she had righteous indignation to keep her company. This time, not only had he not done anything wrong, but he was going out of his way to help her. And he wasn't leaving. She needed to find a way to get her reactions to him under control.

Casey checked in with her regularly. She'd called her friend soon after Cole left and told her about the fake engagement. After the initial shock, Casey agreed it wasn't the worst idea, especially if it helped Mia's case. Then she told Casey about the kiss. That shocked her more. "I probably shouldn't ask, but how was it?"

"Horrible," Mia said, because in some ways it was the truth.

"Really? Isn't that a good thing then? You can resist him."

"Horrible because it was wonderful."

"Ah, sorry. That makes more sense. And makes things more complicated."

"Because that's what my life needs more of right now, complications." Why couldn't he have kept his sexy lips to himself? Why did she have to give in to them?

By her next day off, Mia was ready to get away from the hospital. It was exhausting being the center of attention and speculation. She spent time over the next several days visiting with her father, working on a quilting project, and making plans to help Casey at the senior center for Thanksgiving. As a senior staff person, she'd been able to get the upcoming holiday off, but it changed the flow of the coming week. Her schedule was typically three days on, three days off, which made for a different schedule at home each week. But it was subject to change based on the hospital needs and days she wanted off. The calendar on the refrigerator kept everything clear, so Dean knew when she'd be around all day and when she wouldn't be home until dinner.

On Tuesday, her last day off, she hoped that since it had been over a week since Cole showed up, hospital gossip would have moved on to a new topic. There must be something more interesting in town to talk about than their resident rock star.

As she was putting dinner in the oven, Bowie gave a sudden bark, making her jump. "More squirrels? I thought we agreed you didn't need to bark at all of them." He'd go days without alerting her to everything outside the house, then start noticing every little movement all over again. It was usually amusing, but she was too tired to be amused. When the doorbell rang a moment later, she apologized to the dog, realizing he must have seen the person approaching. She opened the door to a stranger who immediately had Mia wishing she wasn't dressed in a baggy sweatshirt and leggings. The woman had a polished look Mia was never able to achieve, even with hours of time to get ready. Her brown hair was in a sleek bob that Mia imagined always fell properly, her pants and blouse fit perfectly, and her low-heeled shoes looked expensive. Whoever she was, she must be at the wrong house, or she was selling something, which meant she was definitely at the wrong house. "Hello. Can I help you?"

The woman stood a little taller and looked a little offended when she said, "You don't recognize me, do you?"

There was something familiar about her face, but Mia couldn't place it. "No, I'm sorry. I don't."

"I'm Heather Buckley." Ashley's sister. Dean's aunt. They had the same eyes. She was here. Why was she here? She wasn't expected until Friday afternoon when she was coming to get Dean. Mia had been dreading the weekend and was thinking of picking up extra shifts so she wouldn't have to be at home with nothing to do but think and worry while Dean was gone. She didn't realize she was staring and standing still until Heather asked, "May I come in?"

It took Mia another beat before she trusted herself to say anything. "Of course, please." She stepped back, held on to Bowie's collar, and allowed Heather to enter.

"I've never been here," Heather said, walking into the living room and looking around. Mia and Ashley had been in and out of each other's houses constantly — until Ashley moved in permanently — but there'd never been a reason for Heather to come by Mia's. "It's... cozy." If Heather was trying to hide her derision, it wasn't working. The way her head tilted back as she glanced at photos and furniture literally put her nose in the air. Mia could almost feel the distaste rolling off of her. Heather walked to the fireplace and picked up a picture on the mantle of Ashley, Mia, and Dean taken when Dean was seven. Mia loved that picture. She'd gone to Florida to visit after Christmas, and they'd posed in front of a palm tree covered in Christmas lights. "You saw my sister more recently than I did. The last time I saw her was the day she packed and left to live here."

"Because your family threw her out." Mia had been with Ashley when she told her parents the news of her pregnancy and had helped her pack when they turned their backs on her. "You could have visited her here. It's not like we lived far apart," she said. Her tone was clipped. She needed to relax and not let Heather know how upsetting her arrival was. "Why didn't you come over?"

Heather shrugged. "When you're fourteen and your parents are madder than you've ever seen them, it doesn't occur to you to do anything that might make them more upset." A reasonable explanation. Still, there had to have been some time in the years after Ashley left that Heather could have reached out to her sister and rebuilt their relationship. Of course, if she had, Ashley might not have left custody of Dean to Mia. Mia couldn't be sorry that things turned out the way they did. Heather put the picture back and turned to face Mia, who couldn't help but recognize the Michael Kors logo on Heather's bag. It didn't look like a flea market rip off.

"I'm confused," Mia said as Heather continued to look around the room as though she was expecting something to jump out and bite her. Fortunately, Bowie stayed next to Mia. "You weren't supposed to be here until Friday. I know my days blur together, but last time I checked, today's Tuesday."

"Then I'll get right to the point. I heard you're engaged and, frankly, I don't believe it."

Oh fuck. Lucas had to update Heather's lawyer on the change in Mia's status since it potentially changed her standing with the court. Mia had hoped the news would have Heather backing off. Then, after a reasonable amount of time — whatever that might be — she and Cole would "break up" and that would be the end of it. She certainly didn't expect the woman to appear on her doorstep.

Apparently, she wasn't that lucky. Hoping she sounded calmer than she felt, Mia said, "It doesn't matter if you believe it. It's true."

"Must be very recent. What did you do, convince some guy you were dating to make it official sooner rather than later?"

"Absolutely not." This was not good. Mia hadn't "convinced" Cole to do anything, but Heather couldn't find out what was actually happening or Mia would be in a worse position than before. "And I don't have to prove anything to you."

"That's where you're wrong, and I am not leaving until I have some more answers."

"Then have a seat." Mia said curtly and gestured to the couch. She didn't like feeling uncomfortable in her own home. She needed to get herself and this conversation under control. "Can I offer you some coffee or tea?" Heather agreed to coffee, and Mia left her in the living room to make two mugs, grateful for the reprieve but aware it wouldn't buy her much time. She needed help. Fast.

Pulling out her phone, and glad she had his number, she texted Cole.

Chapter Thirteen

♥

I need you to come over as quickly as possible.

The text was startling not only for the request, but because it was the first he'd gotten from Mia in over twelve years. He had a moment of joy followed by one of panic. There were other people she could reach out to if there was a problem. There had to be a reason she'd chosen him. Was everyone else busy? He responded, *OMW Is everything ok?*

Had something happened to her or Dean? He looked at his watch. Dean should be in school, but anything was possible. He was halfway to the car when his phone buzzed with her reply, *Yes. But pull into the driveway and kiss me when you get here. Will explain after.*

He didn't need an explanation. Anything that gave him an opportunity to kiss her sounded good to him. Still, it was an oddly specific request. He assumed it had something to do with their pretend engagement, but he'd wait for her to tell him. It didn't take him long to get to her house from the Sinclairs where he'd been sitting in his room playing with the lyrics to a song he'd thought of that morning. He'd been grateful for the wisp of an idea, the first he'd had in ages, and he was enjoying what was coming to him.

The first thing he noticed when he got to her house was the white Mercedes with Massachusetts plates parked out front. Could this be a reporter? Did someone track him down and decide to go to Mia for information about him? No, they usually drove junk. He parked his car next to Mia's and went in through the side door that led to the kitchen. "Hi honey, I'm home," he said in a joking voice.

"We're in here," came the response.

Cole dropped his keys on the table by the front door and went into the living room where he saw Mia sitting stiffly on the couch, Bowie at her feet, with an unfamiliar woman sitting on the loveseat where Lucas had been the other day. He didn't make snap decisions about people, having had too many made about him over the years, but he instantly didn't like the woman. He took in her expensive clothes, sleekly styled hair, and pearl earrings and necklace along with the way she sat ramrod straight, her face pinched and serious. She looked as though she didn't want to touch anything. So, this is what fastidious meant. If she recognized Cole, she gave no notice of it. When Cole looked at Mia, he saw concern in her eyes and hoped that his being here could help whatever was bothering her. As their eyes met, Mia jumped up and came over. He opened his arms, and she walked into them like it was something she did every day.

God, it felt good to have her close. He gave her a quick hug, breathing in the scent of her shampoo and when he let her go, he looked into her eyes and gave her a soft lingering kiss. He intended it to be quick and appropriate.

That wasn't how it stayed.

The moment he touched her, the moment he tasted her, he wanted more. He hadn't stopped thinking about their kiss a few days ago. No matter what else he was doing his mind would go back to her being close and how much closer he wanted her. Keeping one arm around her, he put his other hand behind her head and deepened the kiss, giving her lips a gentle flick with his tongue. She responded by opening her mouth to him, and he tightened his grip around her waist. He was aware of her breasts pressed against him and considered stopping before he made a fool of himself, then decided he would kiss Mia for as long as she'd let him.

He was a breath away from carrying her to her bedroom when the woman cleared her throat impatiently, and they broke apart. He liked her less and less. Mia kept her arm around Cole's waist. He enjoyed the feel of her leaning against him as they walked the few steps to where the stranger waited, and Mia made introductions. "Heather, this is my fiancé, Cole Hanson. Cole, this is Dean's aunt, Heather Buckley."

Oh, holy hell. Heather stood to shake his outstretched hand and then sat down again. Cole kept his arm around Mia and said, "Sorry to have gotten carried away there. I've only been back in town for a few days, so we're still making up for lost time." He gave Mia another quick kiss to emphasis his point — and to kiss her again—and they sat on the couch together. He motioned for Bowie to sit next to him and was grateful the dog took the cue. Hopefully that made his presence seem more normal. He owed the pup a treat. "What brings you to Fable Notch, Mrs. Buckley? Was this a scheduled visit?"

Before Heather could answer, Mia said, "Heather heard from her lawyer about our engagement." Now he was putting things together. Mia's lawyer must have passed along the change in Mia's status because it strengthened the case. This explained not only the text, but the request. Their lie was spreading, and the consequences were starting.

"Quite frankly, I didn't believe it." Her tone suggested she still didn't. "My lawyer pressed for more information about when this happened, since originally we were told Mia was single, and when none was offered, I decided to drive and see if it was true."

"As you can see, it is," Mia said. Cole didn't think she sounded very convincing, but hopefully Heather didn't hear it. "We've kept our relationship private because of Cole's fame and our history. We don't want people prying into our lives."

Heather looked at Cole, "I thought you lived in Colorado."

The downside to living in the public eye. Strangers knew more about him than he'd like. He was going to have to be very careful about what he said so this lie didn't trip them up. He'd never forgive himself if he put Mia's custody of Dean in jeopardy. "I have a place there, yes. But I've been thinking about moving back since my brothers returned. The bus accident changed my timetable when the tour was postponed."

"Well, this must be a recent change in your relationship. You aren't even wearing a ring."

Mia covered her left hand in an automatic gesture, as though that could fix the issue. Cole took her hand in his and gave it a squeeze. He would not let this woman get the best of Mia. Thinking quickly, he said, "Not that it's any of your concern, but the ring is at Prince's because I didn't get the size right. Even the best of plans don't come together perfectly." He hoped Mia knew all he was trying to say. This situation was his fault. He would do whatever was necessary to make it work out. "Does your husband know your ring size?"

Heather changed the subject. "So, you're saying that you two stayed in touch even after Mia was dumped from the band? I remember that was big news around here for a while."

"Circumstances changed, not our feelings," Mia said. Did she mean that? When she looked at him, he thought he saw care in her expression, but she could be putting that on for Heather's benefit.

"Things were out of our control back then." Cole put a hand on her thigh and continued, "We didn't speak for a long time, but I've never stopped caring for Mia." That was the truth. It wasn't the way he intended to tell her, and given the context, she might not realize what he was saying, but he'd worry about that later. "Her leaving the band had nothing to do with our feelings for each other. She had no say in what the record label decided after she left to take care of her mother when she got ill. Family is important to both of us."

"Yes, well, family is important to me, too. And Dean is all I have left. My parent's died three months ago."

If Mia felt bad for Heather's loss, it wasn't enough to keep the annoyance out of her voice. "I'm sorry to hear, but Ashley's been gone for over a year. Where have you been in that time? Where were you before that and when she was sick? She could have used family then."

Mia's tone had gone from angry to accusatory, and Heather had the grace to shift uncomfortably. Her voice was shaky when she responded. "As you said, I didn't have a relationship with my sister. After my parents passed, I wanted to find the only family I had left. When I did, I learned Ashley was gone. I decided then and there I would do what I could to find my nephew and give him the home he deserves."

"That's exactly what he has here," Mia said, and Cole heard an edge of desperation and anger in her voice. If she was trying to hide her concern, it wasn't working. At least not with him. "Ashley wanted him with me. It was a hard transition after Ashley died, but he's settled and doing well. Why do you want to change that?"

"He may be settled now, but you're engaged to a rock star. That news is eventually going to come out and then both of you will be splashed across the entertainment news. What's going to happen to Dean when people learn about this? Or when you're back on tour? Mia will be alone, and the press will be looking for ways to prove that you're cheating so they can get a story. Have you thought of the consequences of that?" Of course they hadn't. As far as Mia was concerned, Cole would only be her fiancé until the custody was settled. Cole, however, had to wonder about Heather's words. Would Mia want to stay with him knowing that the press and headlines were a part of their lives? Before he could respond to Heather's question, she continued, "I'll be honest. I don't know what the two of you are playing at, but I still think this engagement is awfully convenient. It isn't anything more than a scheme you've cooked up, Mia, to keep Dean away from his real family now that we've reached out. And I don't know why Mr. Hanson is going along with it."

"I am his real family," Mia said with conviction. "He's been with me for over a year. You can't show up and think you can take him. He's happy here."

"He'll be happy with us, too. You seem to forget, I know this town. I grew up here, too. And it's... fine, but in Andover he'll be able to go to one of the highest rated school systems in the state which could open all kinds of doors for him for college and beyond. Don't you think he deserves that?" Mia didn't answer, and Cole didn't know what to say. He'd already been the one to put them in this position, and he didn't want to make things worse. Heather stood. "I am staying in town for the rest of the week and then taking him with me on Friday for our scheduled visit."

"Fine. It's your time. I can't stop you."

"No, you can't," Heather said with a finality Cole didn't like. "I'd also like to take him to dinner tomorrow night. Give us a chance to meet and talk before he spends the weekend." Mia nodded. Cole assumed she didn't trust herself to say anything. "I'll see myself out."

They sat there until they heard Heather drive away, then Mia said derisively, "I'll bet she's staying at the Castle on the Hill."

"Given her outfit and car? Most likely." The hotel was the nicest in the area.

Mia stood up and started pacing. She reminded him of Theo, who could never sit still when there was something bothering him. "His 'real family'? What the hell does she mean by that?" Cole kept his distance as Mia stormed around the room, picking up the mugs and taking them into the kitchen. He and the dog followed and watched as she practically dropped them in the sink. He was amazed they didn't break. Bowie gave a whine at the noise and stomping. Cole agreed with his concern. "Since when did anyone in that family act as though they gave two shits about Ashely or Dean? I was Ashley's only family before Dean was born. And after."

"I remember," he said. "You were always there for her. She was lucky to have you."

"What are we going to do now?" The heartbreak and worry were clear on her face and in her voice. "That horrible woman is going to be hanging around, which means this charade needs to look real for the foreseeable future or she's going back to her lawyer, tell her we've been lying, and I'm going to lose Dean."

He'd given her enough space. Putting his hands on his shoulders and forcing her to face him, Cole said, "You will not lose Dean. I haven't seen you two together much, but as you said, this is what Ashley wanted, and it's clear how much you love him."

Mia sniffled and nodded. "We have to make sure Heather believes our engagement is real."

He hoped whatever she suggested included more kissing. *Focus, Hanson*. Now was not the time to think about her mouth, no matter how good it felt. "Agreed. Any ideas?"

She was thoughtful for a second then said, "Yes, but it's going to be awkward as hell."

He was curious. "I can handle awkward. I got us into this situation, so I'll go along with whatever you think will help."

"You need to move in with us."

Chapter Fourteen

♥

She couldn't believe what she'd suggested, but as soon as she thought of it, she knew it was the only thing to do. Now that Heather had shown up and questioned the validity of their engagement, they needed to appear engaged. She didn't want to think about what they might have to do to keep up those appearances, but having Cole move in was necessary.

Oh, but that kiss... his kiss... had melted her insides to the point where she'd forgotten Heather was sitting a few feet away. And for the rest of that awful woman's visit, Mia found her thoughts bouncing between wanting to lunge at Heather and rip her eyes out and lunge for Cole and rip his clothes off.

And now he was going to live here?

She covered her hand with her mouth and took a steadying breath. She could manage this. She was an experienced ER nurse. She handled stressful, life-and-death situations all the time. Of course, those didn't affect her directly, but there was no reason she couldn't find a way to make this work. Dean was worth it. "Tonight," she said.

"What about tonight?"

"You need to move in tonight. As soon as possible. Now. We can't take a chance on Heather finding out you're living with the Sinclairs."

"I've been in town for over a week. People already know where I've been staying. They'll tell her if she asks." He was right. There was no way someone as famous as Cole came back to town without people noticing and talking. They needed more of a plan, more of a story.

And then it occurred to her. The situation itself gave them the perfect situation. "Have you told anyone about the engagement?"

He gave a shrug and looked embarrassed. "I may have mentioned it to my brothers. I know we said we'd keep it under wraps, but it felt odd not to say anything to them. If it helps, I did say it was a setup."

"That's fine. I told Casey the same thing. I need you to tell Martin and Millie, too. Let them know the truth, but tell them all to spread the word that we've been keeping our relationship a secret and even though we've been engaged for a while, you didn't move in immediately because we wanted to let Dean get to know you first. That's a plausible idea, and once people know you're living here, they won't be too clear on when you moved in."

He seemed to think about it for a second before saying, "That could work."

"It *has* to work. Dean is my son, and he belongs with me."

"Yes, he does," Cole said, and he pulled her into his arms. She couldn't stop herself from leaning against him. She needed the extra strength. He stroked her hair, and she took a deep, shuddering breath. God, this was hard on so many levels. "I don't know what it is exactly, but there was something about Heather I didn't like. And it's not because she's someone who likes to flaunt what she has or because she wants to take Dean. I just don't get a maternal feeling from her."

"I agree." She was glad Cole saw it too, because given the circumstances, she couldn't trust her own impressions. Her dislike could have come from bias, but if he sensed something, Mia felt better about her instincts. Time to focus on the next step. Triage. Logic. She stepped away from him and said, "You can use the downstairs bedroom. It used to be the television room. We made it Dad's room when the stairs became too much for him." She was going to need to put as much distance between them as she could if he was staying in the house. There was a free room upstairs, but having him sleep down the hall would be too hard.

Cole gave her a knowing smile. "I remember where that was."

Her pulse quickened. Naturally he remembered that room. It was where they'd hung out anytime they were at her house. Her parents didn't think it was appropriate for her to have a boyfriend in her bedroom, so they insisted she and Cole stay there when he was over. It didn't matter. It gave them plenty of privacy, and it was easy to hear if anyone was coming. The two of them spent hours kissing—and so much more—on the couch in that room. And now she couldn't get images of those times out of her thoughts. No, she had to concentrate on the situation at hand and make it work. Shifting her focus to the logistics of having him here, she asked, "Do you have much stuff at the Sinclairs?"

He shook his head. "About two weeks of clothes, a few books, a laptop, my guitar and a portable keyboard."

"The washer and dryer are downstairs in case you run out of underwear." Oh my god, why did she say that? Great, he hadn't even moved in and already she was tripping over her words and needing to watch what she said. She hoped her embarrassment and horror didn't show on her face. Something he said made her think of a question. "How long were you planning to be here?"

"I hadn't thought specifically. Definitely through Thanksgiving, possibly beyond. The tour doesn't pick up until sometime in January, so I was considering staying through the December holidays."

The holidays. With Cole. This was going to be hell. Maybe she could sign up for a few extra days at the hospital so she wouldn't have to spend as much time with him. That would make some of the other staff happy. It was always hard to find people to work on special occasions. Of course, if Heather found out Mia was working more, she'd use that against Mia. Probably claim she wasn't there enough for Dean or use it as proof that the engagement was false. This was so unfair. It was bad enough that she had to fight to stay Dean's mom, but now she had to fight her traitorous heart as well? "Why does doing the right thing have to have negative consequences?"

His expression turned serious. "I wish I knew." She looked at him and knew he was talking about more than their current situation. Between them were years of decisions and consequences of doing the right thing. Her returning home to take care of her mother and leaving the band. His choosing the band in order to take care of his family. "I'm sorry. It does seem like every time one of us has a responsibility, there are casualties."

They stood there staring at each other, years of conversations waiting to be spoken. She wasn't certain if there was anything she was ready to say now. It was a lot taking in the change in their living arrangements. Until tonight, she'd been able to avoid him even if she couldn't avoid the talk about him. That would no longer be an option.

Before she could think of how to respond, he saved her the trouble by saying, "We need to put things in motion. Let me go to the Sinclairs, tell them what's happening and get my things. Should I pick up something for dinner on my way back?"

Dinner? Mia glanced at the clock on the stove. It was almost four. Dean had stayed after school to work on the school newspaper, and he'd be home soon. She could defrost something in the microwave, but, truthfully, she didn't have the energy to think about that and get things ready. "That would be great. One less thing to worry about."

"On an ever-growing list." Before she could respond, he stepped closer and gave her a quick kiss. She assumed he meant it to be reassuring, but it stirred her insides. "I'll do everything I can to make this as easy as possible for you. For you both. And before you know it, this will all be over, and you and Dean will be fine."

All be over. She and Cole would be over. Again.

Yeah, like that was going to be easy.

Once Cole was gone, Mia sat alone in the living room, not knowing what to do next. What she wanted to do was go to her room, hide under the covers, and not come out, but that wouldn't help anything. Only a few weeks ago, everything was going smoothly. Dad was happy in the assisted living facility. Dean was doing well at school, and she was... fine. Sadly, she couldn't come up with a better word than that.

She couldn't stop herself from thinking about all that had happened since Cole had left her life. It hadn't been what she'd once imagined, and she'd never expected to stay in Fable Notch, but it hadn't been so bad.

For the first two years, her time was taken up by caring for her mother until she finally beat cancer. That was when Mia's mom taught her how to quilt to pass the long days. After, she took a few classes at the community college which, combined with helping her mom, got her interested in nursing. If her dad hadn't needed her, she might have moved to Florida to take care of Ashley when she got sick, but her friend wouldn't allow it until the very end. And the next thing she knew, Dean was living with her. She loved being his mom more than she expected.

And she intended to be there for him as long as he needed her. Forever sounded good.

She gave herself a mental shake and stood up. If she was going to create forever for Dean, she needed to get the spare room ready for Cole. Since her father moved, she used the space for her quilting stuff. She started moving her things out, her arms filled with material before deciding she'd make space for it in a corner of the living room. Bowie followed her as she went back and forth, finally getting bored after a few trips and curling up on the newly uncovered bed. She gave a thought to putting it all in an upstairs bedroom so that Cole wouldn't see everything. As much as she enjoyed it, part of her was embarrassed by the hobby. There was something so "old lady" about it, although the women she'd met at the Artists' Cooperative the few times she could join their quilting nights were all different ages. But putting things upstairs would also mean moving the sewing machine, and she didn't want to have to carry it. Ultimately, she decided it didn't matter. What did she care what Cole thought of how she spent her time?

She received an exasperated look from Bowie when she shooed him off the bed so she could put on fresh sheets. She placated the dog by taking him out for a quick walk when he was done. When she came back, Dean was home, head in the refrigerator. "Hey there. Good meeting at the paper?"

Without looking at her, he said, "Pretty good. I'm getting the hang of things. They give freshman mostly grunt work, but it's not so bad. What's for dinner?"

She hung Bowie's leash on its hook and said, "Whatever Cole brings."

Dean turned to look at her, the door still opened. "O-kay. I'm sensing there's something more going on besides dinner."

"A lot more. Have a seat." He turned back to grab a cheese stick, then joined her at the kitchen table where she told him everything. When she was done, he said nothing, just stared at her, the snack half eaten. "Any questions?"

"Probably, but I don't know where to start. Let me be sure I've got this right. Because you told your lawyer you were engaged, my aunt arrived early. Now she's staying in town to check out your story, and Cole is moving in to make the engagement look real."

"That's about it. He'll stay in Grandpap's old room." Dean was taking this remarkably well. Mia supposed compared to his mother dying, this wasn't a big deal. "I'm sorry. I know this is an awkward situation, and I feel like a fool for letting Cole say what he did, but it's too late to change it. We'll make the best of it, and hopefully this will all be over after the gateway hearing."

"Do you know when that is?"

"No. Lucas thinks it should be before Christmas, but if not, it will be soon after the new year." She really hoped before. She didn't want this hanging over their heads for the holidays.

"I'm sorry you have to go through this," Dean said. "I know it's a hassle."

Mia recognized the expression on Dean's face. She'd seen it often enough in the mirror. He wasn't thinking the situation was a hassle. He was worried *he* was the hassle. It was something she'd felt all too often growing up. "It's not. Don't think that for a moment."

"But if it weren't for me, you wouldn't have had to lie."

She was not letting him take this on himself. "No, if it weren't for your aunt. She's the one creating a situation where there shouldn't be one."

He nodded as he popped the rest of the cheese stick in his mouth. He swallowed and asked, "Is there anything else?"

"She'd like to take you out for dinner tomorrow."

"Jeez, really?" She let him process the request without interrupting. Finally, he said, "I guess that's okay. Not like I have any big plans. I do have some homework though." He stood up and gave her a hug. Still holding her, he said, "Thank you."

"For what?"

"Because you're doing all of this — including having Cole move in — for me. So I can stay."

Mia bit her lip, but that didn't stop the tears. "You're not going anywhere. Not if I can help it." Her phone buzzed, and she gave him an extra squeeze before she let go to look at it. "Cole's going to DeMarco's and wants to know what we want on our pizza."

"Meat," Dean said. "And if you insist on vegetables, no mushrooms. They get gross."

"Agreed," she said as she texted back. When Cole responded with an eggplant followed by a question mark, Mia laughed. Did he know what that referred to? Regardless, she liked DeMarco's eggplant pizza, so she sent a thumbs up. Maybe she'd tell him later what his text was suggesting.

Maybe not.

Having him so close when his kisses already turned her into a puddle would not be easy. She was going to need every wall she'd ever built to keep an emotional distance, or she was going to be a mess when they had to return to their separate lives.

She was watching television and channel surfing, unable to focus on anything, when Cole's car pulled into the driveway a little while later. He brought in the pizzas first, which had Bowie dancing around his feet, and when Mia saw the stack she said, "Three? Large? How much do you think a teen eats?"

"Sorry, been a while since I needed to feed more than myself. I figured better too much than too little. Besides, it's been years since I've had DeMarco's pizza, and everything sounded good." He held up a small paper bag. "I got cannoli, too."

He knew she had a sweet tooth. He knew too much about her. "There will definitely not be any leftovers of those."

"I'm going to get my bags. Come help me, Bowie."

The dog followed him, probably thinking there was more food, and Mia said, "Traitor," to the empty room.

She called Dean down and opened the boxes, breathing in the comforting smells of good pizza. "Meatball and sausage. Cheese. Eggplant," she said, pointing at each one when Dean came in.

"Where is he?" Dean asked as he grabbed a big plate out of the cabinet and helped himself to three pieces.

"Getting his stuff from the car." She assumed Dean would take his meal into the other room where he could watch television as he ate and sneak pieces to Bowie, but he waited.

Cole came in with two pieces of luggage and his guitar across his back. "I've still got one more bag and my keyboard in the car," he said as he tried to maneuver into the room with the bulky bags and even bulkier dog next to him.

Dean put his plate down on the counter and grabbed one of the bags. "I'll show you where you're staying."

Mia couldn't help but smile at the slightly imperious tone in Dean's voice. Cole gave her a questioning look, but Mia shrugged and watched as the two of left the room.

This was going to be interesting.

Chapter Fifteen

♥

C ole knew exactly where he was staying. The room, he'd once been told, had originally been a garage. Then when Mia's mother discovered she was unexpectedly pregnant with her third child, they'd converted the space into a bedroom for their son. Mia's sister moved into the vacated room and gave Mia what was known as the "little bedroom." By the time Cole met Mia, both siblings had moved out, and the space was used as a family room. He and Mia had made out — and more — for hours on the couch. Today, as Mia said, it held a queen-size bed covered with a few pillows and a blue and green comforter, a dresser, and a small desk. In the corner was a sewing machine.

"I see Mama Mia cleared everything out for you," Dean said as he put the suitcase on the bed. He held his arms out to the side. "This is it. Bathroom's across the hall, although I guess you know that. Make yourself at home."

"Thanks. I know this is a little strange," Cole said.

"Yeah, you could say that." Dean shoved his hands in the pocket of his hoodie. Cole couldn't tell if he was pissed or resigned. "I mean, you haven't seen each other for years, then you're back in town for a little over a week and now you're living here. What gives?"

He hardly knew himself. The opportunity to be close to Mia on a daily basis was wonderful, but if this backfired, if for some reason Heather got custody of Dean, Cole would lose her forever. "It all happened kind of fast. I stopped by to talk to your mom, see if maybe we could find a way to be friends again since I'm planning to move back. When I heard about what your aunt was doing, I wanted to help Mia, in part because of how shitty she was treated by me and the label when she was cut from the band. It didn't occur to me that we might have to make it look real and what it would mean if we did."

"What's the other part of the reason?"

Damn, the kid was perceptive. Cole considered his answer before saying, "Can I be honest with you?"

"Don't know, but under the circumstances, it might be a good idea if you were."

He appreciated the boy's protective streak. It reminded him of himself when he was younger. "My relationship with Mia didn't end because something went wrong. There wasn't some big fight or months of problems. When she left Emporium to take care of her mother, I expected to see her again in a few months. We talked and texted all the time. I was still in love with her when everything blew up and changed."

"When she got replaced." Cole winced. Even after all this time, it was hard to hear. "I gotta be honest. I understand why you're doing this — why you're both doing this — and I'm grateful, but I don't like it. She's been jumpy as hell since you've been back, and I doubt your moving in is going to help her relax. I don't know a lot about your history together, but I can see that where you're concerned, she's got some soft spots. Are you going to hurt her again?"

It was odd getting grilled by a teenager. Cole had never been interrogated by the father of a girl he was dating — Mia's parents had been the only ones he'd ever met — but he imagined this is what it felt like. "That's kind of a loaded question." Dean was about to argue, but Cole put up his hand. "I know what you're asking. No, I don't want to hurt her again. Between you and me, I'd rather this engagement was real, but I don't think that's something she's ready for. And until she is, I hope you'll keep that between us. But even if we stay together, chances are I'll do something stupid at some point and, yes, she'll get hurt. It happens in the best of relationships. Does that make sense?"

"Yeah. It does." Dean gave him a small smile. Cole counted it as a win. "Thanks for getting dinner."

"No problem." He'd passed inspection, at least for now.

"Cool guitar," Dean said as he walked toward the door.

"Thanks. You play?"

"Nah, never had a chance to take up an instrument."

"I could teach you." Great, more spur-of-the-moment ideas that could land badly. He'd never taught anyone, but as soon as he said it he found himself hoping Dean would say yes.

Dean gave him a measured glance. *He's trying to see if I'm buttering him up.* Cole liked the way the boy didn't accept things at face value. He wasn't as instantly suspicious of adults as Cole and his brothers had been, but he was cautious. "That could be cool," he finally said. As he left, he turned and added, "Don't eat my cereal."

Cole was about to call out, "Which one is that?" then decided tonight wasn't the night for flip remarks. He looked around the room and started unpacking, then decided it could wait. Pizza was better hot. He passed Dean eating pizza in front of the television in the living room and joined Mia in the kitchen, where she was staring at her slice. She'd poured herself a glass of wine, but unless it was her second, she hadn't touched it. It was still full. He took a slice from each pie and sat across from her. "I noticed a few missing businesses since I've been back, but I'm really glad DeMarco's isn't one of them."

She looked up from her food as if she'd been in a trance. "No, it's still here. Still just as good." She took a bite, chewed slowly, then put the piece down again. "Cole, what if this doesn't work? What if Heather finds out that this is a sham?"

"How could she? You know this town. The expression 'word travels fast' could have been invented here. I've already spoken to Theo, Nick and the Sinclairs. Everyone is happy to start the buzz about you and I being engaged. It will be the hottest topic around in no time." When he'd gone over to the Sinclairs to pack, Millie made it clear that she hoped this wouldn't be pretend for long. He'd told her he agreed, but she couldn't share that with anyone. "The only thing they were upset about was you having to go through this in the first place."

"I appreciate that. Will you thank them for me?" He nodded, and she went back to studying her meal as if the answers to their situation could be found somewhere in the melted cheese.

"Did I get the wrong toppings? I thought you said eggplant was okay."

"Eggplant is great, but I'm not very hungry. I'm sure it won't surprise you to know that I've got a lot on my mind. But that reminds me. You do know what an eggplant emoji means, don't you?"

"Yeah, it means.... Oops." He laughed and scrunched up his face. "Sorry about that. I was only thinking about dinner." Or at least he was then. Now he was thinking about more than pizza. Images of her, naked in his arms, kissing her the way he ached to, flashed through his mind.

As if she knew where his thoughts had gone, she broke eye contact, took a sip of her wine, and kept her focus on her food. Deciding not to press after the day they'd had, he did the same and finished his three slices before she managed her one. When she finished, she went to a cabinet drawer and rifled through the mess. He heard an 'ah-ha' when she found what she was looking for. Turning to him, she handed him a key. "For the front door. The side door is usually unlocked, but just in case."

A lot of front doors were left unlocked in this town. He stared at the key, thinking about what it meant. For the next few weeks, her home was his. He'd wanted a chance to get close to her, to see if there was a future for them. He'd gotten his wish. It looked nothing like what he thought it would, but he was determined not to blow it. "Thanks," he said, taking the key and trying not to notice the tingle he experienced when he touched her hand. He went to his coat and slid the key on the ring. When he came back to the kitchen, she was clearing and cleaning. He moved in to help her, not offering conversation, just support.

When there was nothing else to put away, she brushed her hands down her sweatshirt and said, "I'm going to make it an early night."

He heard the resignation in her voice and hated that he was part of it. "My being here isn't chasing you upstairs, is it? I know it's going to be awkward for a while, but I don't want you to be uncomfortable in your own house. I can stay in my room if you want me out of your way for the next few hours to do what you'd normally do."

She smiled at him. "Thanks, I appreciate that. Truthfully, I wouldn't be doing much more than watching television or working on a quilt. I go to bed early on nights before a shift. Make yourself at home. You know where everything is." He did. One more oddity to add to an already strange situation. She leaned against the door frame and said, "Depending on how deeply you sleep, you'll hear me leaving by 6:15. Dean gets up for school at seven and he's out the door about a half hour later. After that, you'll have the place to yourself. Any plans?"

He gave a disparaging chuckle. "Nope. I don't have much on my schedule, and they're not hiring at the Emporium."

"You could always try playing pool for twenties at the Varnum," she teased, and he smiled. They had so much history together, so many memories, and most of them good. He hoped this arrangement would give them the opportunity to create more.

As hard as things had been back then, there was a part of him that wished he could slip back into his old life, go back to a time when things between them had been easy. When she was a part of everything he did. Before he'd hurt her. Before they were both alone. "I may have to look into that. If I go out, can Bowie come with me?"

"Sure, he'd love it." She showed him where the leash was kept. Bowie got excited for a second, then had his hopes dashed for getting another walk. "His days are pretty quiet when I'm at work now that my dad's not around. Those two were pals. I bring him along when I visit Dad, but I think Bowie misses the interaction. He loves being in the car. He's even okay if you can't roll down the window for him. There's a dog park next to the veterinary clinic. You can always take him there to hang out with his friends. You'll probably see Dani if you go."

"Could be nice to spend a little time with one of my future sisters-in-law. You heard that Theo and Eden are already engaged, right?"

"I did. I guess you're right about news spreading quickly around here. It's been a surprising year for the Hanson brothers."

"In a lot of ways," Cole said with a smile. He was so damn happy for his brothers. A year ago, none of them would have imagined what their lives looked like today. What Cole hoped for most was that a year from now he would still be having dinner with Mia. But first, they had to get through the next few weeks. "What time do you get home from work?"

"My shift ends at seven, so I'm home by seven thirty unless I'm in the middle of a case."

"Do you want me to make dinner?" She looked at him quizzically. "I figure if I'm around, I may as well make myself useful. I'm not the one who has a twelve-hour shift."

"Sorry, I'm not used to having anyone offer to help. But no, that's not necessary. I've got meals in the freezer. I'll take one out in the morning, and we can heat it up when I get home. It'll be the two of us since Heather's taking Dean out to dinner." Hours together, just the two of them. It may not be how he'd wanted it to happen, but this was exactly what he'd hoped for. Mia looked less than thrilled. She ran a hand through her hair and said, "God, this is a nightmare. It was bad enough knowing he was going to be spending time with her, but having her hanging around for the next three days? That's going to be weird."

Probably more stressful than weird. He hated that he was more a part of the problem than the solution, but he was going to do whatever he could to change that. "What time is she coming to get him? I'll make sure I'm here. Remind him to mind his manners."

"Thank you. I'd appreciate that." He watched some of the tension leave her shoulders and wished he could do more. She looked as though she might say something else, then changed her mind and simply said, "Good night."

"Sweet dreams." He wanted to give her a hug. Fine, he wanted to kiss her again and feel her melt against him, but he was willing to be patient. He listened to her moving around upstairs and imagined her getting ready for bed. Changing out of her clothes and into.... No, he couldn't let himself think about that, about how close she was. About how much he ached for her. He scrubbed his hands over his face. He probably deserved the torture.

One step at a time. His was a long-term plan that got a momentum boost from this situation. It would take time for her to trust him again, but he was going to do whatever it took to make that happen. Building bridges was a slow process, but it would be worth it.

Chapter Sixteen

♥

The next morning, Cole stayed in bed when he heard Mia come down the stairs. Part of him wanted to get dressed and join her for coffee, but his being there had thrown off her life enough. There was no need to ruin her morning routine, too. Besides, if she had slept as badly as he did, she wouldn't be in the mood for company. He fell back to sleep when he heard her car leave but woke again when Dean was in the kitchen. He threw on a long sleeve t-shirt and a pair of joggers and joined him. The teen was scrolling through his phone and barely acknowledged Cole's being there. Cole looked at the cereal box next to Dean's bowl and made a mental note not to eat that one. Bowie was a little more enthusiastic, walking around Cole and giving him longing looks.

"He's hoping you'll share whatever you have for breakfast," Dean said through a mouth of cereal.

"What's the house policy on that?" Cole didn't know what it was like living with a dog, and he didn't want to do anything to upset Mia. Well, to upset her more.

"One bite per person per meal, no more. And nothing with a lot of sugar. If he's persistent or too much of a pest, you can give him one of his cookies." Dean tipped his head toward the top of the refrigerator where a barrel shaped container held the treats. Bowie clearly understood the topic of conversation because he put both front paws on the refrigerator and barked. "Sorry, should have spelled the 'c' word. Don't say t-r-e-a-t either unless you plan to give him one."

Cole decided to get on the dog's good side and gave him what he was asking for, then made himself some coffee and joined Dean at the table. "Mia said you're having dinner with your aunt tonight." Dean shrugged. It had been years since Cole spent time with a teen and those were his brothers, but apparently, they still didn't communicate much. Unfortunately, Cole didn't know what to say to coax more information out of him. "You okay with that?"

"I guess so. Don't have much of a choice."

Wanting to keep the conversation going, Cole asked, "Do you know anything about your aunt?"

"Just that she was my mom's younger sister, and they stopped talking after Mom got pregnant with me. Gotta say, I don't understand what her deal is. She's got two kids. Why does she want another one she hasn't met?" It was a good question. Cole had wondered about it as well and now wondered if Heather had other motivations. Maybe he could give Lucas a call and see if there was anything they could do to find out more about this woman. Cole didn't know what a private investigator cost, but if it helped Mia keep Dean, it would be worth it. "Did you know my aunt when you lived here?"

"No. I think she would have been in my younger brother's class, but I can't say I ever said more than hi to her if she came to talk to Ashley, and I was around. I remember your mom because she and Mia were close. She was funny and smart and a really good softball player."

"Yeah, she tried to teach me, but sports aren't my thing. I'm more of a word guy. That's why I'm on the school paper."

Cole was pleased that Dean was talking about himself. "Your mom also loved books. I was the one who got her into Stephen King. Have you read any of his stuff?"

Dean's face lit up. "Yeah, I'm loving it so far. Mom said there were some I shouldn't read until I got older, like *The Shining*, but I've read *Carrie*, *The Dead Zone*, and *Christine*, and I just started a book of his short stories." Cole was relieved to have found a conversation-worthy topic. They talked a little more about their favorite books until it was time for Dean to leave. As he stood and put his breakfast bowl in the sink, he asked, "Did you mean what you said about teaching me how to play the guitar?"

Cole was glad Dean remembered. If he was going to have a long-term place in Mia's life, he needed to have a good relationship with her son. This could be a good place to start. King wrote a lot of books, but they'd need more than one thing to talk about. "I did. We could start whenever you want. Tonight?"

"Maybe. I'll see what time I get home." He stood and put his breakfast bowl in the sink, then gave Bowie some attention before saying, "I'm off."

Minutes later, Cole sat at the table, the dog at his feet, his coffee almost gone. Alone in the house, he realized he was facing another day of not knowing what to do. He'd never felt so useless. There were only so many times he could call his brothers and ask them to meet him for breakfast. They had lives.

He thought about Mia and Dean and how he could help them while he was here. A meal was defrosting in the sink, so cooking wasn't necessary, and he had no idea if Mia needed anything done around the house. Even if she did, he wasn't particularly handy. He'd probably make things worse, which, for all his good intentions, was what he was doing anyway. When Theo had come back, he'd jumped into helping Martin with an arson problem, and Nick had kept busy by working construction with Ed Franks and then volunteering for the summer festival. Cole needed something to focus on or he was going to go crazy.

He went to his room to get dressed and saw his guitar propped up against the wall. When he was fourteen, Millie taught him to play piano and read music, and then a year later he'd asked her about learning guitar. She'd shown him the basics and the rest he'd learned from watching other performers, eventually YouTube videos, and hours of practice. Playing had been his escape for years. When things were rough at home or school, music was his solace. That had changed in the last few years. When he'd started, he'd been grateful to make money doing something he loved. Now he still made money — more than he'd ever imagined — but the love wasn't there. Maybe teaching Dean would help him get that back.

He waited until a reasonable hour, even though the Sinclairs woke early, then headed over, hoping Millie could give him some help. As he drove, he passed the Stewart Inn and Cabins where a white

Mercedes in the parking lot caught his eye. Curious, he pulled in to get a closer look. Sure enough, it had Massachusetts plates. Interesting. She wasn't staying at the Castle on the Hill. If he had to recommend any place in the area, the Stewart's would have been his top choice because Valerie and Roger Stewart made the place feel more like home than a hotel, but it didn't seem like what Heather would prefer. Maybe the Castle was booked.

Martin had left for work at the fire station, but Millie welcomed him in. When he asked, "Can you show me how to teach Dean to play guitar?" her face lit up. Seeing her expression, Cole realized that, like Theo, who'd gone into arson investigation, he'd gone into the other family business. Since drinking and leaving were the examples set by his birth parents, this was a better choice. That made him think of Dean again and wanting to do what he could to set a good example for the young man.

He followed Millie into her music room, and three hours later, his head was spinning. He had a newfound respect for the work she did. It wasn't that he thought teaching kids was easy — especially since most of her students were there because their parents told them they had to take lessons — but he never appreciated the patience and focus it took. Even so, it was the most fun he'd had in a long time, and he was looking forward to showing Dean what he'd learned.

To thank her, Cole offered to take Millie out to lunch. She suggested the Just Right Café, one of the newer options in town. He didn't know why she'd chosen the place when he saw how busy it was, but as they were waiting, the reason became clear. Everyone knew Millie and came up to her to chat.

Each time she'd say, "You know Cole Hanson, don't you? And did you hear? He and Mia Durant are engaged. Isn't that exciting?" The first time she did it, Cole cringed, but before lunch was over, someone stopped by their table to chat and congratulate Cole on his good news. As he expected — and hoped — word traveled fast in Fable Notch.

"You are a sneaky old broad," he said when they were alone again.

"Who are you calling old?" she replied with a smirk as she finished her sandwich. He couldn't stop the laugh that bubbled up from his chest. She didn't deny the sneakiness. "Mmm, so good. Don't you dare tell Rosie, but I like the grilled cheese here better than at the diner."

"It's the bread," said a new voice with a hint of Southern in the accent. Cole looked up and saw a curvy woman with a riot of blond curls standing next to the table. "And three different cheeses. I'm going to offer a special grilled cheese each month in the new year."

"I think that's a wonderful idea," Millie said. "As if I needed another reason to come by. Cole, this is Sheridan Behr, owner and chef. Sheridan, I'd like you to meet Cole Hanson."

He took her outstretched hand and said, "Nice to meet you. Guess your last name explains the name of the place."

"Just call me Goldilocks," she said, fluffing her hair. "At first, I balked at giving it a cute name. But after weeks of collecting ideas, I had this long list, and nothing fit. Finally, I said to Laurel 'Is it too much to ask for something that's just right?' As soon as I said it, we both knew I was done searching. And I've come to love our little bear." She fanned her hands out to display her t-shirt with the cafe logo, a bear eating a sandwich.

"It works. Laurel as in Laurel Stewart?"

"It is. We went to college together. I came to help her when the brewery opened and decided to stay. And no, I'm not from around here, which you probably guessed. Born and bred in Alabama."

He liked the woman's genuine openness. "Winters must have been a shock," Cole said.

"Damn near froze my little southern ass off the first year, but then I discovered skiing and now I can't get enough."

"Have you heard Cole's good news? " Millie said. He smiled. She was relentless. And efficient.

"How could I miss it? The whole place is buzzing. Congratulations. Can I bring you something for dessert to celebrate?"

Millie put a hand on her stomach. "Not this time, but soon. And I've got to get over here early enough one day to get your cinnamon rolls." She looked at Cole. "Worth every calorie."

"I can never hear that too often." Sheridan put a hand on Millie's shoulder and said, "Tell you what, when the craving gets bad, call me in the morning, and I'll put one aside for you."

"You're a dear. When are we going to get you married off?"

The woman laughed, making her curls bounce. "Darlin', first I've got to find a man who's 'just right,' and is okay with a woman who works the early shift. So far, I'm still searching."

"You know, my Ryan is single and very hand-some."

Cole hoped he didn't roll his eyes too noticeably. "And in California, Ma. That's a little long distance even with today's technology."

Millie waved a hand, brushing off the observation as unimportant. "If you three boys can move back here, then so can he." Cole felt the urge to message Ryan and warn him. If Millie wanted to see him settled and married, Ryan needed to keep his distance if he didn't share her plans. "Thank you for a wonderful meal, Sheridan."

"Any time. Hope to see you again," she said to Cole before visiting at another table.

"Stop," Cole said when they were alone again.

"Stop what?" Millie's face was all innocent, but Cole knew that look. She got it whenever she needed Martin or one of the boys to do something for her. "I don't care where she grew up. That girl fits in this town. She needs someone she can make a life with."

With a hand on his stomach, Cole said, "And who has a fast metabolism."

"Wasn't this the perfect place for lunch?"

"You know it was," he said, then grew serious. "Thank you. I know it's a lot to ask of all of you, covering for my mistake with Mia. Making this work for her."

She reached out and gave his hand a squeeze. "We're glad to help you any way we can. Which reminds me, Thanksgiving is next week. We're expecting you, Mia, and Dean to join us." Millie looked giddy with excitement. It made him glad that he'd come here instead of having her come to Colorado, where she'd be cooking for a much smaller group and in an unfamiliar kitchen. "It's going to be the biggest crowd we've had in years."

For a change, he remembered not to answer for Mia. "I think she has plans to spend the day with her father at the senior living center."

"Then he should come, too. You know there's always room for more."

"What if you don't have enough food?" Cole managed the question with a straight face that lasted a second before they burst out laughing. Like that was ever going to happen. He thought about the rest of his day and remembered something he wanted to do. "Do you have to get back home right away?"

"No, I don't have a student until 3:30. Why? Did you decide you wanted dessert after all?"

"I could use your help. Would you come to Prince's with me and help me pick out a ring for Mia?"

Chapter Seventeen

♥

Mia's hospital shift had been ungodly long. To start, she was exhausted from a lousy night's sleep. Even melatonin hadn't helped. Knowing that Cole was in the house made her restless, and in the morning, she found herself being careful not to make too much noise as she got ready, so she didn't wake him. Seeing him at dinner would be soon enough. And as the day went on, they had almost no patients to treat. Nothing made time go slower than little to do and too much to think about. Her thoughts were a constant jumble of Cole, Heather, and Dean. If she wasn't worried about one, it was the other. She didn't wish emergencies or drama on anyone, but she really could have used something else to focus on.

She wasn't even looking forward to the end of her shift because when she came home, Dean wouldn't be there. When the clock said five, she pictured him getting picked up in the Mercedes and driven who knows where for dinner. Would Heather take him some place he wanted, like Varnum Bar and Grill which had the best burgers in town, or would she take him to the dining room at the hotel so she could tell him to order whatever he wanted and impress him with her Gold American Express card?

He'd probably still order a burger.

She didn't want Dean to have a miserable time, but she couldn't help but worry. What if he connected with his mother's sister and then looked forward to his weekend away? She knew Dean loved her, but there was a possibility that he'd prefer this new, ready-made and larger family to being with her. Would he prefer to live with his aunt?

It was possible. After all, there were limits to what she could offer him. Mia had looked up Heather's address. Google Earth showed her the Buckley's lived in a large, new home in a well-off neighborhood. She was pretty sure his room would be bigger and what would he think of the pool in the backyard? When she was being logical, she told herself he wouldn't want another move now that he had finally settled in at the high school, but moments later her fears would go into overdrive. He was a teen, and he might be influenced by what the Buckley's could offer.

It took him a while to open up and get comfortable around her, but it had taken no time for her. Within a week of his arrival, she couldn't imagine her life without him. The thought of losing him now was too painful to think about.

And when she thought of losing people, her thoughts circled around to Cole. Thinking about him was almost as distressing. He wanted to move back to Fable Notch to be near his family, but that meant being near her. They'd already kissed twice, and she couldn't be the only one who'd been affected by it. It may have been years since she'd seen him, but she could still recognize desire in his eyes. They'd both gotten lost in the one yesterday, and her quick response to the first one took her completely off guard. Could his being back mean there was a place for him in her life? Did she even want that?

Of course you do. The voice in her head was no help. She couldn't deny that she never got her heart back after things ended. She couldn't say she'd even tried or had a good reason to. Living with a broken heart was easier than living with the possibility of it breaking again. But with him here and his willingness to do whatever it took to help keep Dean in her life, she could feel herself being drawn to him as she had been all those years ago.

As if the day weren't tough enough, in the afternoon she heard someone listening to an old Emporium song as she walked by an office, and she was pulled back in time to the day they met. She'd been a freshman in high school and aware of him for weeks. The hot sophomore who played guitar and entertained everyone at lunch and after school with two of his friends. He'd been gorgeous and unapproachable. Sexy and a little dangerous. He might never have noticed her if she hadn't been sitting on a rock singing one of his songs in the woods behind the high school.

"A little bird is singing my song," he said, making her jump.

She'd been embarrassed. Singing was something she did on her own, never with other people. Ashley had heard her a few times and told her to try out for the chorus, but she refused. She wasn't comfortable with people noticing her, usually because when they did, she got roped into helping them do something. "I'm sorry. I didn't mean to..."

"Are you kidding?" he said, his smile making goose bumps break out on her skin. "Don't apologize. Damn, *that's* how that song is supposed to sound. I knew it was missing something, but I thought it was a better bass line. Turns out it was a better singer. I'm Cole."

It took weeks before she agreed to join him and his friends at the Souvenir Emporium to sing with them and longer before she was willing to sing in public. The applause when she finished was great, but it was the smile on Cole's face that had made it worthwhile. They hadn't had their first date and already she was in love with him.

If she closed her eyes, she could see that smile still.

And he'd be waiting for her when she got home tonight and for as long as this custody case took. What if the judge determined they needed a full hearing? He could be living with her for months, and she was having trouble getting through this first day.

By the time she pulled into the driveway, she was worn out from the storm of worries that had occupied her head when patients hadn't kept her busy. Fortunately, when she went inside, she was greeted by a very happy Bowie and the smell of lasagna. The comforting aroma gave her a moment of calm as she and Cole exchanged greetings. Then she saw he was making a salad, and the calm disappeared as her thoughts turned to what it might be like to come home to him every day. When he turned and smiled, her heart skipped a beat. Stupid heart. She could have been back in high school for the effect he had on her. She needed to put up better walls or when this make-believe engagement ended, she was going to be a mess.

Then she saw the small velvet box stamped with the Prince's Jewelry Store logo next to her place at the table, and her heart did more than skip a beat. When he turned and served the salad, she asked, "What's that?"

"The word is getting out that we're engaged. Millie is a genius, and no one questions her. I don't want anyone to make comments like Heather did. Open it."

She didn't want to, and she longed to at the same time. How many more simultaneously conflicting emotions was she going to go through in the next few weeks? She wished her hand wasn't shaking as she opened the box. When the light caught the gem, she couldn't stifle the gasp. "Is this a pink diamond?"

"It is. I was going to get something simple and traditional, but when I saw this, I knew it was the right one."

It was more than right. It was the most beautiful ring she'd ever seen. The center stone was round and, while she didn't know a lot about rings, probably at least a carat in size with two clear diamonds on either side. "It's gorgeous."

"I'm glad you like it, and before you say I shouldn't have and that this was crazy, don't. I said all of that to myself and more, but if we want people to believe this engagement is real, then this is important. I even got it at Prince's so what I said to Heather about the ring being there isn't a lie. Mrs. Prince said we can come in tomorrow to get it sized if necessary." She continued to stare, not quite believing it was real. "Put it on and see."

Put a fake engagement ring on her own hand. Not what she pictured when this moment came, even if she was with the man she'd always dreamed of. She took it out of the box and slid it on. It stopped for a moment at her knuckle, then settled at the base of her finger. It fit perfectly. Damn him. "I don't know what to say."

He took her hand in his and looked at the ring. "Me either. It seems as though I should say something, but I'm at a loss. I hope you know I will do whatever I can to help you and Dean stay a family."

She teared up and tugged at her hand, but he held tight until she looked at him. Finally, she whispered, "Thank you."

He brought her hand to his lips and kissed her knuckles above the ring. Her skin heated, and she hoped he wouldn't notice. "We'll make this work." He let go, and when he turned to get the salad dressing, she went to the other room to get a bottle of wine, needing a moment of distance more than the drink. She stared at her hand, not believing what she was seeing. It wasn't weirder than him living with them, but it was a very dramatic symbol of what they were doing. She took a deep breath before heading back to the kitchen. No matter how odd it was to wear, it would be worth it when she got to keep Dean in her life.

And she would do what she could to ignore the teen girl squealing for joy in her head.

She and Cole had just finished eating—their second meal a little less awkward than their first thanks to keeping the conversation focused on her work and his lunch with Millie—when she heard a car pull into the driveway and a minute later Dean came in. She barely said hi before asking, "How was dinner?" She hoped her tone sounded casual, because that wasn't how she felt. She wanted to give him the classic maternal third degree and, more important-ly, ask him how he liked Heather.

"It was okay," he said with a shrug.

So not helpful, but she didn't expect more. "Where did you go?"

"The dining room at the Castle." *Figures.* "Don't think they liked my jeans much, but whatever."

Mia couldn't decide if she was glad Heather wasn't the kind of woman who took a teen boy's likes into account. "Did you like it?"

"Their burgers aren't as good as Varum's." Mia smiled and gave herself an internal high five for knowing her son so well. "Aunt Heather is one of those women Mom called an Orderer."

"What does that mean?" Mia asked, trying not to show her discomfort at hearing him say "Aunt Heather."

"Mom would wait tables on Friday and Saturday night at this ritzy place near us. The tips were good, and the leftovers were better." Mia knew Ashley worked as a secretary in the local school so she could have hours that matched Dean's days, but clearly the salary wasn't quite enough. "She always made fun of the women who made a big show about ordering something expensive and then not eating it. She would have laughed if she saw the salmon her sister chose and then barely touched. Guess that's why she's so skinny. Seems stupid to me. I've got homework to do. Algebra test Friday."

"Do you need help?"

"Nah, I got this. The class isn't as bad as I thought it'd be. By the way, nice ring." He put an arm around her, gave a quick squeeze, then said, "G'night."

She stared after him with more questions she wanted to ask but wasn't eager to hear the answers to. And if he didn't want to talk or think about his time with Heather, that was fine with her. She put her hand to the spot on her arm where he'd hugged her, wishing he'd stayed a second longer.

"You're not going to lose him," Cole said, breaking into her thoughts.

What do you know? Something could make her forget Cole. "Am I that obvious?"

"You've been staring after him for three minutes."

She made an unsuccessful attempt at smiling. "This is harder than I thought it would be."

"I can tell. It's odd that she took him to the restaurant at the hotel. I don't think she's staying there." Cole explained seeing the Mercedes at the Stewart's.

"Guess she wanted to impress him."

"Yeah, because teens are so impressed by big hotels and place settings with too many forks."

Mia managed to laugh, but it changed into a sob. "How am I going to make it through this weekend when he's with her?"

"Are you working? That would help."

She wasn't that lucky. "No, Friday is my last day this week, then I'm off through Monday." Maybe she could get lost in quilting or take a long hike with Bowie.

She was still trying to come something when he asked, "What if we do something together?"

She appreciated the offer, but couldn't imagine what they'd do. "Such as?"

"I... have no idea, but I've got until Saturday to come up with something. Can I do that for you?"

He was always looking to take care of others. It came as naturally to him as breathing, and today she was grateful for that. Not trusting herself to speak, she nodded her agreement.

They cleaned the kitchen together again, and she went upstairs as soon as they were done. She slept a little better that night, so Thursday at the hospital didn't feel as long, although she spent most of the day with people grabbing her hand and commenting on the ring. She considered taking it off so it wouldn't be such a distraction, but since it supported their story, she kept it on. By the end of the day, she was certain the entire hospital knew of her engagement.

After dinner, she sat in the living room and sketched out the quilt pattern for her next project—a quilt for Dean for Christmas—and made notes about the materials she needed, while Cole said he had a song to work on and Dean did homework. There was something so normal about it. It was as though Cole had been there for weeks, not two days. She was glad Dean accepted the arrangement, but she wasn't certain how she felt about Cole being able to slip easily into their lives.

Hearing Cole's music so close was another memory punch, bringing her back to a time when he played his new songs for her first. He'd read her the lyrics or hum the melody, and she'd tell him what she thought was working or offer suggestions. And unlike anyone in her family, he listened to her and took her seriously.

From the day they met, she'd felt a connection with him. Cole was someone who understood her. Understood her loneliness and her longing. After he was gone, she'd never found that kind of compatibility with someone else. She looked at the ring, which she'd been doing a lot during the day, and wondered if there was a possibility that this was a new start for them? Starting with an engagement was a little bizarre, but what about her life had been normal recently?

But she couldn't think about that now. She had to get through these next few weeks and prove to the judge there was no reason to proceed with a custody battle. Then she'd decide whether she wanted a future with Cole.

With her thoughts still a jumble, she went upstairs without saying goodnight to Cole. Before heading to bed, she helped Dean pack for the weekend and did her best not to let her concern show. "How are you feeling about this weekend?"

He gave a shrug. It was what she expected. "I guess I'm a little nervous. I want them to like me, but I also don't really want to go." She couldn't say she was sorry about that. "I mean, what am I going to do there?" The question made him remember something, and he packed his video handheld. She pulled a charger out of the wall and handed it to him.

Part of her wanted to call in sick the next day and be there when Heather came to pick him up, but seeing him drive off with the other woman would probably bring her to her knees. Having Cole do this was better. "If you hate it and want to come home sooner, call and I'll come get you." So much for not showing concern.

As she surveyed his bag, making sure he hadn't forgotten anything, he said, "Mama Mia, I'm going to be gone for two nights. To Massachusetts, not the outback. If I've forgotten anything, I'm sure they'll have it."

Somehow, that didn't help her. "Sorry, kiddo. This is all a bit weird."

"For me too," he said. They stood in silence, and Mia, having run out of things to say, ways to help, and not knowing what else to do, pulled him into a fierce hug, the kind her parents never gave her. That he let her hold him for so long told her he was nervous, too.

The next morning, she put a hand on Dean's door as she walked by. She was so torn. The selfish part of her wanted to hope that he had a miserable weekend and couldn't wait to come back to her. But she also acknowledged that loving him meant wanting what was best for him, and if for some reason that was Heather and her family, then she would find a way to accept that. She'd handled heartbreak in the past. She could do it again.

Her Friday shift started with a bang when someone who was running late for work caused a three-car accident in his rush to make up the time.

They brought in all five passengers for evaluation. There was nothing more serious than whiplash and cuts from broken glass, but enough to keep her busy going from patient to patient for several hours.

At lunch, she saw she'd missed a text from Cole. *Having dinner with Nick and Dani tonight. Be home later.*

If anything had changed about Cole, it wasn't his innate sense of consideration. Because he'd been more parent than brother to Theo and Nick, Cole was always good at checking in. She wouldn't have worried if he wasn't there, but he knew she would have wondered. She'd pick up something for herself on the way home.

To an empty house.

Because Dean was in Massachusetts.

She did what she could to keep herself busy for the rest of her shift and not think about later. Sure, there were nights when she came home and Dean was at a friend's, but this would be different. She hoped Cole would come up with something distracting to do tomorrow. She was counting on him to make the next forty-eight hours less miserable.

Mia stopped what she was doing when she noticed her thoughts. She was counting on him.

Oh, this was not good. This was what she'd avoided for years. Since the day of the call from the record label telling her they were releasing her from her contract, she'd shut herself down. Why want things when they could be taken away? From then on, she kept her life uncomplicated. Work, a few friendships, taking care of her parents. Then Dean arrived and her world grew in ways she didn't know were possible.

Now Cole was here again, complicating things and simultaneously making them wonderful. She didn't know how she was going to protect her heart.

Chapter Eighteen

♥

Out with Bowie, said the note Mia had left on the table for Cole when he came into the kitchen on Saturday morning. Such a normal, couple-like thing to see. He loved it. Maybe it meant that in the not-too-distant future, they would be a real couple again.

Sitting at the table with his coffee, he noticed the jeweler's box on the lazy Susan. He picked it up and held it, wishing that giving her the ring could have been something romantic, the way it should have been. As he watched her put it on her hand, he swore he felt an ache in his knee from wanting to move into a traditional proposal position but doing that would make it seem as though this engagement was real.

Going to the jewelry store with Millie had been a bittersweet experience. He could sense how excited Millie was, and while part of him felt the same way, another part worried that this was going to doom his long-term prospects with Mia. He'd gone from hoping for a slow build to a fully-fledged bonfire. That's how you burned bridges, not built them. A forced living situation was not the way to win your way back into someone's heart. He was going to need to talk to Nick about how to hold it together when things didn't go according to plan.

He was about to get a second cup of coffee and make something for breakfast when Mia and Bowie came in. Her face was flushed from the walk and the cool morning air, and all he wanted to do was kiss her. Instead, he grabbed another mug, and put it under the Keurig as she took off her scarf and hung her jacket on the rack by the door. "It's going to be a nice one today," she said as she took the mug from him and put in sugar and a splash of milk. "It's already in the forties. Don't even need gloves." No one in Fable Notch would wear gloves until it dipped below freezing. It was a matter of pride.

"Are you okay with taking a drive and maybe doing some walking?" He'd toyed with the idea of going down to Concord, taking in the shops and things and finding a nice place for dinner, but he'd had a better idea if she was up to it.

"Sure, it's supposed to be a mild day," she said. She glanced down at what she was wearing. She looked comfortable in a long sweater and jeans. He wished he could see her ass better. "Do I need to change?"

That was the last thing he wanted her to do. Of course, she was talking about her clothes, so he said, "Nope, we'll be keeping things casual for the day. Do I?" he asked, hoping he sounded playful since he was only wearing a t-shirt and shorts.

Mia tilted her head back and forth. "You may want to put on shoes."

He smiled. The conversation was ridiculously mundane, and he loved it. He was so damn comfortable standing there with her. The only thing that would make it better would be if he could pull her into his arms. Instead, he asked, "Can I make you some breakfast?" She looked at him as though he'd asked if she could fly. "I know how to cook."

"I know. It's like your offer the other night. I... can't remember the last time someone offered to make me breakfast."

Cole nodded. Neither one of them grew up with parents who did much for them. In Cole's case, they were absent or unable. As far as Mia's parents were concerned, as soon as she could do something herself, they were done. Cole remembered her sharing with him that she'd been packing her own lunches since the first grade. The only reason she didn't have to make dinner was because her mother was already doing that for her father. He assumed when she came home to help, she did everything.

It didn't take him long to scramble some eggs and make toast and within the hour, they were off. Because he wasn't sure of the rules in the places where he planned to take her, they left Bowie at home. As they drove out of town, Mia pointed out some of the newer places that had opened since he left. For every long-lasting business like the Emporium and the Kinsman, there were more modern additions, including a smoothie and juice bar and two day spas. They also passed the Seven Brothers Brewery, which he was looking forward to visiting.

They'd been driving for a while when they passed signs telling them they were approaching Davis' Apple Farm & Country Market. Cole said, "That's a familiar sight. What would you think of picking up food for lunch?"

Mia agreed and soon after, they turned onto the Davis property. The sign out front proclaimed that they 'still had pies' which was a surprise so close to Thanksgiving and was probably part of the reason the parking lot was full. They eventually found a spot and went in, going immediately to where the to-go meals were sold. After choosing sandwiches and chips for lunch, along with a few bottles of cider, and cider donuts, they spent as much time in line as they did making their selections.

"We should bring the cider to the Sinclairs on Thursday," he said as they got back in his car.

"We should?"

"Don't you think it would go well with turkey? We can't bring food. Millie would kill me."

"I meant, I wasn't aware *we* were going to the Sinclairs for Thanksgiving."

Shit. He'd forgotten to ask. This is what happened when you jumped into the middle of a relationship. "Sorry. Millie invited all of us, including your dad, to join them. I said yes, but I should have asked you first. Will you come?"

"You're sure it's okay if my dad is there, too?"

"Absolutely. I told Millie you were planning to spend the day with him, and she said to bring him. If my memory serves, he's a traditionalist and watches a lot of football on Thanksgiving. He can join Martin and any others around the television." When she didn't respond he said, "I'd really love to have you there with me." *Be part of my family*, his heart said. *See how happy we are together and then you'll never let me go.*

It took her a few seconds longer than he would have liked before she said, "Dean will probably have a better time there than with me and Casey at the senior living center."

"You should ask Casey to come, too," he said.

"Maybe she'll join us after her shift."

"So that's a yes?" He could have been Dean's age for how hopeful he thought he sounded.

"It is. Now where to?"

"Somewhere we can sit and enjoy these sandwiches." Mia had been right. The day was sunny and in the low 50's. Perfect for where he wanted to take her.

They got back on the road and soon Route 112 became the Kancamagus Highway. Although it was several weeks past peak foliage season, the view was still beautiful. He gave a whistle as he came up to the infamous hairpin turn before the Hancock Overlook. "Man, I forgot how hard it can be to drive this," he said as he slowed his speed to fifteen miles an hour.

"Those people are idiots," Mia said, pointing at a car that had passed by going at least ten miles too fast. "Every year a few tourists end up in the guardrail or nearly going over the edge. I realize speed limits are usually considered guidelines, but when it comes to the Kanc, too fast is dangerous."

He had to agree and was glad the roads were clear and there wasn't much traffic. A few weeks ago, there would have been so many cars that speeding wasn't possible. Today it was an easy drive, but he knew to be cautious. She turned on the radio to a classic hits station and to keep the conversation going, he asked her about her dad and work, hoping it would keep her distracted from thinking about Dean.

A little over ten miles later, Cole got off the highway — really, the word was an overstatement since it was one lane in each direction — at Bear Notch Road, where signs announced it was closed from

December through March. Mia noticed immediately.

"I know where we're going," she said, and he was relieved to hear pleasure in her voice. He was worried that once she figured out where he was taking her, she might object.

They crossed over the Swift River, and it was as though they'd left the world behind. After a few more turns, Cole pulled to the side of the road and parked the car. Silently he got out, taking the food they'd bought with them along with the blankets he'd picked up the day before when he'd had the idea to come here, then walked around the car to join Mia. He reached out his hand and when she took it, his heart jumped. Every little sign of her comfort and closeness mattered to him. As they walked into the woods, he could hear the water getting closer — unlike the Kanc, the Swift River was aptly named — and soon they came to where he most wanted to bring her. In front of them was an old, covered bridge not strong enough for vehicles and only used by pedestrians to cross a tributary of the river. The White Mountain area was famous for these bridges, but this one was special. He couldn't remember how he and Mia had found it the summer after his senior year, but from the first time they'd been there, it became their place.

It hadn't changed much. The red paint, faded over a decade ago, was only a hint of color today. He'd been worried that time and weather might have ruined or destroyed it, but there were no signs telling people not to cross. Hand in hand, they made their way to the other side. When they came out, he stopped, squatted down, and looked. "It's still here," he said, and motioned for her to come next to him.

"So it is," she said as they looked at the "CH + MD" in the wood. He'd carved their initials the day before he left for college. It was a promise then, and he took the fact that the letters remained as a good sign. She traced them with her finger, then stood. "This would be the time to make a comment about a lot of water passing under the bridge since then."

"It would, but then I'd have to counter with one about things that stand the test of time."

She gave him a smile and took his hand as she stood. "Need help to get up?"

"I've gotten older, not old," he said, but as soon as he tried to stand, his stitches pulled. He winced and let her put a hand under his elbow to make standing easier. "You knew that might happen."

With a shrug, she said, "Occupational hazard. It's clear you're healing well, but certain movements are going to get you. Down is easy. Up? That's harder. Do you want to eat in our usual spot or stick to some place sunnier?"

He knew she'd remember this place as much as he did. "Their spot" was deeper into the woods, shaded and more isolated. With several blankets laid out to protect them from the hard forest floor, it had been an ideal place to make out. Emporium's first hit — the one that brought them to the attention of the record label — was written there. Today, though, it was too close to the end of the season, and she was right about needing the sun to stay comfortable. It would be at least ten degrees cooler in the woods. Besides, he liked the idea of being close to the bridge and their initials. "There's no one around, so we could spread out right here."

"That would work."

He opened the blanket, and Mia unpacked their provisions. As they ate, Cole noticed she seemed distracted. Not knowing if it was the place or the situation, he asked, "What are you thinking about?"

"Everything. Nothing. About how long it's been since I—we—were here last. Wondering about what Dean is doing and if he's having fun. And feeling petty because I'm kind of hoping he's not."

"What's it been like having him live with you?" He thought about trying to distract her, but he also knew how awful it could be to keep things bottled up. At first, she was hesitant, but soon her love for Dean had her telling stories that had them both laughing. It was wonderful to get to know Dean through her eyes. She sounded like a wonderful mother, the kind they'd both wished for as kids. Interested, involved, and loving.

Mia finished the last bite of her sandwich with a flourish. "Those were really good. I think the Davis's get their bread at the same place Sheridan does for the Just Right Café." She lay back on the blanket with her eyes closed, letting the sun warm her face, her brown hair fanned out around her. She looked beautiful, and Cole ached to kiss her, but he didn't want to do anything to spoil the moment. He could wait for her to let him know what she wanted. From here on, he'd go at her pace. He lay beside her, listening to the water rushing by, allowing himself to enjoy the moment. There was nowhere he needed to be, no one who needed anything from him. It was perfect.

He didn't know how much time passed before he sensed Mia sitting up. He waited to see if she'd stretch out again and when she didn't, he opened his eyes. She was sitting with her knees bent, her arms wrapped around them. From her expression, he could see something was troubling her, although she wasn't looking at him. "What is it?" he asked, shifting his position to mirror hers. "Is this about Dean?"

"No. Well, yes, of course, that's a perpetual thing, but that's not what I'm thinking about now."

"Then what?"

She brought her knees in closer. "I'm not sure if I should ask."

This didn't sound good, but he wasn't going to avoid the hard conversations. "You can ask me anything, and I promise I'll answer as best I can."

Mia took a deep breath, and he braced himself. Whatever she was going to say, it wasn't going to be easy to hear. Still looking into the distance, she asked, "Why was it so easy to leave me?"

Chapter Nineteen

♥

Her heart was hammering, and her head was screaming, *Don't ask. Don't ask. What if you don't like the answer?* But she said what she was thinking because she had to know.

The question had occurred to her so many times over the years. She vividly remembered the day Brett, a power-hungry weasel of a man, called and told her they were buying out her contract and replacing her with Paxton Jones. That had been awful, but worse had been the four intolerably long days before she'd finally gotten ahold of Cole, who said nothing but "I didn't have a choice," and "I'm sorry." She'd wanted to scream and rail at him back then, but there was nothing to say and nothing that could be done. She'd told him she never wanted to see him again, that he'd better not return to Fable Notch for anything more than a holiday or special occasion and ended the call. They hadn't spoken again until the day he arrived in her emergency room.

He was silent for so long she wondered if he was going to answer. Then he put his hand over hers, and she turned to look at him. She didn't know if the pain she saw was his or if she was seeing hers reflected in his eyes. "Mia, it was never easy to leave you, and it's been hard to be apart from you every day since."

He ran a hand down her cheek and one of the carefully constructed walls around her heart cracked. She needed to keep those strong. "At least you had success to keep you company and the awards to prove it."

"That doesn't mean you haven't inspired nearly every song I've ever written. Couldn't you hear that?"

She considered not telling him, then decided what was one more revelation in the midst of all they were sharing. "I did everything I could to avoid hearing Emporium since the day I heard Paxton sing *Finally Met You.*" It was the song he'd written her senior year of high school, to tell her he loved her. It was also the band's first big hit. Without her.

"I should have never let her record it." He shook his head and cursed. "I'd hoped you'd heard some of the songs, even though I can't blame you for not listening. So many of them were about how I missed you, how I hated myself for what I'd done to you."

Anger flared. "Then how could you let the record label replace me?"

"There wasn't any 'let.' It wasn't my choice." He ran a hand through his hair. "Brett brought us into his office to tell us about recording our next album. He loved the songs I'd demo'd for him, along with the response we were getting on the road. That's when I learned that Paxton filling in for you was a ruse. We were being auditioned to back her up. She was the one they wanted to push to the top. She'd been with two other groups before us, but they hadn't found a fit until Emporium. They were going to put money and publicity behind our next album but only with her as the lead singer. Otherwise, they'd find another band, and we were done. They weren't even going to let us finish the current contract. We'd be released without compensation because you had left, and therefore we weren't the group they signed."

This was nothing like she imagined. She'd always believed he thought Paxton was better for the band than she was and when the opportunity came, he chose music — and Paxton — over her. There was a lump in her throat when she said, "I didn't know."

He took his hand back and ran it through his hair. "It was a nightmare, and a dream come true simultaneously, and I couldn't wake up. The money they were offering for the next album was huge, and doing what the label wanted was the only way to keep helping my brothers. Theo had just lost Eden, and he was a mess. I'd gotten him a job as a roadie with us. If I was out of work, he was out of work. Nick was getting ready to head to college, and I was still sending as much money as I could to the Sinclairs to help with him. It was my job to take care of them." That was a familiar script. Although she came at it from a different perspective, needing to be the responsible one for other people was something Mia knew all too well. Cole stood, paced, and kept talking. It was as if now that he'd started, he couldn't stop. She could see and hear him reliving the frustration. "And then there were Brian and Hugh. If I walked away, they would lose, too. They were so fucking excited, talking about what they were going to do with their first check and wondering if we'd end up with a gold record.

But they weren't the ones faced with an impossible situation."

"That fell on you," she said, understanding.

"It always fell on me. I thought once I was out of Fable Notch and the band got going, I would be done with having to make those kinds of decisions. I mean, it wasn't like deciding how to pay the heat and delay the electricity bill, or should we have cable or internet, or could we get fresh chicken or was it going to be another week of pasta, canned meats, and chicken patties." Mia listened as Cole's pain came out. She remembered the pressure he was under, the times she offered to help him financially. He always refused, always too proud to accept help. It was amazing he'd accepted what he did from the Sinclairs.

She'd been in so much pain at what she'd lost, not so much the music as much as the man, she never stopped to question if he played a role in the change or not. Her parents had made it clear she was unwanted from the day she was born, their "whoopsy baby" who crowded their lives and needed to make herself useful. Being replaced in the band seemed like more of the same. It never occurred to her that maybe he was as miserable about the situation as she was. "I don't know what to say."

He sat next to her again. "There were two things I wanted, and I could only have one. I went back to them the next day to ask if there was any way for Emporium to continue with you as the lead singer. If they wanted some of my songs for Paxton, that was fine, but I wanted you with us. They told me you'd agreed to leave and had accepted a payment to get out of your contract. I thought.... I thought that if you agreed without a fight, it must mean you didn't really want to come back. But that's not what happened, is it?"

She could see how he thought that, especially given the pressure he was under from so many directions. "No, Brett told me the band had already agreed. He made it sound as though the label was giving me this money out of the goodness of their heart."

Cole gave a laugh that had no humor in it. "That's not possible. Brett doesn't have a heart. It's probably why he's been so successful. I hope it was a significant amount."

"It seemed like it at the time, especially since Mom's care was expensive, and I wasn't working yet. But it paid for a lot of what we needed and my nursing school."

"I wish I'd been able to choose you." She could hear the yearning in his voice as he thought back to what had happened. It echoed what she was feeling. "No, it's more than that. I wish I didn't have to make a choice. Family and love shouldn't be an either or."

She sympathized with that and hated it as much as he did. There was no way to know if things would have worked out if she hadn't had to leave. Emporium might have faded into nothing. They might have broken up for other reasons. The past couldn't be changed. Cole was here now.

As if he read her thoughts, he reached out and cupped her face in his hands. The warmth of his hand on her cool cheek sent a swirl of pleasure through her. She didn't know who leaned forward first, but a moment later, they were kissing.

Like the last times they kissed and the first times years ago, they fit together perfectly. Her hands started on his chest, then moved around so she could hold him to her. Even through the layers he wore, she could feel the strength of his chest. She ached to touch him without the barrier of clothes. She shifted against him, and the cool air brushed her skin where her jacket moved up. She shivered at the contrast of the icy chill against her overheated body. So many contrasts, so many sensations. She could get lost in him.

Again.

And this time, he wasn't planning to leave. Did that mean she could take a chance on seeing if things could develop for them? She didn't have an answer yet, but for the first time, she was willing to find out.

The sound of an echoing giggle and someone clearing their throat had them stopping. When Mia sat up, she saw a family coming out of the bridge. She'd forgotten about the rest of the world or its ability to intrude. She smiled at the couple as they went by, then turned to Cole who had his face averted. Was he embarrassed to be caught kissing her? "What's wrong?"

Her tone must have been harsh, because when he faced her again, he kissed the tip of her nose to ease the tension. "Habit. It's not you. I don't like to be recognized when I'm out."

She'd never considered that. "Is that always the case?"

He shrugged. "I don't worry about it back in Colorado, and I haven't since being here, but when Emporium's on tour, and I go into the city for any reason, yeah, I try not to attract attention. It was fine when we were at the orchard earlier. People were too busy shopping to notice me, but lying here with you, if they recognized me, there's the possibility of it getting to the press. I own a lot of pairs of sunglasses."

"That's got to be hard. To not be able to be you. To want to be invisible."

"I only recently realized how exhausting it's been," he said, wrapping an arm around her. She put her head on his shoulder, hoping he'd go on, let her get close the way they used to be. "When I'm on stage, I'm Cole Hanson, the rock star. No one in the audience knows me and they don't want to — just my music and whatever I stand for to them. Off stage, if they see me, it's the same. They expect me to be That Guy. When I'm in my studio composing, then I can be myself."

"That's not a lot of time to be you." It sounded awful. And lonely.

"I'm pretty relaxed when the band and I are putting together a new album, not including worrying about whether it's going to work. It takes hours in the studio even before we start to record, but it's my favorite part of the process. That feeling when it all starts working." Mia remembered a few of those moments. Watching him struggle with a lyric or melody for days until something clicked, and the song spilled out the way he wanted. "But once a release date is set, I know it's only a matter of time before I have to slip into my role again. Be who they want me to be."

No wonder he was ready to come back and be with family, be with people who saw the real him and with whom he could be himself. "It will be easier when you move home."

He looked at her as she said the word 'home' and dropped his forehead to touch hers. "I hope so.

It's been hard for longer than I've realized." They stayed wrapped in each other until a breeze blew in, making her shiver. "Time to hit the road," he said.

Part of her didn't want to leave. This place, which had held so many special memories, now had one more, but clouds were blocking the sun and the temperature had dropped. They packed their things and headed to the car, once again hand in hand, but this time she felt closer to him than she did when they arrived.

They drove to the other end of the Kancamagus Highway, then went where the road took them, driving leisurely until they were back in Fable Notch, completing the circle. Cole had been willing to indulge her and stop at her favorite fabric store in Ferncroft, where she bought more than she needed but enjoyed every moment. As the day went on, they continued to talk about everything and nothing. His brothers, one of the new nurses she was working with who had a lot of potential but still got crazy nervous as soon as a patient came in, his bandmate's new baby, the song that he'd been trying to write. After the intensity of their earlier conversation, it was good to talk about the everyday things.

Rather than eating out, they stopped at the Seven Brothers Brewery and picked up dinner to go so Mia could get home to walk Bowie. After dinner—and after he was shocked by how good Laurel's beer was—they decided to watch a movie. It took fifteen minutes of scrolling through the streaming service's choices before they agreed on *Top Gun 2: Maverick.* As Cole put a package of popcorn in the microwave, Mia took out a bag of chocolate chips and poured them into a bowl. "You still eat your popcorn with chocolate," he said with a smile.

"I do. Dean thought I was crazy at first, but then he tried it, and now he's hooked, too."

When it was ready, he filled the huge bowl with the popcorn, and they went to the living room. She pulled a quilt down from the back of the couch and curled up next to him. Bowie joined them and a few minutes into the movie, they had to turn the sound up to cover his snoring. She enjoyed the movie, but she hadn't been able to focus on it much with Cole so close. She was more aware of him than she could ever be of Tom Cruise. The scent of his skin, the warmth of his body next to hers. His arm was around her, and his hand stroked her waist periodically, making her ache for more.

When the credits rolled a little more than two hours later, Mia didn't want to move. She couldn't remember the last time she'd had such a wonderful day or felt so close to someone. Hearing his side of their breakup had shifted her understanding—and her emotions. No matter what else happened, there was a part of her that could heal, and she was grateful. A few minutes later, the channel started offering trailers of what they should watch next, so she reluctantly unwound herself, stood, and folded the quilt. Cole brought the empty dishes to the kitchen. When he returned, she went over to him, put her hand on his chest and said, "I'm going to bed. And before this gets awkward, and so we don't waste time standing around wondering.... Yes."

He looked at her for a second, confused. Then she took his hand and pulled him close. His eyes opened wider as he understood what she was saying. "Yes? You're certain?"

"Yes. Yes, I want you. Yes, I'm sure." She kissed him softly and pressed against him. "Yes, take me to bed." His smile went from happy to hungry in the blink of an eye, and he looked at her the way Casey looked at chocolate cake. A breath later, he'd scooped her into his arms and was heading for the stairs.

Chapter Twenty

♥

"Careful. You broke a rib four weeks ago. You probably shouldn't be lifting anything too heavy." She couldn't believe she was clear-headed enough to think of that.

He was nearly at the top of the stairs when he silenced her with a kiss then said, "You aren't too heavy. And I'm supposed to do exercises that help expand my chest and lungs. Trust me, if I'm sore after this, it will have nothing to do with what happened in the accident. Which bedroom?"

"The master," she said.

He turned left and said, "Like when your folks were at work, and we used their bed 'cause it was bigger than yours."

"Except now there's no need to listen for anyone pulling into the driveway."

"And even better, no need to rush." He pushed open the door with his foot and stepped in. As was her habit, she'd left the nightstand light on, which lit the room dimly and made it easy for him to see where he was going. "This doesn't look the same at all. No ruffles. No florals."

"Thank goodness for that." Her mother's style had never been hers. "I knew that if I were going to sleep here, it had to look like what I wanted it to. I didn't want to be in my parent's room." She'd painted the room a soft rose and added bedding in a slightly darker shade with cream-colored pillows. The old heavy furniture was replaced with light woods and clean lines.

"You could sleep on a cot, and I wouldn't care as long as we fit." He put her in the center of the bed and joined her. In no time, they'd kicked off shoes, removed sweaters and pants and were naked. There was a part of her that couldn't believe she was here, that this was happening.

And another part which knew it was inevitable from the day he showed up at her door.

As he brought her close, she took in the tattoos covering his arm and chest. She hadn't seen them since the emergency room and then she'd been too worried about his health to notice how beautiful they were. The music staff and keyboard in the sleeve on his arm. The giant hawk that took flight across his chest. Before she could look more, he rolled on top of her and kissed her deeply. Once they were close, there was no room for thought, only feelings. If this was the wrong time, if it was too soon, she would deal with the consequences later because there was no stopping this.

As they kissed, his hands roamed her body. His touch was both new and familiar. It had been so long — a lifetime — since they'd been in bed together and yet she felt an unexpected sureness about being with him. She knew what he enjoyed, what excited him, what drove him wild, and he knew the same about her. With every other man, there was always a moment of insecurity. Would he like what he saw? Were her breasts too small or her thighs too big? But with Cole, there was none of that. Only desire, sure and strong, and she let herself be carried away by all he was doing to her.

The feel of his hands, warm and rough from years of playing guitar as they cupped her breasts, had her body singing in ways that had nothing to do with music. He shifted from laying on top of her, settling by her side, giving them more access to one another. The tips of his fingers brought her nipples to hard peaks before moving lower. She shivered as his hand ran down the side of her hips, over the curve of her ass. He continued to move lower and when he brushed over the swell of her stomach, then between her legs, she gasped at the intensity of her response to his gentle touch. "So wet for me," he said against her lips.

His tongue explored her mouth as his fingers continued to touch and tease. As she enjoyed everything he was doing to her, she relearned his body. The muscles of his chest and back, the feel of his ass as she dug her nails in and made him gasp. He could have taken her then, and she would have been ready.

When he shifted and broke the kiss, she looked at him and said, "No, don't stop." Could he hear how she was practically begging?

His wolfish grin suggested he did. "Don't worry. You'll be saying yes in no time. I promise."

His mouth traveled from her lips to the edge of her jaw, to the sensitive spot below her ear, making her shiver. Then he moved lazily to her breasts, where he drew a nipple into his mouth and sucked hard. She moaned, the sensation radiating through her body making her shift her legs and point her toes. As his touch moved lower, she tensed in anticipation and was rewarded when he rolled between her legs and his mouth joined his fingers in stroking her pussy.

Her moans became louder and longer, and she was grateful they were alone in the house and hoped Bowie didn't think this was a good time to interrupt. She couldn't manage more than Cole's name and the word yes, but that seemed to be enough for him to know to keep going.

And he did. She ran her hands through his dark hair, then let go to grip the sheets. Every stroke set her on fire. Every touch made her want more. It had been so long since she'd been intimate with someone and even longer since she'd desired someone the way she did Cole. He'd been the first man to touch her this way. There had been a time she thought he'd be her only, and then years of never expecting to experience this again. Sharing this with him after so long added to the intensity of it all.

"God, Mia, I can't get enough of you," he said, and the warmth of his breath and the heat of his words added to the pleasure already building inside of her. As he licked and fingered her, sliding one, then two inside of her, her legs began shaking and her body convulsed, but he didn't let up, instead increasing the pressure and speed until her body arched off the bed. And even then, he held her hips and never broke contact. Finally, there was no stopping the building of pleasure. "Cole, I'm.... I need... I want..."

"I know," he said, and there was something about the truth of his words that sent her over the edge. Her hand gripped his head forcefully as her climax hit, and she let out a scream that only partially conveyed the power of her orgasm. Wave after wave of sensation coursed through her and for a moment, she thought she might burst into tears as a way to release some of the fervor.

The pleasure continued as he slowed his touch, bringing her down as her body shuddered. But even as her breathing returned to normal, she ached for more.

She was about to grab his arm to shift their positions when he moved from between her legs and kissed his way up her body, stopping to lick at her breasts again before finally getting to her lips. "I need you," he said against her mouth.

She knew the feeling. "I'm here."

"Don't move."

"Don't think I can, but where are you going?"

Cole rolled off the bed. "Looking for my pants and my wallet. I better have a condom in there."

"If not, I think I have some in the back of the nightstand drawer." He gave her a look. She almost laughed at the thought of him being jealous. "From a while ago. Habit, not necessity."

"Got one. Ooh, even better. Got two." Her eyebrows raised. "What? Do you really think that once is going to be enough?"

As he yanked the pile of covers completely off the bed, she pulled him close and answered from her heart, "Definitely not."

He ripped the condom package open with his teeth. She took it from him and loved the way he moaned as she wrapped one hand around his shaft and the other covered him with the latex.

As soon as the condom was in place, he pulled her legs apart, rolled over her, and settled between them. She could feel his hardness pressing against her swollen clit. It was maddening and wonderful. "What are you waiting for?"

"Tell me," he said, his voice tense as he held himself back. "Tell me you want me."

It was the sexiest request for consent she'd ever heard. She looked into his eyes and said with clarity and passion, "I want you."

And she did. God, how she wanted him. She ached for him. How could she have kept so much need bottled up for so long? How could it not have burst from her like a soda bottle that had been shaken? Because now that she didn't have to hold back, she felt as if she were exploding with desire.

Chapter Twenty-One

♥

The words were barely out of her mouth before Cole thrust into her, sheathing himself inside her, loving her body's tight embrace. Maybe there would be a time for going slow, but tonight wasn't it.

He hadn't been celibate in the time he and Mia had been apart, but he also hadn't been emotionally connected to any of his partners. Not the way he was with Mia. For all the years that had passed, in this moment, it felt as though nothing had changed for him. He loved and wanted her as much today as he did the day they said goodbye. Maybe more, because now he knew how special what they shared was.

At the feel of her wet heat he gasped, and she arched, taking him fully within her. Seeing her come apart as he licked and touched her had been beyond exciting, but it had worked him up into a frenzy. He dropped his head, gave her a tender kiss, then said, "Do you remember our first time? The rehearsal?"

She chuckled. "Is it wrong that we call it that?" They had both been virgins. He was eighteen and for more than a year he'd been aching to have sex with her. After endless months of heavy petting, by some miracle, they'd found themselves alone in this house. She'd turned seventeen a few weeks before, and they both felt ready.

Maybe too ready. He'd lasted only seconds and while he was hard again in no time, her mother came home and the opportunity to continue was gone. Cole had been so embarrassed it was weeks before he could even think about trying again. Then they were able to plan a bit. Knowing when her parents wouldn't be home, they made sure to have more time. And it had been wonderful. Everything his young heart had hoped for. After, Mia said she would always think of the other time as a rehearsal.

"Not wrong, but I'm worried that I'm in a similar situation. I don't know if I can last."

"Then lucky for you, there's a second condom," she said as her hands moved down his back to grab his ass and pull him deeper.

And that was the gift of being with Mia. Yes, he wanted this to be good for her, for them both, but she knew him in a way that no one else ever had, ever could. If he lasted a minute or an hour, it wouldn't change anything other than how long it would be before they started again.

As she brought her knees up on the side of his hips, he pulled out, then joined with her again and gasped at the feel of her.

"Are you hurt?" she said, concern moving across her features. "Is this too much?"

His injuries were the furthest thing from his mind. He ran a hand through her hair and kissed her. "My little bird, always worrying about others. I'm fine. I'm better than I've been in years. Let me show you."

It wasn't long before they found a rhythm. Their bodies came together as they always had — perfectly. He couldn't take his eyes off of her and her gaze was locked on him as well. He ran a finger over her beautiful, full lips, and she bit it gently then sucked it into her mouth, adding to the overwhelming pleasure he was already experiencing. Letting out a hiss, he decided two could play at that game and he took his finger back, slipped it between their bodies and found her sensitive clit. Her body contracted around him, and they both cried out.

Deciding he'd lasted long enough, he increased the pace of his thrusts and the swirling of his finger. She begged for more and he gave her what she demanded, what he wanted as much as she did, and when his orgasm ripped through him, he came shouting her name. Seconds later, he collapsed on top of her, hoping she wouldn't mind the weight of him because he didn't think he'd be able to move for a few minutes.

"That was..." he started.

"Agreed," she said and took his face between her hands and kissed him. He stayed there, nuzzling her neck and nibbling her ear, which made her giggle, before finally rolling to the side and taking her with him. He let go of her to grab a tissue and take off the condom. Then he turned off the light, wrapped his arms around her again and kissed her. She put her head on his chest, reminding him of all the times he'd held her like this and all the time since he'd been able to. The emotion of it caught him and he took a shuddering breath. Her head lifted, and she asked, "Everything okay?"

"More than okay. Everything is perfect." And it was. He wanted to tell her this was where he always wanted to be, but he wasn't certain she was ready to hear it. Things between them had moved much faster than he'd expected and although he couldn't bring himself to be sorry about it, he knew she might need more time. He'd give her all the time she needed.

And she was right.

A few hours later, they used the second condom.

The next morning, Cole woke a little disoriented, but as soon as he remembered where he was, he couldn't stop the smile that spread across his face. This was his third different view since arriving in Fable Notch, but it was definitely the best. Bowie was asleep at the foot of the bed. He liked seeing the big fur ball. This must be what Theo and Nick had with their pets. He looked around the room, now lit by sunlight. He liked the changes Mia had made, the way the room now reflected her. The comfortable chair in the corner with a quilt over it and a full bookcase next to it. He could imagine her curled up, holding a mug of hot chocolate and reading. He wondered if she'd made that quilt or if it had been one of her mother's.

Cole didn't think he usually slept badly, but this morning he woke feeling so rested, he wondered at how he managed all those other days. It had to be the woman in bed next to him and not just the sex, which allowed him to relax so deeply. She'd rolled over in her sleep, so he curled against her, molding himself to her back. When she reached and pulled his arm around her, he kissed the exposed part of her neck and said, "Good morning."

He would have gotten them both going again, but for some reason he couldn't stand the thought of using protection she'd bought for another man. Instead, he kissed her and breathed in the vanilla scent of her shampoo. God, he loved having her close. As they continued kissing, someone's stomach growled but he couldn't say whose. "What do you say to breakfast at the Kinsman after taking Bowie for a walk?"

She looked over his shoulder at the clock on the nightstand. "There will be a line already."

"But it will be worth it for blueberry pancakes and bacon we don't have to make ourselves." He knew her favorites in and out of bed. "And it will give people a chance to see us together, see the ring. Make sure that whatever gets back to Heather, she hears we're together."

"It's not a bad idea." He was glad she was feeling better about their fake engagement. Being able to help her keep Dean was the best thing he'd been able to do for anyone in a while. He was thinking about what else she might need to make things easier, when Mia rolled on top of him and said, "If there's already going to be a wait, then we may as well not rush."

They didn't rush, and he forgot his aversion to the previously purchased protection. They were both happily starving by the time they got to the Kinsman. As they waited for a table, a half dozen people stopped to talk to Mia before noticing him and Rosie made the expected fuss over Mia's ring when they were finally seated. He couldn't remember the last time he was so happy to be with someone. The last few days, for all the stressful moments, had also been the best he'd had in a very long time.

It confirmed everything he'd been thinking before he drove to Fable Notch. Being here was what he needed, and now that he'd spent time with Mia, now that he knew what it felt like to have her as a part of his everyday life, he knew without a doubt that this was what he wanted — every day. The only question that remained for him was whether or not Mia would want this as well. His life since coming back was calm, but that wouldn't be the case in a few months when it was time to put together an album. There was the manic intensity that gripped him as he was writing, the stress of recording and getting it right, followed by the tour schedule that would keep him away for months.

Would she be okay with that? Could she accept his crazy life along with his love?

"Did the coffee suddenly get cold?" Mia's question had him snapping back to the present and noticing that he'd stopped drinking with the mug halfway to his lips. "Is something wrong?"

Not feeling ready to say his thoughts out loud until he thought through any consequences, he leaned forward and in a lowered voice said, "I was thinking about how beautiful you look. Naked."

Her eyebrows shot up and he laughed. As diversions went, it was a good one. "I don't think you can say that in a diner."

"I'm in New Hampshire. Live free or die, and I want to tell you that there's nothing like watching you climax."

"How am I supposed to concentrate on my breakfast with you making lewd remarks?"

"You could concentrate on something else." This wasn't where he thought the conversation was going to go, but he liked it.

She took a bite of her pancakes, then said, "Nope, not working. All I can think about is how it feels when you slide inside of me."

He choked on his omelet. "You don't play fair."

"Didn't think you wanted me to," she said and winked.

After that, they finished eating as soon as they could and didn't speak to anyone as they left. He broke a few speed limits getting them back to the house, and they were naked before they got to bed. Turns out he didn't mind using her condoms as much as he thought.

The next hour passed without a single worrying thought going through his head. It was heaven.

As they got dressed, Mia said, "I'm going to work on Dean's Christmas present while I know he can't accidentally walk in on me, which means I need to do some prep work in your room. Quilting takes space."

"Not a problem. The living room is fine for me. I'm working on a song that I want to fiddle with. I'll have the keyboard headset on, so the music shouldn't bother you."

"Your music never bothered me," she said. Except when he wrote it for other people, but instead of saying that out loud, he kissed her. "We'll need to leave here by three to make it to Andover by five thirty."

"I'll be ready." They went to their separate spaces and as he let the lyrics and music weave their magic together, he couldn't help but think about Mia working on her own project only a room away. He loved this. He loved her. He wasn't going to tell her yet, not until they got through the next few weeks with Dean and the first hearing, but as soon as he could, he wanted her to know.

When he took his headset off at two thirty, he was surprised by how much he liked what he'd written so far. He was staring at his notes when he realized he heard singing coming from the other room. He peeked in to see Mia with her head bent over the sewing machine. He expected to see her wearing ear buds, but apparently the song was in her head. "You sing when you work."

She jumped at the sound of his voice. "Sorry, I was in the zone. What did you say?" He repeated it, and she shook her head. "No, I don't." She paused, and he watched as she seemed to struggle with what she was going to say next. "I never sing. I haven't since you left. Well, since I left."

He hated that she'd given that up, or at least believed she did. "You may think you don't, but you were singing. Something by Kate Bush if I'm not mistaken." He sang it back to her, and she blushed.

"I had no idea. I didn't bother you, did I?" She was noticeably uneasy, although whether that was about her singing or possibly disturbing him, Cole didn't know.

"Of course not. I've always loved your voice. I'm sorry you stopped because of what happened between us."

She looked away and refocused on the quilt. "Is it time? Let me finish this piece. I'll take Bowie for a quick walk before I change. Then we can go."

"I can take him out if you want."

"Thank you. That'll give me a little more time to get ready. I'm... I'm nervous."

He crossed the room to where she was sitting and gave her a quick hug. "I know. And I understand." He left her to finish what she was doing, put Bowie's leash on, and went out into the chilly afternoon. They crunched through the fallen leaves on the sidewalk, and Bowie stopped regularly to check for signs of squirrels and chipmunks.

When he came back, she'd changed clothes and was now wearing a silk blouse and skirt. It was clear she'd dressed to make a good impression on Heather's family, but he could see that she wasn't comfortable. "Do I look okay?"

"Yes, but I'm the wrong person to ask because I always think you look wonderful. Hope what I've got on is okay." He'd put on a burgundy button-down shirt, which was the dressiest thing he had. Jeans were going to have to do since he didn't bring any other pants.

"It'll be fine. They already know you're a rock star. They probably expect you to be wearing leather and a ripped t-shirt."

"Nothing like a stereotype to bring everyone together."

The drive to Andover was practically silent. Cole put on the radio—sticking to the classic hits station, not knowing if Mia still didn't want to hear Emporium songs—and the only speaking came from the GPS. Every chance he could, he took Mia's hand, and either gave it a squeeze or a quick kiss, hating that there wasn't more he could do to help her. She needed to see Dean and get him back home. Only then would she relax.

They pulled up to the enormous colonial a few minutes before they were expected. The neighborhood was relatively new and well-lit so even in the early dark of the evening he could see how large the houses were. McMansions, his brothers would have called them. As they walked up the driveway, Cole noticed some unexpected details. First, the car parked next to the Mercedes wasn't another luxury car but a much older Honda Accord instead, and while the neighbors had overly illuminated front yards showcasing perfectly manicured lawns and lush landscaping, the Buckley house only had the porch lights on. As they walked to the front door, Cole could see untrimmed hedges and overgrown flower beds.

Heather greeted them at the door with a huge smile that couldn't have been more fake. She called up to the second floor to let Dean know they were there, then led them to the living room where she introduced them to her husband, Ross.

"So, you're the musician," he said. Cole couldn't tell from Ross's tone if he was impressed or appalled. Probably a combination of both.

Before he could reply, they heard Dean flying down the stairs. He came in with a small, wiggling kid under each arm. "These don't fit in my bag, so they'll have to stay here."

He put down the children, and Heather introduced her eight-year-old twins, a boy, Bradley, and a girl, Bailey. They politely shook hands with Cole and Mia, but were clearly more interested in their new cousin, and they jumped all over him, saying, "You can't go. We had so much fun. When can you come back?"

As Mia made conversation with Heather and Ross, Cole looked around the room. The room was well appointed, which he expected, but there were details that didn't fit. Smoke stains covered the outside of the fireplace and there were burn marks on the rug outside the hearth.

When he tuned back into the conversation, Heather was saying, "Dean fits so beautifully with our family. We had a marvelous time. And you can see, the twins adore him. We can't wait for him to come back again. Maybe during his Christmas break." The twins cheered and offered a chorus of "please, please, please."

Mia looked decidedly uncomfortable, but said, "We'll see what we can plan, weather permitting."

"I'm sure you don't want to keep him from his family," Heather said. To Cole it sounded like a threat. He could almost hear her saying, "Don't make me tell my lawyer on you."

"Of course I don't. It's clear he's made a wonderful connection with his cousins."

They only stayed a few more minutes before saying their goodbyes and piling into the car. Mia was rubbing her hands as though they were cold. She probably didn't notice how she kept playing with the ring. Once they drove away, she asked Dean, "So, did you have a good time?"

"I guess." Great, he was not going to be helpful, but he probably had no idea how on edge Mia was. "The kids are fun. Heather and Ross are kind of stuffy, which I expected."

Trying to get some more information for Mia, Cole asked, "What did you do?"

"Not much. Heather drove me around so I could see the area. She took me shopping, got me a sweater that I'm telling you right now I'm never wearing again." Cole smiled. That was a good sign. "I think she was annoyed that I didn't have the appropriate clothes to wear to go to their club for dinner on Saturday night. I guess I'm lucky she didn't buy me a shirt and tie, too. There really wasn't much to do. I spent a lot of time in my room. Glad I brought my Switch. There are only so many games of Apples to Apples Junior a guy can play with little kids. Or how much I want to hear about how great my life could be if I tell the judge I want to live with her."

Cole looked over at Mia. He'd noticed her flinch at Dean's use of the phrase "my room," but he didn't think she had anything to worry about. If Dean had enjoyed his time or wanted to go back, they would be hearing a different kind of story about the weekend. Heather's pushiness wasn't going to win Dean over. Truthfully, Cole didn't think anything would. Dean loved being with Mia, but until this was over, she would be concerned.

When they got to the highway, Dean asked, "Could we stop at the Varnum for dinner? I know it'll be late, and I've got school tomorrow, but I'm starving. I need something that takes up the whole plate. Aunt Heather is really into portion control." Interesting. Cole had always been careful about portions when he wanted to make sure that his brothers got enough to eat, but it could be a weight thing for Heather. "And she serves cardboard pasta."

That sounded horrifying. Cole said, "What is cardboard pasta?"

"I guess it's whole wheat. It's supposed to be healthier, but it's brown and tastes like you're eating the box the pasta came in."

There was silence, and then all three of them burst into laughter. Mia said, "I've always wondered if it was any good. Guess I have my answer."

"Never, ever buy it. So, Varnum? Please?"

Cole looked at Mia, who gave a small nod. "I can get us there in two hours."

He got them there in less. Cole had mixed feelings about the Varnum Bar and Grill. It was where his mother once did most of her drinking — Cole had driven her home more nights than he cared to remember — but he'd also gotten a weekend gig bussing tables there, and Ken, the manager, let him play pool for money. At $20 a game, Cole could bring home an extra $100 on a good night.

As they walked in, he saw the place hadn't changed much. It was still dimly lit, with the bar area on one side and casual dining on the other, no tablecloths and baskets of peanuts and popcorn that customers could fill themselves. It was late on a Sunday, so it was easy to get a table.

Dean ate as if he'd been starved for the last two days. He demolished his burger along with most of the pizza fries they ordered for the table. Cole and Dean's chairs faced one of the enormous televisions. They watched the Celtics and talked about whether they had a shot this year. Mia participated a little, but he knew she was still concerned.

Back at the house, Dean dropped to the floor to play with Bowie and the dog acted as though Dean had been gone a month. A few minutes later, Dean headed upstairs, Bowie at his heels.

Cole walked up behind Mia, who was staring after her son. He encircled her with his arms and said, "He's happy to be home."

"I think so. I hope so," she said, leaning back against him. He liked the feeling that she was using him for support.

"I know so," he said. Now that they were alone, he had another topic to bring up. "I didn't want to say anything in front of Dean, but I get the feeling that all is not right in the Buckley household."

She turned to face him. "What do you mean?"

"As someone who grew up with so little, I spent a lot of time noticing what other people had that I didn't. I think Heather's family is having some money problems."

"You lost me," she said, and he explained what he noticed about the second car, the landscaping, along with what Dean mentioned about the food portions. "The food thing sounds like something a skinny woman like to control, but the rest is interesting. Do you think it means something?"

"I'm not certain, but if financial security is something Heather is using to bolster her case for custody, then I think she's lying."

"I had to disclose my finances, so I assume Heather would have done the same. Lucas would have said if anything didn't look right."

Cole hadn't thought of that, but still, something didn't seem quite right. "What if we hired a private investigator?"

"It's not a bad idea." He was glad she was considering it. "I could pull some money out of my 401K. That could cover the cost."

"I'll take care of it." He saw she was about to argue, and he put a hand up. "We'll call Lucas in the morning and tell him my suspicions. We'll see if he thinks they have merit and if an investigator can help. Please let me do this for you and Dean." *For our family*, he thought, but kept that to himself.

"I've got a shift tomorrow. I did only two days off this week so I could have Thanksgiving."

"Then I'll make the call and let you know how it goes."

She put her arms around Cole and hugged him. "Thank you."

He kissed the top of her head and breathed in the scent of her floral shampoo. Being in bed with her had been wonderful, and he wasn't looking forward to sleeping alone again, but being able to do something more concrete that could help her keep Dean was even better.

Chapter Twenty-Two

♥

While Mia got ready for bed, she thought about what Cole said and his offer to pay for the private investigator. If his suspicions were correct, it could give her what she needed to end this battle before it began. Having had money situations of her own throughout her life, Mia hated the idea of using financial difficulties against someone, but if it meant Dean could stay with her, it would be worth it. She hadn't noticed anything in the Buckley's home beyond how out of place she felt there and how everything looked new and expensive compared to what she had here. She knew that wasn't what made a home, but she couldn't help but worry that it might influence Dean.

But Cole was right. Dean seemed happy to be home. Over dinner instead of talking about the Buckley's, he talked a little about his classes and more about the boring work they gave freshman to do on the school newspaper. It was clear from his tone that even the boring parts made him happy. Mia could have listened to him ramble all night.

Before he went to bed, he asked her to review the algebra he'd done over the weekend to see if he'd made any glaring errors. It was the one class where he regularly asked for help. As they went through the problems together, it occurred to her that he could have asked either Heather or Ross to do this with him but didn't. She took that as another good sign that while he may like them, there was no real connection being formed.

Later that night, with most of her worries about Dean at bay, she found her head filled with thoughts of Cole. She got into bed early, but as she read the latest book by Lisa Bouchard, she found herself unable to fall into the magic or murder of the paranormal cozy mystery. They'd only spent the one night together, but it felt odd to be alone. She missed him. She wanted to put her head on his chest, feel his arm around her as she fell asleep, have him next to her when she woke in the morning.

Have him wake her in the middle of the night, as hungry for her as she was for him.

Things had shifted between them this weekend. It wasn't the sex, although that was wonderful. It was the time together and discovering that their connection hadn't gone away after so many years apart. That they could talk or be silent and both were comfortable. She understood his longing for connection and family. He understood her intense desire to do whatever it took to care for Dean and make sure he knew he was wanted. It was the same reason he'd done all he could to keep his brothers safe and out of the foster care system, even though it meant leaving her.

Love and commitment. That's what made a home. But what next?

She looked at the ring on her finger and wondered whether it could mean something long term.

She hadn't thought about a life with Cole in so many years. After he chose Emporium, it wasn't possible. It felt possible now, and that scared her. Her life has been molded by situations where she'd been told or shown that she wasn't wanted. As a response, she'd made choices which allowed her to be in control as much as possible and be needed for what she could do. Needed might not have been as good as wanted, but she accepted it. Now there was Dean, who definitely needed her.

More and more, she saw he was happy and hoped this was where he wanted to be. But Cole? There were so many questions. Could he want her to be a permanent part of his life? If so, what would that look like with his commitment to Emporium? After he'd broken her heart, she'd kept it very safe and made sure it was never broken again. Was she willing to risk loving him again? She didn't feel any closer to the answers when she finally fell asleep.

Before her shift started the next morning, Mia sent a quick text to Cole telling him to get in touch with her as soon as he finished speaking to Lucas. She would have left a note, but she didn't want Dean to see it and wonder what was going on. She spent the next few hours glancing at her phone to see if she'd missed his call. And a little before eleven, she was at the nurses' station reviewing charts when her phone finally buzzed. She skipped the hello. "How did it go?"

"Really well," he said, and she released a breath she didn't know she was holding. "Lucas agrees that there could be something to this. He's got a few PI's he works with, and he'll see who can get started on it the soonest. I told him the cost was no object which I think will help. He said it could take a while, especially with the holiday coming up, but hopefully someone will be able to find what we need. I have a good feeling about this."

"I'll let you hold that for both of us. I'm too nervous to hope." She'd lost too many things that mattered to her over the years — including the man she was talking to. This time, she wanted a legal guarantee.

"I understand. Anything you need from me around here today?"

It was a lovely offer, and she appreciated it, even though there wasn't anything. "Nope. All good. You could take Bowie out if you want. He'd like that."

"We've already discussed it. I wanted to take a drive, but he said something about needing to go to Significant Paws."

The pet store in town. Mia laughed. "Don't let him con you into going there. You'll end up buying more than you — or he — need. Trust me. I speak from experience."

A beeping sound told her that a patient hit the nurse's call button. "I have to go. Thank you again for calling Lucas and for being willing to fund this. It means a lot to me." She didn't need to tell him that, but she wanted him to know his support mattered.

Shortly after her lunch break, Mia's phone buzzed in the pocket of her scrubs while she was helping a patient who'd had a severe allergic reaction to some medication. She hoped it wasn't anything serious, since she couldn't stop what she was doing. It buzzed three more times before she finished, each time making her wonder who was calling. It couldn't be Cole again, unless he'd already heard from Lucas, but that seemed unlikely. Had something happened to her father? Was Casey trying to reach her?

When she was finally able to look at her phone, her heart raced when she saw she'd missed four calls from the high school. Ducking into a supply closet for privacy, she called back then sank to the floor as the secretary put her through to the Vice Principal. Mia couldn't decide if that was better or worse than being transferred to the school nurse. The Vice Principal meant Dean hadn't been hurt, but he was in trouble.

"Ms. Durant? This is Dr. Pike." As if the woman needed to introduce herself. "Dean's been in a fight with another student."

"What happened? Is he ok?" Dean had some issues with bullies when he started at the middle school last year, but nothing physical. He wasn't that kind of kid.

"He's fine. A few scratches, but nothing more. From what I can tell, he's not the one who started it, but we have a zero-tolerance policy for fighting. Both boys are being suspended for two days and the other student is also being put on probation from extracurricular activities for the rest of the semester."

She was glad Dean didn't lose extracurriculars. He'd miss the paper. "When does this suspension start?"

"Immediately," said Dr. Pike. Great, Dean was going to be home for the week since school was already closed Thursday and Friday. He was probably going to be bored out of his mind. "That's why I'm calling. Someone needs to come pick Dean up."

The one other time Dean had needed to be picked up during the day — because he'd gotten sick — Mia had been working, and Casey had gotten him. She thought of calling her friend then remembered someone else. "Cole Hanson will be there shortly to get him." There was silence on the other end. Yeah, Cole's name was unexpected and instantly recognizable. "Is that okay?"

"Oh, yes. Absolutely." Mia could almost hear the woman fixing her hair in preparation for meeting Cole. She should warn him that there might be some fawning when he got there.

As soon as she hung up with the Vice Principal, she called Cole. He answered quickly and agreed to get Dean. "Do I need to administer a stern, fatherly speech after I bring him home?"

"Probably not," she said. It's not like the role was actually his, but there could be an advantage to having Cole there. "But ask him if he wants to talk. He might say something to you he's not as comfortable sharing with me."

"Do you want me to tell you if he does?"

"No, he should be comfortable saying whatever he wants to you without fear of you reporting back." Sure, Mia didn't know if Cole was going to be a part of their lives going forward, but he was someone she trusted, and that was enough for now. "You could tell him about the time you were suspended."

"Proving I'm a less than stellar role model?" Cole had been suspended for arguing with and then throwing a book at a teacher.

"Proving that things happen, people make mistakes, and move past them." Her words hung between them. It was a summation of their life together and apart. Before they hung up, he promised to keep her posted. Less than an hour later, she got a text. *We're home.*

Free to respond, she typed, *All good?*

She watched as the three dots appeared. *Wouldn't say good. He's worried. And sorry.*

She understood. Dean was a caring kid who didn't look for trouble, although it seemed to find him more often than he'd like. They'd talk when she got home and, hopefully, he'd be okay with what happened. He was probably worried about this affecting the custody case. She'd wondered that as well, but these things happened to lots of kids from every type of home. And he hadn't started it, so that had to count for something.

The rest of her shift dragged, and she drove home as soon as it ended. The side door hadn't closed behind her before Dean ran up to her from where he and Cole were sitting in the kitchen, and said, "I'm sorry. I'm so sorry."

Mia had been more worried than angry and seeing the misery on Dean's face increased that. She opened her arms, and he sank into them. After a tight squeeze, she said, "Let's talk in the living room." Cole stayed back as they walked to the other room and sat on the couch. She brushed his hair away from his face and saw a few scratches. He was probably bruised in places she couldn't see. "I'm sure you did this already with Cole, but tell me what happened."

"Joe Rennery happened," he said, as if that explained everything. It almost did. Dean had had problems with Joe the year before when he'd been new. Neither she nor Dean understood why the boy didn't like Dean, but he'd taunted him for months until one of Dean's new friends threatened to report the bullying. "He heard about Cole being here, and you two being engaged. He made comments about how Cole must be slumming, and why would someone choose you when they could be with Paxton Jones? I didn't let it bother me — well, I tried — but then he said you two would probably start a family of your own and then where would I be?"

"Oh, Dean, that's awful. I'm sorry." All her feelings of having been replaced by Paxton and an unfortunate addition to her own family came roaring to the front. She couldn't stand the thought that this kid made Dean think he might not be wanted. "Besides the fact that this engagement isn't real, you know you would nev—"

"Yeah, I do," he interrupted. "Which makes what happened next even worse. I learned something about Joe since last year, and I was so angry I used it against him and started the fight."

"The office told me you didn't start the fight," she said.

"I didn't throw the first punch, but I started it." He paused, and she saw his reluctance to tell her. "I said 'Just because your mother left to start a new family, doesn't mean mine will.'"

"Holy shit," Mia said before she could stop herself. She didn't know the Rennerys or their family dynamics, but that didn't sound good.

Dean nodded. "It was a really low blow. Joe's folks divorced when he was in seventh grade, then a year later, his mom remarried. When she got pregnant, she and her husband moved to be near his family. They claimed they didn't want to 'upset Joe's life' by making him start over in a new place, so both Joe and sister stayed here with his dad. I knew his soft spot and went right for it." Mia heard the hurt in his voice, and she blinked back tears. Her son had a good heart. "I saw what was coming before it happened. His face changed, and he lunged. Then we were on the ground fighting. Someone got a teacher. Most people filmed the fight on their phones, so if you want to see what happened, I can probably get you a copy."

"I'll skip that, if you don't mind." She put an arm around him, and he leaned against her. "I feel like I should say something wise and meaningful here, but I've got nothing. You know what you did was wrong and why it was wrong. I understand why you said what you did, but my guess is you hurt him more with your words than he hurt you with his fists."

He cursed. "I gotta find a way to apologize to him."

"Probably a good idea. And, if possible, before you're both back in school on Monday."

He sat back heavily against the couch. "Yeah, I can do that. Maybe you could drive me over or something?"

"I'm off on Friday. Let's give both of you a little time."

"This won't hurt the custody case, will it?"

"I don't think so." She wasn't positive, and her worry hadn't stopped, but there wasn't anything she could do about it. For now, she'd give Dean her love and understanding. "These things happen and according to the official report, it wasn't your fault, so that's got to count for something."

He gave her a hug. "I'm sorry."

"I know." She breathed in his familiar scent. God, she loved having him in her life. And she hoped with all her heart this incident wouldn't change that.

Chapter Twenty-Three

♥

Dinner was a quiet affair. Cole watched Mia and Dean as they sat with their thoughts and wished there was something he could do. Not being able to offer anything was a challenge for him, but as much as he wanted to help, it wasn't his place. And there wasn't much that could be done.

As they were cleaning, Mia put her mother hat back on and said, "You brought all your books home, I hope."

"Yeah, I pretty much emptied my locker."

"Good, because you're not going to spend the week playing video games." Cole almost laughed at her imperious tone. "Use the time to get a jump start on reviewing things for the end of the semester. High school isn't middle school."

"Will do," Dean said, giving her a salute.

"I could give you a guitar lesson or two," Cole said. It would fill the time and give them a chance to get to know each other better. "If you're still interested."

Dean looked at Mia, who nodded. He smiled. "That would be really cool. I'm gonna go upstairs to read. Been a long day."

Mia went into the living room and slumped on the couch as soon as he was gone. "You don't think I was lying, do you? This isn't going to affect the custody case, right?"

Cole sat down next to her so she could lean against him. He put his arm around her and said, "No. Like you said, these things happen, and it wasn't his fault, which Dr. Pike stressed to me when I picked him up. She said suspending Dean was more procedure than punitive. I was told the policy is," he put on a formal voice to mimic the vice principal, "to suspend both parties to discourage students from instigating fights and then claiming it wasn't their fault."

"Which is pretty much what happened here. Dean was right about being partially to blame."

Dean had given Cole the details of the fight on their drive home. "He was, but I assume you're happy to see he recognized that and took responsibility for it."

"I am. This parenting thing is tough." She rubbed her eyes and sighed. "There's almost nothing you can control, which totally sucks. In the ER I know what to do, what steps to take. Here I'm at a loss nearly all the time, and I almost never feel confident. Was this what it was like for you when you were a kid and had to take care of Theo and Nick?"

He thought back. "At times. The worst was the two years after my dad left and before we met the Sinclairs. Mom was doing less and less, and there always seemed to be something that needed to be done. As soon as Theo had what he needed, Nick would have a problem. Fortunately, by the time her income really fell off, I was already earning money and Martin and Millie were there to do some of the parental things. I doubt Theo would have stayed in high school if it hadn't been for them. Or that it was a chance to see Eden. Nick was easier, but I knew that could change at any minute."

"I saw how much you worried about them, but I didn't understand. Not like I do now. Knowing that someone's wellbeing depends on you is a huge thing. I was thirty-one when I became Dean's guardian. I thought I was adult enough to handle what was coming, and I was still unprepared. You were...." She looked at him as the truth hit her.

"Younger than Dean when things got bad."

Her eyes were glassy with tears. She continued to stare at him with a mixture of concern and care, and he imagined she was reviewing his life with her new filter. She confirmed that when she said, "Oh, Cole. I am so sorry. And not just for what you had to do and give up for your family, but for not recognizing why you *had* to make the decision you did when the label made Paxton the lead singer. You really didn't have a choice. I would do anything I could to keep Dean safe and happy no matter what it meant for my own life. I was ready to move my dad and I to Florida if Dean wanted to stay there. I'd change jobs and wait tables if Lucas told me it would help my case. That's what you had to do for your brothers."

He didn't think he could love her more than he already did, but having her truly appreciate and accept his choices was a gift he never expected to receive. He put his forehead to hers. "It killed me to hurt you. All these years, I stayed away not only because you asked me to, but because I couldn't face what I'd done to you. I will always be sorry for having to make that choice."

She turned her head and kissed him, not a kiss intended to excite but to acknowledge their new understanding. He drew her close and deepened the kiss, aching to show her the connection he was experiencing. Passion and orgasms were great, but this.... This was a magic all its own. Knowing things could get out of hand, and not wanting to get to that point, he broke the kiss and tucked her under his chin. "Whatever happened in the past, I'm here now and however I can help, I will."

Her whispered "Thank you," was all he needed.

The next morning, Cole set his alarm so he could be up before Mia and assure her that he and Dean would be fine for the day. The smile on her face when he handed her a mug of coffee was worth waking at the ungodly hour. "I'm happy to check in with you," he offered. "Tell you how things are going."

"I appreciate that, but it's not necessary. But make sure he doesn't play video games during what would have been school hours. Otherwise, I trust you. And you don't have to stay cooped up all day supervising him."

"I've got songs to write. I'm sure we'll think of something." When it was time for her to go, he kissed her goodbye, and it felt like the most natural thing in the world. If they stayed together, would this be what mornings were like? He could think of worse ways to start the day.

Dean spent the morning reading stuff for school, and Cole took them to get sandwiches to go from the Triangle General Store, where Claire Fisher made a fuss over them both and insisted he take a jar of her bread and butter pickles with him. When they got back, Dean did a little more work while Cole reviewed his work from the morning. Later in the afternoon, Cole found him sitting on the couch with Bowie and a thick book. "For school?" he asked.

"Nope, it's *Different Seasons*." Ah, Stephen King, Cole thought. "These are the first short stories I've read of his. Did you know three of the stories in here were turned into movies? Don't wanna see them until I read them, though."

"I can understand that. When you come to a breaking point, would you want a guitar lesson?"

Dean smiled. "Hell, yeah. Let me finish this chapter and take Bowie for a walk, and I'm good."

While he was out, Cole got a call from Lucas telling him an investigator had been hired. Cole was grateful to hear and hoped there would be some news sooner rather than later. He sent a quick text to Mia to let her know but didn't hear back, and he assumed she was busy.

Dean's cheeks were still red from the chilly afternoon air when they sat facing each other in the kitchen a little while later. Cole thought chairs would be better than the sofa for learning to hold the instrument properly. It wasn't long before he realized that teaching someone something that came easily for him wasn't easy, but Dean was a willing student and understood that this was as new for Cole as it was for him. An hour went by before he knew it.

"This is a lot harder than you guys make it look," Dean said after needing several tries to get a note right.

"I said the same thing when Millie taught me piano. Part of me thought you picked up the instrument, put your hands in the right spot and poof. Turns out there's a lot more to it."

"It stings, too," Dean said, giving his hands a shake. "How do you do it for so long?"

"I've built up a tolerance over time, but at first it was awful. You're also using my guitar, which has metal strings. Most people learn on nylon. If you think you want to continue, we'll get you one of your own. But even if you use a pick, you'll end up developing callouses on your fretting hand," he said, miming making chords at the top of an invisible guitar, then holding his hand out, palm up. "I, of course, have them on both hands."

Dean leaned forward to look. "Damn, it looks like you do construction." Cole looked at his fingers. He'd never thought about it since this is what his hands had looked like since he was in his teens. Did it affect how his touch felt to Mia? She hadn't said anything, but he couldn't help but wonder. "Will you show me more tomorrow?"

He liked the boy's eagerness. "I will, but you'll have to tell me when it gets to be too painful. Been years since I felt that, and you're my first student, so I don't know what to expect."

"Deal. This was fun. Man, if anyone ever asks me how I started playing guitar, I'll get to say that you taught me. How wild is that?" Cole knew what Dean was saying, but that wasn't what hit him. He'd loved showing Dean how to play, sharing what he knew. There were a few moments of frustration where he couldn't figure out how to explain what he wanted Dean to do, but those passed quickly, and he didn't think Dean noticed. After only an hour with Dean, he could see himself wanting to do this more. He couldn't see himself being a seventy-year-old rock star like the members of Rolling Stones or Aerosmith. Could he be a music teacher instead? He smiled to himself, picturing the way Millie would tear up if he told her.

He took the guitar from Dean, still wondering about this new idea, when Dean said, "Can I ask you a question?"

"I'm guessing from your tone it's not about music."

"I read that you weren't much older than I am when you lost your mom, right?"

Interesting subject and a bit unexpected. "Yes, but because of her problems with alcohol, I lost her long before that. My brothers and I were pretty much raised by Martin and Millie Sinclair. She taught me to play piano, then guitar. I don't know where my brothers and I would be without them."

"Well, that's how I feel about Mama Mia." Ah, that was the point of the question. Cole had been wondering if they might have this conversation. He liked that Dean loved Mia enough to worry about her. "I don't know if you realize, but these last few months have been rough for her. Grandpap moved into that senior place, you had your accident, and she was the one to tell your family, then the custody thing and you showing up here. And now I'm suspended. She tries to make it look like she has it all together, but it's been a lot."

He knew all these things, but hearing it laid out like that made him realize how much stress Mia had been under and how he'd added to it. "I imagine it has been. What's your question?"

"You haven't been around long, but I can see that she means a lot to you. When you got here, you said you didn't want to hurt her again. Now I want to know if what the two of you have is temporary or serious."

Cole couldn't answer for Mia, even though he hoped he knew what she would say, but he knew his response immediately. He considered giving a vague answer, not knowing if he should admit what he was feeling to a teen, then decided Dean deserved the truth. "For me, it's serious. I love Mia. I always have, although I haven't told her that yet, and I'd appreciate it if you kept this between us. If she feels the same way, I'm planning to stay with her and with you. Are you okay with that?"

Dean considered Cole's answer and then nodded. "Yeah, I am. For all the weirdness of the past week, Ma's also seemed happy. I'm glad about that."

If Dean saw that, it gave Cole hope. "So am I."

Dean gave a single nod and left. He was a good kid. Alone in the kitchen, Cole kept his guitar out and strummed the song he'd been working on, now finding himself thinking about writing one about the challenges of a boy becoming a man and needing the right teacher. He was looking for paper and pen to write down some lyrics when Dean popped back in. "One other thing. If you guys want to sleep in the same room, I'm cool with that."

He left before Cole could do more than sputter. Cheeky kid. As Cole sat at the table jotting notes and humming, he couldn't stop the smile that spread across his face. He was going to like watching that boy grow up.

Chapter Twenty-Four

♥

The next two days were some of the toughest Mia could remember having in a long while. The emergency room itself was pretty quiet, except for two cooking accidents, one from someone losing several layers of skin to a mandolin accident and another with second-degree burns. Unfortunately, she felt as though she was always on a personal kind of high alert. On the few occasions her phone buzzed, she nearly jumped out of her skin. It was worse when it didn't buzz. Several times a day she checked to make sure she hadn't missed something or that her phone wasn't suddenly on low battery. It was hard to accept everything was fine and there was nothing she needed to do.

She didn't know what she was expecting. Good news from the investigator? Bad news from Heather? Check in texts from Cole? He did send those on occasion. A picture of Bowie and Dean playing. A question earlier that day about what to do for dinner when they'd forgotten to defrost something — she told him to order in. It was all so perfectly normal and completely different from what she was used to.

Nights when everyone was in their rooms were a little tough. She wanted to go to Cole, wanted him to come to her, but there hadn't been a way to tell him and with Dean down the hall, she wasn't sure if it was a good idea. No need to make things more complicated than they already were.

On Wednesday night, she came home to Cole and Dean laughing in the kitchen. Classic rock was blaring from a speaker somewhere. Cole was cooking and Dean was standing next to him, stirring something. Bowie was keeping a careful watch to make sure if anything dropped, he'd clean it up. Seeing them together made something in her want to burst with joy. The moment after she felt it, she tried to rein it in; there was something too risky about relaxing. "I thought we were having take-out for dinner."

Cole looked over from the pan he was tending on the stove and smiled. Seeing the happiness in his face had her forgetting about being scared that the sky was about to fall. Maybe, for this moment, she could let herself feel wonderful. He turned down the music and said, "No, you said 'Whatever you want is fine. Take-out menus are in a drawer in the kitchen.' I looked through what you had and found enough to make a meal."

"Wait until you see, Mama Mia," Dean said, peaking around Cole. "He pulled out a whole bunch of different things, a few leftovers, and a bag of tater tots. I'm working on the gravy. All it takes is beef broth, butter, and flour. Pretty cool, right?"

In a moment of panic, she asked, "You didn't use what I need for my scalloped potatoes, did you?" The last thing she wanted was to go to a grocery store the night before Thanksgiving. After learning they would be spending the holiday at the Sinclairs, Mia had called Millie to ask if there was anything she could bring. Millie insisted they had enough but, if Mia wanted, she could bring something she enjoyed making.

Mia got as close as she could to the stove to see what he was cooking. Whatever leftovers he was using had become some sort of amalgam that looked like a mess but smelled good. "It looks like you haven't lost your touch."

"I'm out of practice, but it's all coming back to me. And your refrigerator and cabinets are fairly well stocked."

Dean said to Cole, "Guess you don't cook much."

"No, not often. Things are done for us on the road and even when I'm home, I've gotten used to those meal delivery services," Cole said. "But that's not what your mother means. I grew up with very little and my special talent was making dinner out of whatever I could find or afford." Cole had been a master at making meals out of almost nothing. He used to joke he could stretch a food budget like a stereotypical 50's housewife.

"That served us well on our first tour," Mia said as she popped a bag of frozen peas into the microwave. At least some part of dinner would be healthy. "The label doesn't do much for opening acts. Cole used his talent for what we called 'rest stop cuisine.'"

Dean made a face. "That sounds horrifying."

"Oh, I don't know," Cole said, taking the tater tots from the oven and spreading them over the bottom of a baking dish. As he poured the contents of the skillet over them, he continued. "It's amazing what you can make from Doritos, condensed soup, and beef jerky."

Dean's eyebrows went up and one side of his lip did as well in a perfect Billy Idol imitation. The expression was comical, and Mia couldn't stop the laugh. "Amazing, yes. Tasty, no."

"Okay, not all of my creations were good." She said nothing. "Fine, some of them weren't even palatable, but it wasn't all bad."

She looked at him and memories hit her hard. Uncomfortable nights on the bus. Shabby hotels. Audience members who wanted them to be done so the "real" concert would start. Wondering if they'd be successful or if they'd dropped out of college for nothing. And through everything, she'd been ridiculously happy. In a soft voice she said, "No, it wasn't all bad."

He leaned forward and kissed her on her nose. It was a silly gesture, yet it settled in her heart, filling a piece that she hadn't realized was empty. Turning to Dean, he said, "Time to pour on the sauce, dude."

Mia watched as every inch of the meal was covered then topped with grated cheese and popped under the broiler to melt. She supposed as long as the gravy was tasty, the meal would be too. She could almost feel her arteries clogging. As Dean set the table, Mia gave Bowie a scoop of food. Cole opened a bottle of wine, then they sat down together to eat. After taking the first tentative bite in unison, there was a long pause. Dean broke the silence. "How the hell is this so good?"

Cole grinned. "It's magic."

"It's luck," Mia countered.

"Actually," Cole said, "it's really hard for anything to taste bad when there's gravy and tater tots involved."

Cole had a point. Regardless, this was exactly what Mia needed, and she was grateful for his help. She was a little concerned about accepting so much support, worried about what it might mean when he was gone. Then she decided that, like the happiness, she would let herself enjoy what she could when she could because they both knew how things could change in a moment.

The next morning, she woke at her usual time, but lingered in bed until Bowie barked at her to get up. She was slicing potatoes when Cole came in looking bleary-eyed. "When did you get to sleep last night?"

He put a mug under the Keurig and started a cup, staring at it as though he was willing it to brew faster. "I think it was around two."

They'd watched television until 10:30, when she'd said good night and gone upstairs. "Everything okay?"

"Can I be honest?"

No. Here comes that other shoe. "Of course."

He waited until the coffee was ready, then took a sip. She could have screamed. "First, I was laying there trying to will you to come down the stairs. Then I was trying to decide if you would be okay with my joining you. And then I had an idea for a song."

"If it makes you feel any better, I've considered coming to you every night since Sunday." The last few nights had been the toughest since he'd arrived. Her body tingled with need and awareness.

As if sensing this, he put his mug down, stepped closer and put his arms around her. "It makes me feel a little better, but not as good as having you in my bed would be." He kissed her softly, then moaned and deepened the kiss, making it clear he wanted more. She responded by leaning into him, loving the warmth of his body and firmness of his muscles she could feel through the soft shirt he was wearing.

She was about to put her hand under the shirt's hem when she heard Dean coming down the stairs. She turned away quickly and started working on the dish again. "He knows I've kissed you," Cole said.

She suspected as much. "That doesn't mean I'm ready for him to walk in on us kissing."

"Go ahead and kiss," Dean said as he entered the room and headed straight for the cereal, then the milk. "Kiss away."

As quickly as he entered, he was gone. She and Cole stared at each other for a moment before chuckling. "What really amazes me," Cole said as he put bread in the toaster, "is Dean is the same age you were when we met. It doesn't seem possible. Were we really that young?"

"We were. It's strange to think about. Eighteen years have passed."

"A lifetime," he said.

Before she could answer, Dean popped his head back in. "What's the schedule for today?"

"We're going over to help Casey at the Senior Center at noon." She'd changed their dining plans, but not helping her friend. "Then we'll leave with

Grandpap and head to the Sinclairs. We need to be there no later than 3:30. Dinner is at four. And—"

"We'll be eating for hours after that," Cole interrupted. "Don't wear jeans. You'll pop a button. There's gonna be a lot of football and food."

"Sounds like a plan," Dean said and left again.

Thinking about the day, she offered him a chance to back out. "You sure you want to come to the Center with us? Dean and I could come get you before heading to the Sinclairs."

"Stop asking me as if I'm being forced to do some sort of horrible, assigned community service work." He came over and gave her a reassuring hug. "It'll be good to see your dad for a bit before we're in a crowd, and I'm looking forward to meeting Casey."

He was so comfortable doing what she needed. She didn't always know how to feel about that.

Once the potatoes were in the oven, she went upstairs to shower and get dressed. Cole was right — it was a day for leggings and a sweater. She was putting on earrings when she noticed her hand. Thinking about Cole's family, and how Theo and Eden had recently become engaged, she decided to take off her ring before heading back to the kitchen. Her growing — or were they returning? — feelings for Cole were real, but their engagement wasn't.

As she covered the piping hot potatoes with tinfoil, Cole came into the room. It took him only seconds to notice the change. "You're not wearing your ring."

She shrugged. She wasn't going to tell him how much she didn't like removing it. "We're going to be doing messy food prep and serving work at the Center, and I don't want to risk it coming off." Okay, that was at least partially accurate. "Besides, it's not like everyone at the Sinclair's doesn't know the truth. I figured it wasn't necessary."

He didn't say anything, and she couldn't read his face. She thought he looked disappointed then annoyed, but ultimately, he nodded and went to get Dean and their coats.

Once they got to the Senior Center, they were thrust into a flurry of activity. Casey had work for them all. She handed them aprons, gave them instructions, and the next several hours flew by. It was fun and hectic. Another family whose mother was a resident was also helping, and they had a daughter Dean knew from school. Unless she missed her guess, Mia had a feeling there would be a date between the two before Christmas. She smiled at the thought.

When they had a moment of calm, Casey came over to Mia and asked, "How are things going?"

Mia had kept Casey up to date on what was happening with the custody case, but that wasn't what her friend wanted to know. "It's a lot. It's comfortable and fun and stressful and... I'm scared to death that when it ends, it's going to be unbelievably hard to put the pieces back." She took a deep breath and admitted, "It's been wonderful living with him. Everything I once dreamed of."

Casey gave her a hug. "Are you sure it has to end?"

"I'm not sure of anything at the moment, and you know how much I hate that." The unknowns of parenting were tough enough. Adding the unknowns of a relationship was overwhelming.

Before Casey could say anything, she was waved over by a resident and Mia got back to work. Busy was better. Kept her thoughts from running away.

When they were done mid-afternoon, Casey thanked them for their help and said she'd see them for dessert at the Sinclairs. Mia had been touched that Millie had invited her. They piled back into her car, this time with her father, went to the house to pick up the potatoes and Bowie, who had also been invited, and headed back out. If the cars in the driveway and on the street were any indication, there was a crowd inside.

When they walked in, they were greeted by dogs before people. Bowie was in heaven seeing Dani's dog, Otis, who he knew from the dog park — and vet visits — and meeting Theo's dog, Harlow, and Nick's new puppy, Lola, who looked as though she was in awe of the larger dogs around her. Somehow, they managed to step around fur and paws and greet everyone else who was there. As Mia and her family slowly made their way into the house, she found herself overwhelmed with hugs and introductions. First there were Dani's aunts, Rosie and Helen, then the recently retired veterinarian, Doc Wheeler, and his wife, Leslie, followed by Ed and Ruth Franks and their son, Gordon and his wife and three kids, one of whom, Brandon, was a year older than Dean. Mia was glad there were other kids, so Dean didn't feel "stuck" with the grown-ups.

A few minutes after they arrived, Janelle Novak showed up bringing the total number of people over twenty and the amount of food to mountainous. Mia thought there may have been less to eat at the Center. She was initially overwhelmed by the bustle, but soon found herself buoyed by the energy and the connection. This is what family felt like. She was grateful she, Dean, and her father had been welcomed.

It wasn't long before they all found places at the huge table. Appetizers were served but eaten carefully so as not to fill up before the main course. The biggest turkey Mia had ever seen was carried in by Cole and was greeted with applause. Martin did the carving, and everyone helped to make sure food was passed around. It didn't take long before Mia's plate was too full to add anything, and not long after that, she was equally full. Conversation was a lively blur. She glanced over at Dean several times to make sure he wasn't feeling left out, but both Helen and Dani had him and Brandon engaged in talk about movies and video games, and he appeared to be having a great time. Cole, who was sitting next to her, took a break from eating on several occasions to give her hand a squeeze or feed her something from his plate that she hadn't put on hers.

It was perfect.

An hour later, the table looked as though it had been attacked by a hoard of locusts and folks began shifting in their seats, rubbing full stomachs. Millie said they'd take a break and come back for dessert around 6:30 when more guests were expected. Mia couldn't imagine where everyone would fit, but figured Millie had a plan.

People broke off by interest as one group went to the living room to watch football and another headed into the kitchen to put away food and prepare for the next course and the additional round of guests. Mia and Dani took the four dogs for a walk. Mia used the opportunity to ask Dani what it had been like to reconnect with Nick when she saw her first love again a few months ago. "Were you glad to see him?"

Dani groaned. "God, no. I thought I was being given some sort of horrible test. Here I was, finally getting my life together in the town I've always loved, but before I could be certain I was doing a good job, in walks Nick. It was awful. Like when you run into your ex, when you look dreadful."

Mia understood. Cole's arrival was not good timing, given everything going on. Then again... "Is there ever a good time for someone to walk back into your life?"

"Absolutely. When you're tan, rested, perfectly dressed and confident about every choice you've made since leaving them and have some hunk on your arm." There was silence, and they looked at each other and laughed. "Yeah, there's no good time. You make the best of what you have."

Mia hoped that's what she and Cole were doing. She and Dani didn't stay out too long—the cold brought them inside. They hung up their coats, then went and found Eden and Janelle in Millie's music room. For a minute Mia considered joining the group watching the game since she didn't know these women well and wasn't certain she'd feel comfortable, but it wasn't long before she was laughing with them about everything from indecent yoga poses Eden found, to hideous bridesmaid dresses that Janelle had in her shop, to unusual names people gave their pets. By the time Casey arrived, Mia was at ease and enjoying herself. Soon after, Laurel and Sheridan joined them, which let Mia know that the members of the Stewart family had descended.

"Are all of you here?" Mia asked. Laurel's family of ten was an instant crowd. Mia gave some thought to where everyone was going to sit.

"No, Gabriel is with his girlfriend's family," Laurel said, naming her oldest brother and giving a shudder, "and the sooner he gets rid of her the better. And Drew and Jeremy are off skiing in Utah for the week, so we're *only* seven tonight."

"Eight if you include me," Sheridan said, bumping Laurel's shoulder with hers. Mia liked Laurel's college friend. The woman, and her café, were a welcome addition to the town. "We brought lots of desserts, so I hope people left room."

There were groans all around. Mia asked, "Did Adam bring ice cream?" Adam owned The Bright Spot ice cream shop, which served some of the best Mia had ever had.

"He certainly did," Laurel said. "Classic vanilla and pumpkin spice, which is rapidly becoming one of my favorites."

"Maybe we should take the dogs for another walk," Dani said to Mia. When a yell came from the living room telling them something had happened in the football game, Mia could hear her father's voice among the cheers and was glad he was enjoying himself. He liked the living center, but coming here for the holiday was a good choice.

"Mia, do you mind if I ask," Eden said, breaking into her thoughts, "how are things for you? It can't be easy living with Cole or having this custody situation hanging over you and Dean."

"And if anyone knows how hard it is to find yourself living unexpectedly with a Hanson, it's Eden," said Janelle, referencing what had happened to Eden when Theo came back.

Part of her wanted to gloss over the truth, but she was willing to trust these women and decided to be honest. "It's not the easiest arrangement, as you can imagine, but it's working better than I expected. And Cole is teaching Dean to play guitar."

"I saw those looks you two were sharing at dinner," Dani said, batting her eyes. "I'm guessing that's not the only thing making it worthwhile."

Mia wished she could deny it, but no one would believe her. "Yes, a lot of the old heat is still there, along with something new I'm not sure what to do with."

"Yeah," Eden said looking at Dani, "we get that. Do you think Cole will stay? Has this become something more than a charade?"

Mia looked at her hand and touched the space where the ring usually was. When she looked back at the women, it was clear they'd noticed. "I don't know. Sometimes I think that's where this is heading, but then I remember his commitment to the band. I know he wants to be here, and, for the time being, he wants to be with me. More than that, I couldn't say for sure." Even if she knew what she wanted.

Mia hadn't noticed how much time had passed until Rosie Kinsman stuck her head in the room. "Time for dessert, ladies."

They filed out and headed back to the dining room. Eden gave her a quick hug as they walked side by side and she appreciated the gesture of understanding.

Once everyone was seated — somehow Millie had managed to place enough seats — Nick stood up and clicked his glass with a spoon. "If I could have your attention for a second. When Dani and I were talking about today, I realized nearly everyone we love would be here. I wish Ryan were here," he nodded to Millie and Martin, who took his wife's hand and gave it a squeeze, "but I can't remember the last time I had both of my brothers and the Sinclairs in the same room."

"Not including the day I arrived and collapsed," Cole offered.

"True. And I'm glad that worked out," Nick said, taking in Mia as he glanced at his brother. "With all of us together, it seemed like the ideal time to do this." He pushed away his chair and got down on one knee. Dani gasped and her hands covered her mouth. "Dani Vaughn, I love you with all my heart. I let you go for too long and although the circumstances sucked at first, I am truly thankful we have found a way to be together again. Would you make me the happiest man in the world and marry me?"

He opened the Prince's jewelry box where an elegant diamond solitaire was nestled in the black velvet. Everyone held their breath while Dani was speechless for a minute then sniffled and said, "Yes. Most definitely, yes."

Nick put the ring on Dani's finger, and she leaped into his arms. He stepped back from the chairs enough to spin her around, then gave her a kiss that had the temperature in the room rising and wolf calls coming from a few of the attendees.

Mia couldn't stop herself from tearing up. Their happiness was palpable, and she was thrilled for them. They'd been through a lot to get to this moment. She was glad she'd made the decision not to wear her ring. As people applauded, she looked over at Cole and saw him staring at his brother with love and... something else.

It took her a second to identify what she saw in his features. It was longing. There was an ache in him, and she wondered if anyone else would recognize it. As though he felt her looking at him, he turned to her. The emotion remained for a blink longer before it was gone, hidden behind a lazy smile. But Mia had seen it and she knew.

What Nick had, Cole wanted. And unless Mia was reading Cole wrong, he wanted it with her.

Chapter Twenty-Five

♥

C ole couldn't be happier Nick and Dani were officially engaged or that he'd been here to see it happen. As much as he'd appreciated the video from Theo after he proposed to Eden, this was better. But a moment after Dani said yes, he locked eyes with Mia and something in him shifted.

Hard.

All he wanted to do was cross the room, take her into his arms and proclaim to her in front of everyone that he loved her and wanted their engagement to be real. For the first time in a long time, he was clear about what he wanted — a life with her and Dean, time to write his music and a chance to teach. As for the band, he had more questions than answers, but he was willing to figure those out as long as he could be here and with her to do it. The understanding had come to him less than an hour ago when he had some time with his family. He wasn't ready to say any of it out loud, but the desire was clear.

As everyone crowded around Nick and Dani, Cole thought back to earlier when he was hanging out after dinner on the three-season porch with his brothers and Gordon Franks. Martin joined them, bringing a six-pack of beer from the Seven Brothers Brewery. They stood and talked about the Patriots, who weren't supposed to be good for a few more years since they had a new quarterback, and snow predictions for the upcoming season. Conversation soon turned to work.

"I'm glad we have so many indoor projects lined up for the winter," Gordon said. Gordon was the "Son" in the Franks and Son Construction company. Nick had worked for them when he was in high school and then again when he came back to Fable Notch. It was because of Gordon's father, Ed, that Nick got into home redesign. "Gonna be a good few months. Something to be thankful for, that's for sure."

"If the house I'm working on goes according to plan, you'll have some work from me in the spring," Nick said. Cole loved the excitement in Nick's voice when he talked about his new business. "They want to add a second floor to a ranch. It'll be a good-sized job."

"Don't tempt the gods with talks of possible contracts," Gordon said, waving a hand around as if to push away bad vibes. "Nothing is set until it's set and even then—"

"It's not set," Nick finished. "Yeah, I know. But I've been a planner for too long to let the habit go."

Cole still marveled at the changes in his brothers' lives. Hoping Nick would be around for the next few weeks, he asked, "Do you think you'll be traveling to New York a lot during the winter?"

"Not sure yet," Nick said. "Definitely not for the next month or so. Things are slower now that the holidays have started, but they'll pick up in January.

I'm hoping I'll be able to do most of my work remotely, so I don't have to deal with weather issues."

Theo added, "And so you can be on the slopes more?"

Nick nodded as he took a sip of his beer. "That's the plan. The last few years I've barely been able to ski more than once the whole season. Things are going to be different."

"Never did see the point of racing down a mountain and freezing," said Theo, shaking his head, "but to each his own."

"Soon as you move back, you'll join me, right?" Nick asked, tapping his bottle to Cole's. Cole had been Nick's first ski instructor, but it wasn't long before his little brother was shooting down the mountain on his own.

"I've skied less than you in the last decade, but I could give it a try," Cole said. He didn't even own skis anymore, but he liked the thought of learning again alongside Nick. Maybe they could teach Dean. This was only his second New England winter. "Nice to see you thinking of ways to have fun."

"I like having my own business. Turns out, I'm a terrific boss, and I know how to give myself time off." That was a huge change for Nick, who had been working ridiculously long hours since he graduated from college. "If you find a place to buy soon, I could fly out to Colorado and help you pack. Get in a few runs on that fluffy western powder before we drive back here."

"Three days in a car with you? I don't know about that." Cole shook his head and made a face, but his voice was teasing because he thought it would be a great idea. Of course, if he waited until summer to make the move, Nick would miss the skiing, but

Dean could join them. That could be an amazing trip.

Cole drank his beer and pictured what he wanted to do and when. If Mia was feeling what he thought she was, he didn't need to buy a new place. He'd be happy to stay in her home. He'd need to build something for studio space, but that shouldn't be too hard. Maybe something with both a place to record and space for a new idea — a music school. Working with Dean had been more gratifying than he expected, and the idea of doing more was appealing. He could hire people to teach other instruments. Would Millie be willing to teach some students there?

He'd zoned out of the conversation and was enjoying his own thoughts when his phone buzzed twice and brought him back to the present. Since there were very few people who had this number, and he'd exchanged holiday greetings with the band earlier in the day, he took it out to check only to be sorry the moment he did.

Two texts from Brett Searle. *Happy turkey day. Need to talk to you and all of E this week about the new contract. Gonna be huge. Hope you're writing.*

It was as if the universe decided to remind him he couldn't only think about his needs. He should have expected it. The Grammy nominations proved they were still a bankable act. Their last contract had been for four albums. Would the label want that many again? Four albums, eighteen months apart, was six years. Tours were at least three months, usually four, sometimes five, which meant a minimum of a year on the road, probably more. What if the contract was for five albums?

A hand on his shoulder broke him from the math he was doing in his head. He looked over to see Martin standing next to him and the others staring. "Son, are you okay?" He didn't know what they saw, but from Martin's expression, he assumed it was worrying. "Did you get bad news?"

That was a good question. "A text from our manager about the band's next contract. He expects it to be big."

"Shouldn't that have you smiling?" Nick's was also a good question. Cole put down his beer and put away his phone. "Shit, I know that look. Theo, pull over a chair."

Cole didn't know what Nick meant, but a moment later he was being helped into a seat as he dropped his head into his hands. His pulse was racing, and it was hard to catch his breath. It was as if there was something wrong with his lungs again, but he knew that couldn't be the case.

"Deep, slow breaths," Theo said. Cole raised his eyes to see Theo squatting in front of him. "Follow my breathing." It sounded ridiculous, but Cole did as his brother said and, after a few minutes, his heartbeat slowed, and he found himself feeling a bit better.

"Sorry. Guess I can't hold my beer anymore."

"That had nothing to do with beer," Nick said. "You've never had a panic attack before, have you?" Cole looked at him, brows furrowed. "Your thoughts take over, loud and lousy. It's like a storm inside your head that you can't get out of."

That pretty much described what had happened. One minute he was thinking about his life here, and the next, years of work and commitment stretched in front of him. "I had no idea that's what was happening."

Theo said, "The first is always the toughest. I'd been warned about them when I was in the army, but even that didn't help."

"My first one was so bad I ended up in the hospital," Nick reminded them. Cole almost laughed at the competition, even if that's not what Nick intended. There were definitely places where you didn't want to outdo someone. Putting a hand on Cole's shoulder he said, "Yours didn't seem too bad."

"Didn't feel so good, though. Guess I wasn't expecting to have to think about this right now. I can't even wrap my head around going back on the road for our current tour, let alone what it's going to take to do the next albums." Hell, he'd just begun writing songs again.

Martin handed him a glass of water. Cole hadn't even seen him leave to get it. "Maybe you shouldn't sign. Maybe you should leave the band."

Cole took a swallow of the cool liquid. "Yeah, right," he scoffed, "like that's an option."

There was a long pause before Theo said, "Why wouldn't it be? Why can't you do what you want?"

Cole looked at him as though he'd spoken another language. "Let's see, there are three other members of the band who might not be so thrilled at that decision. And what about the other people who need me to be part of Emporium? Like Alan Harris, over at the souvenir shop. When I visited, he said he would have closed years ago if it weren't for the group. How could I do that to him and his family?"

Martin gave a sharp laugh that had them all turning to him. "You misunderstood him. Alan's wife has been trying to get him to retire for years, but he held on to the store because you guys started there. If you left the band, he'd probably sell it and finally retire to Florida the way she wants to."

Cole stared. He'd assumed responsibility where there was none.

Theo went back to leaning on the porch rail, took a swig of his beer and said, "I've always been curious. Did you ever *want* to be a rock star?"

That was not a question anyone had ever asked Cole, but he knew the answer immediately. "No. I liked the song writing better than the gigging, but performing was necessary to make that lucrative. I never expected anything to come of it until it did." And because it let him take care of his family, it was too important to turn down, even when it cost him Mia. "Once we hit big, I couldn't stop. I mean, who's crazy enough to walk away from something you're good at that makes you so much money.?"

Nick pointed a finger at himself. "I did. I mean, I lost a lot of money, too, but when I got offered the chance to go back to my job, I turned it down."

"Not entirely," Cole reminded him.

Nick tipped his head in acknowledgment and said, "True, but I'd be raking in a lot more money if I'd gone back full time instead of being a consultant."

"And you'd be on the floor with more panic attacks, too," Theo said.

"Also true. Not to mention I wouldn't have Dani. And to quote an old credit card commercial, that's priceless."

"If Nick could change his plans, anyone can," Theo said, as they all laughed. Nick was known for two things — his commitment to his plans and his priority around making money. But he'd changed. If both Nick and Theo could do something they thought they'd never do, maybe Cole could, too. "Why should you do something that's not making you happy anymore if there are other options?"

"And it's not your job to be responsible for everyone," Martin said. "I know you took that on early, but even then, it shouldn't have been yours."

Maybe it shouldn't have been, but with his parents out of the picture, there was no way he wasn't going to do everything he could to keep his family together. It had become the guiding point of his life—taking care of others. Could it be time for him to leave that behind and take care of himself? "So, you'd both be okay with this?"

"With having you around and seeing you more often?" Theo asked.

"Or seeing you happy?" added Nick. "Yeah, we could be very okay with that."

"It's not like we're getting laid because our brother is a rock star," Theo said. Cole gave a startled snort. He was pretty certain neither of them had ever used his fame to get a girl. "But seriously, of course we'd be okay. We *are* okay. Haven't you noticed?"

He looked at his brothers and allowed himself to take in their happiness and success and the part he played in their being able to find their way. It hadn't been smooth, and there'd been some scary moments, but Theo was right — they were both doing well. Cole couldn't be happier for them.

"I, on the other hand, will be completely heart-broken and never get over it if you leave the band," Gordon said. There was no pause before they all burst out laughing. When the chuckling stopped, he added, "If you need a gig to tide you over like Nick did, come on by and we'll teach you construction."

"Thanks," Cole said. "I appreciate the offer."

"Don't listen to him," Nick said. "As someone who's managed your portfolio, I can tell you that you could sit on your ass for ten years and still be doing okay financially."

"That's good to hear, but I know what I want to do." They all stared at him and for a moment he considered saying he wasn't ready to talk about it, but he decided he needed to say it out loud, make it more real. With a slow smile, he told them about the music school idea. By the time they went in for dessert, Cole was not only feeling better, he was feeling hopeful.

And now he stood in the dining room, congrat-ulating his baby brother on his engagement and wondering how much longer he and Mia had to stay there before he could get her home. He wanted to hold her, tell her he loved her, then tell her about his plans and how he hoped she would be a part of them.

It was another two hours before they finally left the Sinclairs, and even though they'd stopped eating a while before, he was still full. They dropped Mia's dad back at the living facility and made sure he was settled before heading home. He hadn't spoken with Mia's father much, even when they were volunteering earlier, but he could see that he loved his daughter and new grandson.

It was nearly nine when they finally made it home. After finding space in the refrigerator for all the leftovers Millie gave them — Mia wasn't going to need to cook for the rest of the weekend from the looks of it — Dean took Bowie for a walk while Cole and Mia sat on the couch. He loved the feeling of her snuggled against him and he couldn't resist kissing her. Softly at first and then with more passion. She caressed the side of his neck, making him shiver, but they pulled apart when they heard Dean come back. "It's as bad as when your parents were here," he said.

"Guess there are some things that don't change."

He put his mouth by her ear and said, "Including how much I want you."

It was her turn to shiver. He smiled at the encouraging response. Maybe tonight he'd go upstairs after he was sure Dean was asleep.

Dean and Bowie came into the room, both sitting on the other couch. Cole was glad Mia didn't move out of his arms. "Can we watch *Shawshank Redemption*? I finished the story. I want to see the differences."

Two and a half hours later, the movie came to a close as Red joined Andy in Mexico, and Mia was dozing against him. "Movie's done," he whispered to her, and she curled into him more.

He could have stayed that way for hours, but when Dean stood and Bowie jumped up to follow, she woke. "All that turkey finally caught up with me," she said, stretching. "Guess I'll head upstairs and sleep off the rest of the day. See you in the morning." She gave him a kiss and went to bed.

He sat there for a minute longer, listening to the noise above him, finding it comforting. He remembered when he was younger and listening for where his brothers were in the house, not falling asleep until they were both home and safe. In the span of only a few days, the same thing had happened for him with Mia and Dean.

It was - almost – everything he wanted.

He headed to his room, then changed into sleep pants and laid on top of his covers with a book, hoping he'd feel tired soon. Instead, all he could think about was what he'd learned while talking with his brothers and what he was going to say to the band about leaving. A few more hurdles, and he could have what he wanted.

Mia.

That was the other thing keeping him from sleeping. Thoughts of going upstairs and ravishing her, but she'd seemed exhausted, and he didn't want to bother her. Too restless, he took out his guitar and the notebook he'd been writing in and started to play. He was fiddling around with some lyrics that weren't right yet when he thought he heard a knock at the door. "Come in?"

Mia pushed the door open, and he was instantly hard. Lyrics and music went out of his head as he looked at her. The last time they were together, she went from clothed to naked, nothing in between. Now she stood wearing a dark red night shirt that wasn't meant to entice and she still looked sexier than anyone he'd ever known. In a whisper she said, "I thought I heard you playing. Is everything okay?"

He held out his hand, and she came to him. "It is now." He put the guitar on the floor, letting it lean on the nightstand, then kissed her, letting loose all he'd been feeling throughout the day.

"We have to be quiet," she said. They were so close it wasn't necessary to be loud.

"Like when we were kids."

"Except now it's because I have a kid."

That was a definite change, and one he didn't mind at all. As they continued to kiss, he moved his hands to her thigh, just below where her shirt stopped so he could stroke her legs then work his way higher. At the same time, she found the edge of his t-shirt and they pulled apart long enough for him to take it off.

She moved her mouth from his lips to his chest where she traced his tattoos, caressing the wings of the hawk that started on his left side and arched across. She swirled her tongue around his nipple then blew, the cool air making him suck in a breath and close his eyes with pleasure. It didn't take much for her to drive him crazy. When she kissed a familiar spot. She stopped and he wondered if she noticed?

A moment later, she answered his unspoken question with a question of her own. "Is that my name?"

He didn't open his eyes, simply put his hand on his heart where he knew she was looking. Under the wing of the hawk was a smaller bird, and inked into that bird's wing was the word, Mia. How many nights had he put his hand there to calm himself, to help himself fall asleep? "Yes."

"When?"

"When I knew you weren't coming back. When I knew I couldn't leave." It had been his first tattoo, placed in the spot where she'd spent hundreds of hours resting her head. When he'd had the larger ones done, he'd made sure the bird was never covered.

"I can't believe I didn't notice it last time."

"I suppose you were distracted by other things." She gave a small laugh and kissed the image. He opened his eyes and pushed her hair away from her face so he could see her clearly. "I had to have you close. I didn't want to be without you."

"Cole..." Her voice trailed off.

She may not know what she wanted to say, but he did. "It's simple. I love you, little bird. I always have, and if the last few weeks have shown me anything, it's that I always will."

Chapter Twenty-Six

♥

He loved her.

Hearing him say it was more wonderful than she expected. She'd seen it in his actions, felt it the last time they were in bed together, but this was different. She glanced again at the bird tattoo and thought of him carrying her with him all these years. She never would have guessed. She was the unwanted baby in her family and the unwanted singer in the band. But Cole *had* wanted her, even if he hadn't been able to choose her. She kissed him, then said what she hadn't said to anyone since he'd left. "I love you, too."

His arms came around her and she melted into him. As wonderful as his mouth was on hers, she wanted more. Words and actions were one thing, but there was another way she could show him how much their connection meant. She pushed herself up, kissed him deeply, then worked her way down his body. He managed to say, "What are you..." before she grabbed his pants and pulled them off along with his briefs.

She loved having him naked before her. The muscles of his chest and abdomen maybe weren't as tight as when they were teens, but who's were? He was still incredibly sexy. She traced the line of hair that started above his stomach to his groin, first with her hand, then with her lips, and smiled as his cock bobbed up as if to greet her moments before she took him into her mouth. His moan was all the encouragement she needed. She swirled her tongue around the tip as she wrapped her fingers around the base, then used her other hand to cup and caress his balls. This time, the moan was louder. "Shh," she said. "We have to keep quiet if we want to keep going."

"This is torture," he said, barely moving his lips.

"Should I stop?"

"Don't. You. Dare." She gave a soft laugh and continued to please and tease his cock. He brushed her hair away from her face, and she glanced at him. Seeing him watching her gave her a surge of feminine power, and she refocused on driving him crazy. She must have done something right because after a few minutes, he sat up and grabbed her hips. "Come to me."

Now it was her turn to be confused until he pulled one of her legs over his chest, so her pussy was in front of his face. A second later, his mouth was on her as she lay on top of him. Giving and receiving mixed together in a tangle of desire that she willingly surrendered to. It became a wondrous game of pleasure. If he made her gasp, he felt her reaction on his shaft. When he moaned, her pussy vibrated. They drove each other to new heights, each trying to outdo the other until he stopped licking her and put his hand on her shoulder. She took her mouth off him, looked back, and gave a slow smile. "Is there a problem?"

"Hardly, but I want to be inside of you when I come. Turn around."

As she did what he asked, he opened the nightstand and took out a box of condoms. "Aren't you an optimist?" she said with a laugh.

He took one out and ripped open the package. "I was definitely hopeful. Besides, we used my only two last time. I thought of driving over to Littleton to get them and avoid undue notice, but I figured if anyone saw me buying them here, it would add to what people were already saying about us."

She covered her face with her hand. "Okay, part of me wants to crawl under the covers and disappear."

Sitting up, he kissed her below her ear, and she gave a soft sigh. "And the other part of you?"

"Wants you to put one of those on as fast as possible so you can be inside of me already."

He tore the condom open and rolled it over his erection, then turned to her. She threw one leg over him and grabbed his cock again. Holding herself above him, she teased her opening with the tip, feeling her wetness coat his erection and her hand. Putting only the head in, she tried to prolong the tension, but he grabbed her hips and pulled her down, forcing her to let go of him as he filled her. Her head fell back at the sensation of being connected to him. She shifted her hips, adjusting to his girth, letting the pleasure build again. Then she looked at him and gasped. The passion and love in his eyes were so plain, so raw.

So real.

If there were any walls left around her heart, any doubts in her mind, they disappeared.

As she let the emotions consume her, she let her desire do the same. This was the man she'd always loved and would love forever. There was no one for her but Cole.

He reached up and palmed her breasts, his thumbs teasing her nipples. Her body was alive with sensation and need.

She rocked against him, enjoying how full she felt. When she thrust her hips forward, her head fell back.

"God, you're gorgeous," he said. The wonder in his voice was thrilling.

She raked a hand down his chest, pinching his nipples, making him gasp. "Need. More," she said, struggling to be quiet. Fortunately, he knew what she was aching for, and his hand came between them, his finger finding her swollen clit. His mouth had already made her excited and needy. His touch brought that all back, and her body reacted with a flood of desire.

When she thought she couldn't take any more, he grabbed her hips and built a rhythm between them. She saw the change in his expression telling her he was close. She fell forward and covered his mouth with hers, muffling his cries as they came together.

They stayed there kissing and trying to breathe normally until finally his softening cock slipped from her body. He removed the condom with a tissue and held her close. "Well," he whispered, "that was something to be thankful for."

"No argument." As they lay there, relaxed and comfortable, she said, "I liked what I heard you playing when I came in." She almost didn't knock because it sounded so beautiful, but she needed to be near him. "New song?"

"It is, but I'm stuck. It's close, but not quite right. Do you want to hear?" She nodded. He sat up, picked up the guitar, and adjusted the covers so he positioned it right.

"Have you ever played naked before?"

"Nope, this is a first." He played what he had so far, singing along. "And I've never been able to decide, if you're more beautiful in the sunset or the moonlight. If I prefer your smile or your sighs. But I know your laughter is my favorite sound. And I want to kiss you always. Let me back into your heart. Let me back into your life. Let me be the last man you kiss."

"Forever," she said, and he gave her a quizzical look. "Change it to 'I want to kiss you forever.' The extra syllable will make it flow better. And you're playing a D chord. Try a D7."

He made the changes and sang it again. "That's it," he said. "Sing it with me?"

Her heart skidded. He'd shown her that she sang while she quilted, but that was alone and unconsciously. The last time she'd sung with him was more than ten years ago. A lifetime of choices and mistakes and.... It didn't matter. They were together now, and she wanted this. She nodded, and they repeated the verse. "Wow," she said as their voices trailed off. Somehow, she'd forgotten how they sounded together.

He leaned over his guitar and kissed her. "Very wow. I'm promising you now, this song is yours. I'm not sharing it."

She knew what he was telling her. Unlike *Finally Met You*, she'd never have to hear this song with

Paxton's voice on the radio. She took the guitar from his lap, put it on the floor next to the bed, and curled into him. "Thank you."

They laid in bed talking, kissing, then making love once more. When the sky started to lighten, Mia said, "I should get back to my room."

"And I should tell you something Dean told me." He told her about Dean being okay with them sleeping together, and she laughed.

"That boy." It was a little embarrassing to know he'd talked to Cole about this, but she was also glad he was supportive of the relationship.

"He's wonderful."

"I know. Let's get through this custody madness. Then we'll tell him about you staying and change our sleeping arrangements." For the first time, she allowed herself to hope that everything was going to work out. Cole and Dean would be part of her life.

It was hard to get out of bed, but it was the right thing. For now. He walked her to the door, kissed her, and said, "One more thing."

"Yes?"

He picked up her hand. "Put the ring back on."

As soon as she was in her room, she did.

Chapter Twenty-Seven

♥

Mia managed a few hours of sleep in her own bed before coming down on Friday morning. Sex really could tire a person out, especially good sex. When she walked into the kitchen, Cole was already sitting at the table with a mug of coffee and a slice of pumpkin bread, although he'd barely touched it. She wasn't ready for food yet, but there was something else she wanted. With Dean not around, she gave him a lingering kiss, then stole a sip of his coffee before pouring herself a cup.

Dean didn't get up until close to noon. "I think I had a food coma after last night," he said after downing half a glass of orange juice. "Can't believe I'm hungry this morning, but I am."

"Millie sent us home with plenty of food, so feel free to forage," Mia said. She was already thinking about having stuffing and gravy for lunch.

After eating, Dean called and confirmed Joe Rennery was home, and Mia drove Dean to his nemesis' house. Before they left, Cole told Dean he was proud of him for taking responsibility for his part in what happened, and although he tried to hide it, Dean blushed at the compliment. Mia liked seeing the way the two of them connected. It meant everything to her that Cole fit in with their lives.

Once at the Rennery's, Joe and Dean went into the living room to work things out while Mia made small talk with Stanley, Joe's father. It was uncomfortable as Stanley stammered out his own apologies, but she figured if Dean could do the hard work of facing his bully and apologizing for his part in their fight, she could manage a few awkward moments with another parent. It took longer than she thought, and twenty minutes later, they were back in the car.

"Well, we're never going to be friends," Dean said, leaning back into his seat and slouching, "But I don't think I'll be having any more problems with Joe. And he won't have any from me. Neither will you, Mama Mia."

"So, you're going to be perfect from here on?" He gave her a half smile. "Exactly, people make mistakes. Hopefully, we learn so we don't repeat them, but no one gets through life without screwing up. With any luck, you'll continue to have people in your life who help you through those times and love you no matter what." She thought of the bird tattoo on Cole's chest. They'd missed a lot of time together, but knowing he loved her was a balm. They'd both made decisions and mistakes, and she wanted time to build on what they'd rediscovered.

"Love you, Ma."

She glanced at him and saw Ashley in his expression. *You did so well with him, my friend.* "Love you, too."

Back at home, the three of them spent the rest of the day doing nothing, and it was wonderful. Mia worked in the bedroom on Dean's quilt while Dean hooked his Switch up to the television and taught Cole how to play Smash Bros. She hoped the game, along with more guitar lessons, would keep them busy over the weekend since her next work shift started on Saturday.

She couldn't deny that after working twelve hours the next day, she was looking forward to coming home to Cole. She loved sharing about her work (a light day with more paperwork than patients), hearing what he and Dean had done (she'd been right about the video games and guitar lessons), and listening to some new lyrics he'd written. On Sunday night, Dean played her the notes he'd learned and was thrilled when it almost sounded like a song. The look on Cole's face told her how much he enjoyed teaching and how proud he was of Dean. She couldn't remember if she'd ever felt so happy.

Monday was work for Mia, but Tuesday started her next set of days off. After Dean left for school, Mia and Cole gave each other a pointed look and practically ran up to her bedroom where they made love for the next several hours. They were discussing going out for lunch and the downsides of having to put on clothes when Mia's phone rang. Her heart started racing when she saw the ID. "It's Lucas." She tossed on her shirt, feeling awkward about being naked while talking on the phone with her lawyer, then answered and put the phone on speaker. "Hey there. You're on speaker with me and Cole. Have you heard anything?"

"I've heard all I need. Cole, not only were you right, but there was more going on than you could have guessed."

Mia looked at Cole and then back at the phone. Lucas didn't sound upset, so Mia was willing to be cautiously optimistic. "What does that mean?"

"Are you sitting down?"

Mia put a finger to her lips. No need to tell Lucas exactly where they were. "Yes."

"The Buckley's have, in fact, had some financial difficulties in the last two years. They've been spending above their means and recently had some investments that didn't pay off as expected. My investigator turned up information on credit cards the Buckley's took out in their children's names and were not disclosed, as well as some other bills which were recently paid by Heather's in-laws which lowered their liability and made them look better on paper. In addition, they put in an application for a home equity loan after their financials were turned over to the lawyers."

Mia was confused. She understood financial difficulties, but not the Buckley's decision to pursue custody in their current situation. "Then why does she want to be responsible for another person?" Adding a teen was not going to make things easier financially.

"This is where it gets interesting," Lucas said. "It seems Ashley's parents felt guilty for what they had done years ago and wanted to make sure she and her child were taken care of in the future. Their life insurance policies, his pension, and various other financial earnings were put into a trust for Ashley. They didn't know she'd died. With Ashley's death, the trust automatically goes to Dean. However, Dean is still a minor, which means..."

"His legal guardian has control over the money," Cole finished. Heather had been motivated by money, not love. Shocked, and not certain how to take the news, Mia dropped the phone onto the covers. Cole put one hand over hers, picked up the phone and asked, "I assume it's a fairly substantial amount."

"I'm not sure of the exact totals, but from the quick numbers the investigator told me, I'm guessing it's low- to mid-six figures." Cole whistled. "Exactly. Enough to get the Buckley's back on their feet. And as far as I can tell from the documents I've been sent, nothing would have protected that money from Heather. It was set up for Ashley to use as she wanted to take care of herself and her son. If Heather got custody, she could have drained it with impunity. She wouldn't even have to disclose the amount to Dean."

Mia's thoughts were still a jumble. This was good news for her, but both good and bad for Dean. Although the trust was great, he was going to learn his aunt had only money on her mind when she petitioned for custody. That was going to hurt, and she couldn't protect him. "Why didn't anyone contact Dean about his grandparents' bequest? Shouldn't we have heard from the Stevens' lawyers when the will was read?"

"Typically, yes, but when their lawyers learned that Ashley had died, they reached out to Heather to ask if she knew where her nephew was. She volunteered to get in touch with Dean, so he didn't hear about his grandparents from a stranger. Wasn't that nice of her?" Lucas's sarcasm came through clearly.

Rubbing the space between her eyes, Mia said, "So, Heather goes looking for who has custody of Dean. Discovers it's me and decides to pursue custody. To get a hold of Dean's trust." Saying it out loud made it more real, but not more believable.

"That's about the size of it."

She was almost afraid to hope when she asked, "What does this mean for the case?"

"It means it's essentially over. I already called Heather's lawyer who let out a string of very colorful curses — I don't think the Buckley's are going to be able to use him in the future for anything — and he said he would get in touch with his client and strongly advise her to drop her suit. After we get off the phone, I'll be putting these documents in order and sending them to the court. It'll take a few days to be official, but I think it's safe to say you have nothing more to worry about. Take a deep breath and relax, Mia. Dean is staying with you."

After weeks of worrying, moments of panic when she wondered if she'd lose Dean, to have it suddenly over was more than she could take in. The relief, the joy. Her head was spinning. "I don't know how to thank you, Lucas."

"Just doing my job, and I'm glad to deliver good news. Part of the thanks goes to you, Cole. If you hadn't been suspicious and hired the PI, this might not have come out until it was too late."

Mia blew him a kiss as Cole said, "I'm glad I could help. Even more glad for things to have worked out this way."

"Agreed," Lucas said. "I'll be in touch as soon as I can about Dean's trust. I need to reach out to the

Stevens' lawyers and figure out the things we need to do to transfer this over to you both. They're in for a surprise. If Heather's really unlucky, they could press charges against her."

Mia couldn't bring herself to care about what happened to Ashley's sister. "Feels like Christmas has come early."

"Sometimes the good guys win. These are the moments that make my job worth it."

After a few pleasantries and talk of getting together for a drink, Lucas hung up, and Mia and Cole stared at each other for a heartbeat before she flung herself into his arms. She took a deep breath and unexpectedly burst into tears. She'd seen patients cry with relief when she delivered good news, but had never experienced it before. As happy as she was, she needed to get out all the pent-up worry and fear she'd been holding back. Cole held her as she was wracked with tears, and she was grateful for his strength and comfort.

When she calmed to sniffles, the logical part of her brain kicked in and she started to think about what needed to happen next. The first step was going to be the hardest. Still curled in Cole's arms, she said, "It's not going to be fun telling Dean the reason his aunt tried to get custody." It wasn't the same situation she'd been in with her family, but the not being wanted… that had a too familiar ring to it, one she understood the pain of all too well. "Maybe I should tell him the judge looked at the petition and didn't see a reason to pursue it, that Heather's case was too weak."

"You're not going to lie to Dean." He was right. She wasn't, but she was already dreading hurting him. "Let's look on the bright side, though. It's over. There is no chance of you losing your son."

Mia looked at him and let the truth settle in her heart. These last few weeks she'd been living under a cloud of worry about what could happen, and now it was gone. They'd done it. Dean was staying. Her home would always be his home. "I hope you don't mind, but I don't feel like going out for lunch, if that's okay."

"We'll manage with whatever you've got downstairs."

Mia didn't taste the sandwich Cole made, and once it was past the time for the high school to let out, she kept glancing at the clock, waiting for Dean to come home. She hoped there wasn't a reason for him to stay late. Was today a newspaper day? She couldn't remember.

When Dean arrived, they brought him into the living room. Her expression must have looked serious because he asked, "What happened now?" She explained everything they'd learned and why the case would soon disappear. He thought for a while, then said, "I guess this means she never really wanted me."

This is what Mia was afraid of. She sat next to him on the couch and took his hand in hers. "Her motivations have nothing to do with what an amazing person you are. She and your grandparents made their choices, and they lost out big time on knowing a terrific kid. I, on the other hand, am very, very lucky that you're in my life, that you're my family. I'm sorry this is the reason she petitioned for custody, but I am not sorry in the slightest that this is how things turned out."

Dean unexpectedly turned and wrapped his arms around Mia, putting his head on her shoulder, and hugged her fiercely. He held so tightly for a moment she lost her breath. Of course, that could have been the emotions of the day bubbling up. She looked over at Cole and thought she saw his eyes water. When Dean broke the embrace, he said, "Can I admit something?"

She wasn't sure she liked the sound of that, but said, "Of course."

"Heather told me that because of my age, the judge would be asking me where I wanted to live, and my request would carry a lot of weight." Mia noticed he'd dropped the 'aunt' already. She didn't hate it. "She made sure to tell me all the reasons why choosing her would be better for me. But there was nothing she could say to make me choose anyone other than you, Mama Mia."

"Oh, Dean," she said, unable to say anything else past the lump in her throat.

"Losing Mom was awful and, at first, I didn't think I'd ever feel better again. You know I still have some tough days, but I never imagined I could be so happy, so at home. I think Mom knew, and that's why she made you my guardian. She was right."

Mia thought she was cried out earlier. She was wrong. She couldn't hold back the tears, and when she saw he was weepy, too, she pulled him in for another hug. As her tears fell on his hair, she met Cole's gaze and, again, he blew her a kiss. It was a while before she kissed the top of Dean's head and said, "I love you like crazy.".

"Same," he said, moving away and wiping the tears from his face. They sat there, basking in the glow of the good news for a bit before Dean asked, "So, does this mean I'm rich?"

Mia laughed. She was wondering when that part of the information would strike him. "It depends on what you consider rich. It's a good amount of money that will give you a solid cushion. For example, you don't have to worry about paying for college."

Dean seemed less than thrilled by that response, but his face lit up before he said, "Can I get a car?" She loved the typical teen boy request.

"You are going to want to be long-term smart with this money," Cole said. "Take it from someone who blew through almost everything I earned from my first contract in less time than it took to write a song." Mia knew that wasn't entirely true. He'd put almost all of that money into an account for his brothers. Maybe later checks were used carelessly, but she couldn't imagine Cole doing that. "Lucky for you, my brother, Nick, is a financial whiz. He's made me and my band mates richer over time, so if you want, we can meet with him, and he'll tell you the best way to manage this windfall."

"Will he say I can't get a car?

Mia laughed at his persistence. Oh, this was going to be tricky. She couldn't wait. "Driver's license first, then we'll talk car. And something sensible, not sexy."

"Deal," Dean said. He agreed so fast she had a feeling she might regret this. But she was too crazy happy to think about it. She would take the worry that went along with him driving because it meant they stayed a family.

"I think we should go out to dinner to celebrate," she said. It had been forever since she'd wanted to do that. "Cobblestones?"

"Do they have burgers?" Happily, some things weren't going to change.

"Their steaks are better," Cole said, "but yeah, they've got burgers. Great desserts, too."

"Nice," Dean said. The boy had his priorities. "I'm gonna take Bowie for a walk, okay? Got a lot to think about."

The dog perked up at the sound of his name. "Agreed," Mia said, and soon they were out. When they were alone again, Mia held out her hand and Cole came to sit by her. "Well, this was quite a day."

"You have a gift for understatement," he said, and kissed her. It felt so good to have this over and even better to share it with him.

As they sat there, Mia found herself looking at her ring. "I guess this means that we can stop pretending to be engaged."

He shook his head. "Not exactly."

That wasn't the answer she was expecting. "What do you mean?"

"Mia, don't you know by now that I was never pretending?"

Chapter Twenty-Eight

♥

Cole was surprised she didn't know, but he was happy to tell her. "Yes, I said I was your fiancé to help you, but the moment I did, I knew it was what I wanted. You have no idea how hard it was to put the box on the table and let you put the ring on yourself." He didn't break eye contact as he put his hand under hers and lifted the ring to his lips. Could she see how much he loved her? Yes, he'd said it, but he needed her to believe it. "The only thing I was pretending was that it meant nothing. Every part of me wanted to do what Nick did a few nights ago. Get down on one knee and ask you to be part of my life forever." He almost did it as he said it, but the day already had them on an emotional high. He'd propose properly another time.

"I don't know what to say." It wasn't surprising. The last few hours had been a lot.

"Then don't say anything. Just let me hold you." And she did. They stayed on the couch in comfortable silence until Dean came back, and they got ready to go out.

Going to dinner at Cobblestones was the perfect celebration, especially since it wasn't a place he'd ever been able to take Mia when they were younger—too expensive. He and Mia each had a glass of champagne to start, and she snuck Dean a sip. They all ordered the steak and twice-baked potatoes, and Cole and Mia laughed when Dean's eyes almost rolled back into his head at the first bite of his meal.

"Holy shit," he said through a mouthful of his second bite which included a moan. "The only reason I'm not snarfing this down is so I can make it last."

"If we have to order you more, we can," Cole said, and smiled at Mia's horrified expression. "What? Growing teen. Why hold back?" Her eyes narrowed, and she gave him a devilish look that made him think of all the ways he didn't want to hold back.

They didn't order second helpings, but they did order dessert and when she fed him a bite of her chocolate cake, it took all his strength not to make a scene that would embarrass them all. They arrived home sated and happy. It was a perfect night.

Made even more perfect when Mia came to his room.

They made love slowly and tenderly. Stroking and sighing. All the right touches in all the right places may have brought on their orgasms, but for Cole, it was being with the woman he loved and who loved him, which was the greatest pleasure.

She stayed in his room until nearly one in the morning before giving him a kiss and heading upstairs. As he fell asleep, he made a mental note to figure out what needed to be done to change this arrangement. The engagement was real. There was no reason to sleep apart.

In the morning, he worked on a new song and after lunch drove Bowie over to the dog park. He ran into Dani, and they shared a coffee while the dogs played. Cole had been sixteen when Dani spent her first summer in Fable Notch and because he was working as much as he could then, he hadn't gotten to know her. He was looking forward to that changing.

When he and Bowie approached the house after their visit, he saw a half dozen cars parked along the street. His first thought was that his neighbors must be having some sort of party, then it occurred to him that it was Wednesday and who had parties on Wednesday in the middle of the afternoon. Not until he pulled into the driveway and a small crowd of people got out of their cars and charged him did he understand what was going on.

The paparazzi had shown up in Fable Notch.

It was such an incongruous thing to see that his mind had trouble putting the two things together until his car was surrounded and flashes were going off in his face. Bowie, not understanding what was going on, started barking and jumping around the front seat making it even harder for Cole to think about what to do next. Finally, he put a leash on the dog, opened the door and, with a hand in front of his face, made a beeline for the house.

"Is it true you're engaged?"

"How long have you and Mia been together?"

"Is the boy your son?"

"What does this mean for the band?"

Thank goodness the side door was unlocked. He got in easily, but he could hear the press outside.

So could Bowie, who was still agitated. Between the press yelling his name and their questions, and Bowie barking, the noise was overwhelming. He needed time to think. He pulled the shade down over the door's window so they couldn't see in, then raced around the first floor closing blinds and curtains.

How the hell had they found him? Why were they here now? And how had they heard about Mia?

There were only two possibilities, one more likely than the other, given the questions he was asked. He decided to eliminate the easy one first. Pulling out his phone, he called Brett, who answered almost immediately. "Hey there. You're calling me? Does this mean you're ready to talk contract? This could be headline making if you play your cards right."

The man only ever had one thing on his mind. "Not now, Brett. Did you call the press and tell them where I am?"

"You've got press? Did they hear you haven't signed yet?"

That answered Cole's question. "I need your help. Find out who called them. I think it was a woman named Heather Buckley, but I want to be certain."

"What are they asking about?"

Oh, his manager was not going to like this. "Do you remember Mia Durant?"

Brett took a second before answering. "Short, curvy girl. Used to front the band."

"Yes. I've been seeing her, and they've heard we're engaged."

"Are you?"

Cole pinched the bridge of his nose. "It's a long story, and I can't explain now. Please find out who tipped them off."

"I'll call you back as soon as I know anything."

"Thanks," Cole said. Pressing the button to end the call was not as satisfying as slamming down a phone, which is what he wanted to do. Instead, he went to his room, shut the door with a bang, sat on the bed and covered his mouth with a pillow as he screamed so the press couldn't hear. He'd wait for confirmation, but even with it, there wouldn't be anything he could do to make them go away before they got what they came for.

He heard Bowie pawing at his door, so he opened it to let him in. The dog jumped on the bed and laid his head in Cole's lap. "Yeah, I don't like them either, boy, but there's nothing to be done at the moment." He needed to think. It wasn't a big crowd. He'd faced more. Guess they didn't want to drive out to a small town in New Hampshire. A point in Fable Notch's favor. He'd need to warn Mia. Maybe tell her and Dean to stay with Casey until he could get rid of the press.

His phone rang sooner than he expected. "That was fast."

He didn't look at the caller ID, so he was surprised to hear Nick's voice. "I don't know what was fast, but can you tell me why there are reporters outside my house asking about you?"

"What?" Cole said, coming off the bed so fast Bowie barked at him.

"A few minutes ago, there was a knock at my door. I opened it to find four people with cameras and microphones asking about you and Mia, and what could I tell them about your engagement and your kid."

Cole let out a string of curses. This was not good. If they were at Nick's, they could also be at Theo's or the Sinclairs. Or the hospital. "I need to find out who else they are bothering. I'll call Theo if you call the Sinclairs. Tell Dani, too. Just in case. Then call the cops. I know Fable Notch doesn't have much of a force, but it could help."

"Will do. Anything else you need?"

"To have these people gone." His jaw already ached from clenching it.

"I hear that. I won't tie up your phone. Watch for my texts."

"Thanks." They hung up, and Cole called Theo at his Concord office. He told his brother what he could and asked him to warn Eden. Like Nick, Theo asked how he could help, but there wasn't anything to be done. Cole never liked dealing with the press in routine situations, let alone uncontrolled ones like this, but he never imagined his family could get caught up, too.

His brothers taken care of, Cole took a deep breath and called Mia.

Chapter Twenty-Nine

♥

Mia's phone buzzed when she was helping a child with a head injury who'd fallen in school after tipping his chair back. She hoped the call wasn't anything serious, since she couldn't stop what she was doing. It buzzed three more times before she finished. By the time she looked at it, she was panicked about what could be wrong and was sure she was going to see that the school had called again about Dean. When she saw four missed calls from Cole, she relaxed.

Until he answered the phone with, "Are you okay? Have you seen them yet?"

Not what she was expecting. Who was 'them'? "What are you talking about?"

"Where are you? I mean, where are you in the Emergency Room?"

He wasn't making sense and his panic was making her nervous. "I'm at the nursing station by the patient rooms."

"When was the last time you were in the waiting area?" She didn't like how frantic he sounded. She could almost hear him pacing. Was he hurt? Was he *in* the waiting area?

"Over an hour ago. Cole, what's wrong?" This didn't sound like it had anything to do with Dean. She headed down the hall to see what he might be referring to. For a second, she worried that maybe her father was here with Casey, but if that were the situation, it would be Casey calling her, not Cole.

"If you can, peek out and see if—"

Before he finished his sentence, she stepped into the ER's reception. As soon as she did, she was besieged by at least a half dozen people with cameras, all of them pushing toward her calling, "Mia, is it true?"

"When did this happen?"

"How long have you and Cole Hanson been engaged?"

"Is he the father of your son?

"What does the band think? Can you give us a statement?" Flashes went off in her face and she almost tripped in her rush to get away. Wouldn't that have made for a great picture?

As fast as she could, she got back behind the safety of the treatment area doors. What the hell was going on? She heard Cole's voice calling her name from the phone dangling in her hand and put it to her ear. "I'm here. And so are a lot of reporters."

"Fuck, that's what I was afraid of. I was trying to see if there was a way for you to check without walking right into them. I found them at the house when I got back from the dog park. There are seven or eight on the front lawn and a few at Nick's place. How many are there?"

"Maybe six. I didn't have time to count. What are they doing here?" As she asked the question, she remembered what they were asking her. "They heard about our engagement. And about Dean. How did this happen?"

"According to Brett, Heather leaked the story. She was probably pissed that she'd lost her case — and the money — and made a call to the press."

Mia sank into a chair. Just when things started to go well for them. What was going to happen when this made the news outlets? She sat up straighter. "Oh my God, what about Dean? Will they try to get pictures of him, too?"

"Shit, I don't know. They asked me if I was his father, so they're definitely interested in him, but it's another matter for them to go to his school."

What a mess. She needed to think. And they needed a plan for how to mitigate the impact this might have on Dean. Someone tapped her shoulder, and she turned to see a doctor with an annoyed expression pointing in the direction of the waiting area. News of her visitors was getting around. "Can you reach out to the school and see if anything is going on, then call me back? If they're not there, then he's safe for now."

"Give me a few minutes."

As soon as she hung up, she went to the nurses' station and dialed hospital security to let them know about the press. When Cole called her back in less than five minutes, Mia knew it was a bad sign. "They're there, aren't they?"

"Yup. They were about to call you. They've seen three. One came to the office trying to get them to page Dean, saying they had something from you."

"There's no way they got past Mrs. Weiderspiel." The high school's lead secretary was feared by students and parents alike for her no-nonsense manner and adherence to all the rules all the time. The woman would protect the students like the fiercest momma bear, and Mia was grateful. "I don't want him walking into them the way I did."

"I could go pick him up again."

She appreciated the offer but didn't think it was a good idea. "The press at the house will follow you. That will put you in pictures together. Let's try to avoid that until we can get things cleared up. I'm going to get the rest of my shift covered and go get him."

"Keep me posted," he said. "And I'm sorry. It never occurred to me something like this could happen."

"I know. First things first. We'll see you soon."

The next hour was one of the longest of Mia's life. She called the head of nursing and told her what was going on. The woman, a former ER nurse herself, jumped into action, getting Mia coverage for the rest of her shift and the next day. As soon as her replacement arrived, Mia took a back exit out of the hospital to get to her car.

Using the Bluetooth system, she called ahead and let the school know she was coming and asked to have Dean dismissed to the office. She parked in front and made a beeline for the door. Unfortunately, she was recognized on her way in and the same questions as before pelted her. Dean was sitting in a chair waiting for her and looking worried. He jumped up when he saw her. "What's going on?"

She gave him a quick hug, as much to reassure herself as him. "Downside to fame, coupled with a petty reaction from your aunt. Heather told the press about me and Cole, and about you."

"What a bitch," he said. Mia had a few other words in mind, but she wasn't going to share them.

"We need to get out of here as quickly as possible. There are more reporters waiting for us at home, but we'll manage. Are you ready?" He gave her a nod. She appreciated his confidence in her, even if she wasn't feeling it herself. "Put your hood on to cover as much of your face as possible and let's go."

In addition to having his hood up, Mia shielded Dean with her body as best she could as they made their way to her car. She didn't want them to have an opportunity to get pictures of him. Once she got in, the press pulled back. For a second, she was hopeful until she realized they were getting in their vehicles and following her. As she pulled away from the school parking lot, she dialed Cole. "I've got Dean. We're on our way to you."

"That might not be such a good idea," Cole said. She could hear the worry in his voice. "The ones who were at Nick's showed up a little while ago. It's a zoo here. I'm not even certain you can get in the driveway. Is there anywhere you can go? Maybe to Casey's?"

"I suppose I could—Holy hell!" She gave a startled scream when a flash went off from the car driving next to her.

"What was that? Are you okay?"

"Yeah, they're following me, and one asshole pulled alongside my car. This is ridiculous. It's only one lane in each direction, you idiot." Mia took a deep breath to calm and refocus before continuing. "I'm not sure going to Casey's will help. They'll follow us and camp out there. Oh, now what?" Another car with press had pulled out in front of her and was trying to force her to slow down.

"What's happening?" Cole wasn't trying to — or wasn't able to—hide the fear in his voice, and that wasn't helping her nerves. She explained what was going on. "Can you see how many there are?

"One in front and at least three behind us," Dean said. He shifted in his seat and looked out the back. "No wait, four."

"Dean, scrunch down. I don't want them to be able to see you."

She heard Cole curse. They were all going to be doing a lot of that. "Is there anywhere you can get to safely?"

Mia couldn't think of where she could go. Clearly the press had done their research and anywhere she went, they'd follow. It was picturing them following her like an absurd parade that gave her an idea. "I think I have a way to get them off of my tail, but it's a little risky."

"No," Cole said immediately. "I don't care what it is. Don't take risks, Mia."

"I need to do something. There are at least five cars, and one keeps trying to pull alongside me." Making a quick decision, she said to Dean, "Hang on." He grabbed the Jesus bar as she glanced in her mirrors. When it was safe, she pulled into the oncoming traffic lane, then gunned the engine. She'd bought her Subaru for the all-wheel drive in the winter. Today she was glad for the horsepower. She passed the car in front of them, then pulled back into her lane, keeping her speed steady but fast. If only she could stop her heart racing. The pounding made it hard to concentrate. "I'm ahead of them.

I'm going to lead them somewhere they're not expecting or used to."

"What does that—no, you're not." He'd figured out her plan almost as quickly as she did.

"I know how to drive the Kanc. They don't. They have no idea what's coming." She knew every turn and danger spot. She'd be fine. She hoped.

"They won't slow down. They could force you off the road."

Dean glanced at her. She didn't like how pale he was or his grip on the bar. "We're going to be fine," she said to him and took her hand off the wheel to give his free hand a squeeze before responding to Cole. "They can't do anything without endangering themselves. They'll have to slow, and we'll have a chance to get clear. I'm passing Loon Mountain. I'll call you back as soon as I can."

"Don't! Double back. Come home. Please—"

She hung up, released Dean, and gripped the steering wheel with both hands. She hoped he didn't see how white knuckled she was. For a moment, she considered turning around, but forward seemed like the best choice. Taking a deep breath to calm herself, she said, "This is either really smart or really stupid."

"Any bets on which?" Dean asked.

She was going to get them home safely. There was no other choice. "As long as I stay smart, it won't matter if they're stupid. Trust me."

Out of the corner of her eye, she saw Dean gave her a sharp nod. "Let's do this."

Picking up speed, she was still in front of all of them when they neared the hairpin turn by the Hancock Overlook less than ten minutes later. Mia hated that she was scaring Dean, but as she saw the distance between her and the reporters increasing, she was convinced this was the right move. As she approached the dangerous curve, she slowed. The car behind her got closer until she made the turn. Then it slowed significantly. Too significantly and too quickly—and she heard the telltale sound of someone being rear-ended. She cringed, knowing she was the cause and that someone could be hurt, but Dean was her priority. As soon as she was around the turn, she gunned the engine, taking the road faster than she ever had, grateful that the sun was still out.

Five minutes later and no cars in her review mirror, Mia breathed a sigh of relief. "I think we lost them," she told Dean.

"Good, because it turns out car chases are much better on screen than in real life." He let out a sigh and let go of the bar. As he shook his wrist, she knew how tightly he'd been gripping it. "Nice driving, Lightning McQueen."

"Ka-pow," she said and heard the shakiness in her voice. Her heart was still racing, but her thoughts were calmer, and she was hopeful. She needed to call Cole, let him know they were okay. Unfortunately, they were in one of the area's many dead zones, so it was another fifteen minutes before she could reach him. By then she was breathing almost normally.

He wasn't. She was fairly certain he answered before the ring was even complete. "Tell me you're okay."

"We're fine." She told him about the sound of the crash. "I don't think anyone was able to drive past what happened, because I haven't seen them since."

"Where are you?" She could imagine him pacing in her living room, Bowie dancing around him, picking up on his nervous energy.

"Approaching Lower Falls. Should I pull into one of the rest areas?" There were several places along the Kanc for people to park, hike, and enjoy the views.

"No, keep going. They'll get through eventually, and I don't want them to find you. Take the route we did the other weekend."

It felt like months ago. So much had happened since that day by the bridge. She thought about his suggestion. "That'll take me two hours."

"I know, but the first cars to get around the accident are going to be checking every one of those stops, hoping to spot you." He was probably right. He must have been looking out the window because he said. "Two more just pulled up here. I'm guessing they were part of your tail and decided the drive wasn't worth it. Besides, it's me they most want to talk to."

He sounded as weary as she felt. "I'm sorry. I know you don't like to be in the news."

"You have nothing to apologize for. This is my mess. My fault you and Dean were in danger."

There was something in his tone that troubled her. He was taking responsibility for this. It wasn't a surprise, but she hated how fatalistic he sounded. "It's nothing. It's temporary, and we're fine." There was no response. His silence was concerning and all too familiar. "Cole?"

"I know. I'm still trying to accept that you're okay, and it's taking all of my strength not to go out into that crowd and beat in some heads."

She could hear his banked anger. "They're not worth it. And that's not the story you want to give them."

"Or Heather, which is what's keeping me inside. Get home as quickly—and safely—as you can."

"I will. Have the garage door open for us." Without thinking, she said, "I love you." Dean looked at her and gave her a thumbs up.

"I love you, too," he said, and they hung up.

"Glad you two finally said that," Dean said. "It's pretty obvious."

Mia smiled and kept her eyes on the road, hoping that the press didn't suddenly reappear, and not sharing with Dean that something in Cole's tone sounded exactly like their final phone call years ago.

Chapter Thirty

♥

Cole had never been so scared in his life as he had been when Mia called to say she was going to force the press to chase her on the Kanc. He'd promised himself while he paced and waited that if she made it home, he'd do whatever it took to keep her safe, keep them both safe.

After the longest two hours of his life, he heard her car pull in and the garage door close. Minutes later, she and Dean were in the house and in his arms. He hugged them fiercely, never wanting to let them go and knowing that was what he needed to do.

"Well, that was an adventure," Dean said, stepping out of the hug, leaving Mia in Cole's embrace. "Let's not do it again."

"I'm really sorry," Cole said. He couldn't believe what Dean and Mia had to go through because of him. The two of them finally had what they wanted—each other. He wouldn't allow anything to change that. He couldn't believe what he was about to say, but in the last hour, he'd gotten clear about what he had to do. Taking a deep breath, he said, "I need to leave."

"I thought we just established that car chases are no fun."

"Not leave for a few hours," he said. He almost couldn't get the next words out. "Leave Fable Notch."

Mia stepped back and looked at him with an expression of pain and distress on her face he knew he'd never forget. "What are you talking about?"

"You know I want to make a life with you, but if I stay, days like today are always a possibility. If I'm part of Emporium, you and Dean — and even Theo, Nick and the Sinclairs — are targets. One wrong picture of me with someone while I'm on tour and they'll show up here again wanting to know how you feel about my cheating on you, even though I never would." Mia started to say something, but he held up a hand to stop her. He didn't want to hear her logic or belief this wouldn't be a problem. He knew better. "I am not going through another afternoon like today. I was so damned scared that you'd both end up in a ravine. And what about my brothers? They just got their lives back in order. They're happy, settled. I won't let my decisions up end their lives." He turned to Dean and looked at the boy he was coming to love. Fuck, this was awful. "If anything happens to you in school or there's another fight, word will get out and there will be headlines about how my kid is out of control. Neither of you signed up for this. I have to protect you. I have to go."

He walked toward his room, and Mia moved in front of him. "You said you love me. That you always have." Didn't she know how true that was? He wouldn't be hurting so damn much if he didn't. She held up the back of her hand, the ring opportunely catching the light. "Doesn't this mean anything to you?"

"It means everything to me. *You* mean everything to me. You, Dean, Theo, and Nick. That's why I'm going. I cannot be the reason any of you get hurt, and as long as I'm here, there's a chance of that. What if Heather finds out what happened today and uses the danger Dean was in to try to take him from you again?"

"She won't. And this was her fault." But the waver in Mia's voice and the look of concern on her face told him she wasn't certain.

"If it's not her, it'll be someone else trying to hurt you and Dean or someone else I care about to get to me. I can't have that. I won't." He couldn't believe the band was coming between them again, but he wouldn't let his being part of Emporium put anyone he loved in danger. Maybe he could get the label to agree to a two-album contract. Ease the band into the idea of his departure. Give them time to replace him.

He took a step toward his room, but she stopped him with a hand on his chest. Looking into her eyes he thought, so that's what heartbreak looked like. Was the same expression on his face? "Is this really what you want?"

"Of course it isn't," he said, his voice rising as he moved her hand. He missed her touch immediately. "But I don't get to have what I want, do I? I thought I could, I really did, but today proved it's not possible yet. If my being here while I keep my commitments means any of you are in danger, then I can't be here."

He stormed out, leaving them standing there, his heart breaking. As he got to the door, Dean grabbed his arm. "What the fuck, man?" Cole almost said something about the boy's language but stopped himself. "You said you wouldn't do anything to hurt her."

Cole gestured to the front of the house. "What do you think having those people out there will do to her? To you? I go, they go. Then no one's in danger anymore."

"Like there's no danger without them?"

Cole felt a chill. That was a scary statement. "What does that mean?"

"Cancer took my mom. Alcohol took yours. My aunt tried to get custody of me for money. Shit happens even when you try to stop it."

"But this is something I *can* stop. I have to." He was reminded of a lesson he learned when he was young. Responsibility took the fun out of everything.

Dean looked as if he were going to say something else or try to stop Cole. Instead, he said, "This sucks," and left. Cole couldn't agree more. Moments later, he heard footsteps rushing up the stairs, then a door slamming.

Cole understood Dean's anger — hell, he felt the same way — but he was not going to stay where his presence could hurt the people he loved. This was the way it had to be.

He was about to pack, then realized it wasn't a good idea. Carrying out luggage would show the press he was staying here. He grabbed his guitar and keyboard and went back to where Mia was standing with her arms crossed, silent tears rolling down her face. Seeing her pain would have been the worst thing he could have imagined if he hadn't spent the last few hours imagining her getting hurt because of him. "I'm going to the Sinclairs for the night. I'll leave from there in the morning. I won't take my stuff because if the press sees it, they'll have more questions. You can bring it over to Millie, and she'll ship it to me." The look Mia gave him suggested she'd rather set fire to everything he was leaving behind. He wouldn't blame her if she did.

He put on his coat and found his keys in his pocket. Pulling them out, he noticed one in particular. His shaking hands made it difficult, but eventually he got her house key off. He gave it to her. She stared at it for a second, then rubbed her hands together and took it from him. When she did, he felt her press something against his palm. He didn't have to look to know it was the ring. He wanted to say so much, to make her understand why he had to do this. His only consolation was knowing they wouldn't be hounded if he left. "I'm sorry," he managed through the lump in his throat. Once again, the words were hardly enough.

She said nothing, simply went upstairs. She didn't even slam the door. The quiet was suffocating. Pulling his guitar over his shoulder and the keyboard case with the notebooks of his work and laptop under his arm, he stepped out onto the porch to face the consequences and his future without Mia.

Chapter Thirty-One

♥

Mia sat and listened for the sound of the front door closing and Cole driving away. From her bedroom window she could hear the press yelling at him but not his response. Sadly, Cole was right. As soon as he drove away, the press went with him. She assumed they followed him to the Sinclairs.

She curled up in the center of her bed, feeling miserable. Bowie, sensing her emotions, joined her a few minutes later, and she buried her face in his fur and cried. How did this happen? Again. Yes, there would be downsides to living with a rock star, but there were so many upsides to them being with one another. Didn't he see that? They loved each other. Wasn't that enough? Every relationship had its challenges, but facing them together made it worthwhile. Why couldn't he have chosen to stay?

Her thoughts assailed her like a movie she couldn't escape. She replayed every smile, every kiss, every moment of connection. Cole saying he loved her, telling her the engagement was real for him. Discovering the tattoo of her name. How was she supposed to move forward without him when all these new memories would be holding onto her heart?

After a few hours, she got up and knocked on Dean's door to ask if he wanted dinner. She got a brisk, "No, thanks." She considered pushing, but decided he might need to be alone with his thoughts as much as she did. And she didn't feel like eating either.

She went back to her room, turning on a light since it was late. Not knowing what else to do, she checked her phone to see if her run in with the press had made the entertainment news. Sure enough, all she had to do was put his name in the search engine and videos of the interview he gave on the front steps of her house popped up along with headlines speculating on their lives. The worst was *Did Cole Hanson go home for love? Or a love child?* She'd keep Dean home from school tomorrow until it all died down. No need to take a chance some press would linger.

She clicked on one of the links and watched as he faced the paparazzi. The anger he'd tried to control was clear. She could also see the pain, but that was because she was looking. "I cannot believe you guys are so hungry for a story you would jeopardize the lives of the people I care for. And I'm sorry to say you've come all this way for nothing. I came to visit my family for the holidays and recover from the accident. Nothing more."

A voice called out, "So you're not engaged?"

"Are you kidding? The band's about to sign a new contract. That means more writing, recording, and touring. Not exactly the time to settle down." She hated hearing him say it.

"Wasn't Mia the band's first lead singer?"

"Does Paxton know you're here and talking to someone new?"

He kept his composure, which couldn't have been easy. She was fairly certain he wanted to claw someone's eyes out. Preferably Heather's. "Yes, Mia Durant was someone special in my life, and we're still friends." She noticed he wasn't lying, even though he wasn't telling them the full truth. "I might have stayed through Christmas, but you guys have *bleep* that up for me. I'd like to ask you to leave my friends and family alone."

"What about the kid? Is he yours?"

"I should be so lucky as to have a son as great as Mia's." He didn't use Dean's name. Was that intentional? Cole never could stop protecting the people he cared about. "No, he's not mine, and that's all I'm saying on the subject. Now, I recommend you find places to stay in town—the Stewart Inn and Cabins are the best—or drive to Manchester and fly the *bleep* out of here."

She lay there, her heart aching. He didn't have to go. They could have made it work. Maybe it wouldn't have been easy, but it would have been worth it. Damn him and his overactive sense of responsibility. She couldn't believe that after all they'd been through, they were apart again. It would serve him right if she met someone new and moved on with her life.

As soon as the thought hit her, she dismissed it. She hadn't managed to get him out of her heart before. It wasn't going to happen now. She needed to talk to someone.

She texted Casey, *Cole left.*

Three dots immediately appeared. *I'm on my way.*

Mia considered going downstairs to meet her friend but didn't feel like moving. Fifteen minutes later, there was a knock and Casey came into her bedroom, sat next to her, and pulled her into a hug. Bowie complained, then found a space between the women so he could be near them both. "Tell me what happened." Mia explained about the press descending, the car chase, and Cole leaving. "That sounds awful. For all of you. Is Dean okay?"

She loved her friend's priorities. "Yeah, it was scary for a bit on the road, but he's fine. If the stomping I heard earlier is any indication, he's pretty pissed at Cole for deciding the only way to keep us safe was for him to leave."

"There's no being safe and being in love," Casey said, and her words hit Mia in the gut. After she and Cole broke up, she'd kept her heart very safe, allowing few people to get close. Even her choice of work kept people at a distance—no one stayed long enough in the ER for her to get attached. Then Dean came into her life and Cole showed up and there was vulnerability everywhere. She'd say the anxiety of almost losing Dean and Cole's leaving proved her right about the dangers of caring, but there was also joy and connection. Mia couldn't deny it was worth the scary to have the love. "Why did you let him go?"

Mia shifted and gave Casey a questioning look. "There was no 'let,'" she said and realized she echoed what Cole said about their original breakup. "He made a decision and walked out."

"What did you say to stop him?"

"I said..." Nothing. She'd said nothing. Like all those years ago, she accepted that the decision was made for her, and she had no power. "I gave him back the ring."

"Don't you think that told him you agree?"

"I didn't have a choice." She didn't like what Casey was making her think. And she sounded like Cole.

"Are you sure about that?" When she gave him the ring she had been, but with Casey putting the question in front of her, she wasn't as certain. Before she could answer, Casey said, "You have a habit of feeling like you can't be the important one. I'd been hoping after a year with Dean and with Cole here you'd started to see that wasn't true."

She sat up as her friend's words hit her. It was true. She knew how important she was to Dean and believed that Cole loved her, but his leaving threw her back twelve years, and she'd responded as she always had. Passively. Maybe it was time to take what she'd learned and do things differently. Set a better example for her son. Because she knew the truth — Cole did want her. She *was* his priority, so much so that he was willing to be miserable if it meant keeping her safe. The realization shocked and thrilled her. "I'll tell you one thing I've discovered these last few weeks. I like having help. It feels good to not do everything alone."

"So, if I ask you what I can do to help?"

Mia nodded. "I'm going to try to come up with an answer."

"Terrific. Let's practice. What can I do to help?"

Without thinking, Mia said, "Help me come up with a way to bring Cole home."

After a sleepless night, Mia was surprised to find Dean waiting for her in the kitchen when she came down the next morning. She looked at the clock and saw it was barely eight. She considered checking to see if pigs were flying. Before she could say anything, he said, "You need to bring him back." She looked at him, confused. Had he heard what she and Casey had been saying the day before? "What was it you said a few days ago about learning from our mistakes and not repeating them?" Great. Leave it to her to have a kid who listened. "Besides, aren't the paparazzi like a bunch of bullies? You and Cole can't let them win."

She liked his perspective, and she agreed. Time to tell him what she and Casey figured out the night before. She was not letting Cole make this choice for them again. "I was thinking something similar." Dean perked up. She'd never get tired of seeing that smile. "According to Theo, Cole should be arriving in Colorado in three days. Wanna take a trip with me?"

Chapter Thirty-Two

♥

Ten hours after leaving Fable Notch at the crack of dawn — no press to be found, thank God — Cole pulled into a hotel outside of Harrisburg, Pennsylvania. The thought of two or more days of driving brought on anxiety that reminded him of the panic attack he'd had at Thanksgiving. There was no way he was going to be able to do the rest of the trip on his own. He called Brett and told him he needed a driver sent to the nearest major airport. Within thirty minutes, Brett called back and told him someone would be at Harrisburg Airport by eleven the next day.

Before they got off the phone, Brett said, "Having you in the news for a day was great, but you made the right decision. I don't know what was going on between you and Mia, but married rock stars are never as appealing to the fans." Leave it to Brett to say the wrong thing. Cole had no interest in living a life that appealed to his fans. "We'll talk contract once you're back home."

I'm not going home. I'm leaving home, said the voice in his head. God, he needed that voice to shut up. "Can't that wait until after the new year?" Not that time was going to change how he felt, but he didn't trust himself not to blow everything up at this point.

"We could, but why bother? With the Grammy noms, it's going to be your biggest one ever. Label wants to get this nailed down."

The label can suck my... "I'll get in touch with the others when I'm back at my place."

He lay there on the cheap polyester bedspread staring at what the place considered art, and all he could think of was Mia. How it felt to be near her, the way her smile lit her eyes—and the look in those eyes when he left. She'd never forgive him for this.

But I know your laughter is my favorite sound. And I want to kiss you forever.

He'd promised her he'd never let Paxton sing it, but as the song played over and over in his head, he knew the truth. He'd never let anyone sing it. Those weren't simply lyrics. They were his feelings, and he wasn't going to share them if he couldn't share them with her.

God, how was he going to perform going forward with his heart still in Fable Notch? If the band thought he was checked out before, it was nothing compared to what he'd be like going forward. Maybe he could be so bad they'd fire him. That would be great. Because during the drive, one thing became clear. He didn't want to find a way to have a life with Mia and be a part of the band.

He wanted out.

"Leave the band, not us," Nick had said when Cole called his brother from the Sinclairs to tell him what happened and that he was driving to Colorado in the morning. "Can't you do that?"

Still raw from saying goodbye to Mia and not quite over the fact the press had been chasing her only hours before, he'd barked out a "no" and said he'd be in touch before hanging up. He called and left a message for Theo to tell him the same. He hadn't heard back. Theo was probably mad at him, too. May as well have everyone pissed at him.

He took out the engagement ring from his pocket and looked at it, letting it catch the light and thinking about how it belonged on Mia's hand. Lost in his memories and the ache of missing everyone, he jumped when his phone buzzed. He considered ignoring it, but thinking it could be Theo or Nick checking on him, he looked.

Where are you?

Paxton. He was almost surprised it had taken someone from Emporium a day to reach out once the piece about him and Mia hit the news. He hoped she wasn't too upset. *Pennsylvania for the night.*

We need to talk. That sounded ominous. Guess Brett told her he was dragging his heels about the new contract. He had to remember that just because he wasn't anxious to sign the next five years of his life away didn't mean they weren't. *I'm calling you. Pick up.*

Yup, she was definitely pissed. A few seconds later, his phone rang, and he was face to face with his lead singer. He'd barely managed hello when she said, "What the hell is wrong with you?"

The same thing she'd asked him the night of the accident. Interesting. "You're going to have to be a little more specific."

"You left Mia. Again." Ouch. Nothing like being smacked with your own decisions. "Are you a complete idiot?"

Possibly. "The jury's still out on that."

"No, I don't think they are. I think they are unanimous. Why did you leave her?"

He swung his legs off the bed and matched her frustration with his own. "Did you not see what the press almost did to her and Dean? And my brothers? If I stayed, the next time they might not be as lucky."

Paxton blew a loud breath in exasperation. "We're not a K-Pop band. Our fans don't follow us like that and neither does the press. When was the last time we got hounded?" She stopped and held up her hand. "Yeah, I know, the accident. Which makes this twice in a really short period, but before that? Come on, Cole. We saw the pictures you sent from Thanksgiving. You were happy. Like, really happy, and we know you haven't been in a long time." We. Did that mean she'd talked with Brian and Hugh?

"I didn't have a choice." He sounded like a broken record, but every time he closed his eyes, he saw the look on Mia's face when she came running in the door after they'd chased her and Dean. It was the longest three hours of his life. He was so damned scared for the next call to be from the police, telling him they'd been in an accident. "There was something I could do, so I did it."

"And you're miserable because of it," Paxton said. "I saw your interview, trying to look all angry, but I know you too well. Tell me the truth, Cole. What do you want? And never mind about anyone else. For once, think about you."

She did know him. His instinct was to make the decision that was right for others, that supported or helped them. But for himself alone? He couldn't remember the last time he'd done that. He sighed and rubbed his forehead, then said what he truly felt. "I'm out, Paxton. I can't keep doing this, and I don't want to."

"It's about damn time," she said with a satisfied smile. "I've been hoping you'd say that."

Not the reaction he was expecting, but he was grateful for it. "Can you help me figure out what to do next?"

"It's not that tough. Finish the tour with us. Don't sign the next contract."

"It can't be that simple." Could it? Had he been seeing blocks where there was a path?

"Well, Brett's going to freak—which I'm kind of looking forward to seeing—and then the label will offer us more money than we've ever made in our lives. It'll be crazy tempting, so you'll have to be very sure this is what you want." It was. Now that he'd admitted the truth, he felt lighter. Hopeful. "And in the meantime, you need to find a way to get Mia back."

He winced. Yeah, that might not be as simple. Would she even see him after the way he'd walked out? Maybe not at first, but he would do whatever he had to win her back, one last time.

And the process of convincing her could be a lot of fun, he thought with a smile.

The next morning, he canceled the driver without explaining anything to Brett—and damned if that didn't feel great—and drove back to Fable Notch. He took almost no breaks and made the trip in a little more than eight hours. It was late afternoon and nearly dark when he drove up to Mia's house. Heart hammering, he couldn't make himself get out of the car. Coming back was the right thing to do, but it wasn't going to be easy.

What was he going to say? He needed to include an apology and an admission he was an idiot. Maybe some well-placed groveling. It had only been two days since he'd left, but he'd been obstinate and adamant when he walked out. He didn't like to admit it, but there was a chance he'd burned his last bridge with her.

He was still sitting there when she stepped onto the porch with Bowie, just as she had the first time he'd shown up and lingered in the car. There were shadows under her eyes he knew he was responsible for. If she let him, he would gladly spend the rest of his life making certain she never looked that way again. Taking a deep breath, he got out and walked to her.

She had her hands in the pockets of her coat and not crossed in front of her. He took that as a good sign when she said, "What are you doing here?"

Another echo. The same words she'd used the day he ended up pretending to be her fiancé. He stopped at the bottom of the porch steps and held his hands out to the side. "I made a mistake. I should never have left you. Or Dean." The dog came down to greet him. "Or you, Bowie."

"We all agree." Did that mean she was going to forgive him? He was ready to hope. "What made you realize it was a mistake?"

"Oh, I knew it was a mistake the minute I walked out the door, but I realized I didn't have to live with it after I talked with Paxton. I'm leaving the band."

Her brows went up. It may not have surprised Paxton, but others were not expecting this. "That's a big step. Can you really walk away?"

"Our current contract is done when the tour is, and we haven't signed the next one. What I can't walk away from is you."

She looked at him stunned, but before she could say anything, Dean bounded out of the house, flew down the stairs and gave him a hug. At least someone was immediately glad to see him. "You're here! Are you back?"

"I am," he said, his arm around Dean but his eyes on Mia. He explained the change to Dean and added, "I'm thinking of opening a music school and teaching guitar and piano. Wanna be my first official student?"

"Absolutely. Guess that means our trip is canceled." Now he looked at Dean, who answered the question he must have seen on Cole's face. "We were planning to fly out to Colorado tomorrow. To bring you back."

"You were...." He couldn't finish the sentence. She'd been planning to come to him?

As if reading his thoughts, Mia gave a shrug and said, "After you left, I had a long talk with Casey and then the next morning with Dean." She came down a few of the steps to stand in front of him. "While you were here, I didn't only learn how much you mean to me. I saw and felt how much I meant to you. I wasn't going to let your overactive sense of responsibility get between us again. We were young and foolish once. I didn't think we had to do that again."

The breath left his lungs. It was almost like when he woke from the accident, except this time everything he'd ever wanted was in front of him. No one knew him like she did. Knew and accepted and loved him. He reached into the pocket of his coat and took out the ring box he'd held for most of the drive, then stood in front of her and opened it. She kept her eyes on him and said, "If this ring goes on my hand again, it's never coming off."

"That's what I'm counting on. I've wanted to do this since the day I bought it." Getting down on one knee he said, "I love you, little bird. I can hardly remember a time when I didn't love you, when you didn't have my heart. I gave it to you years ago, and I've never wanted it back. I hate that we had to spend so much time apart, but now I won't let anything keep us from being together. Share your life with me. Let me share mine with you. Mia, will you marry me?"

Her eyes bright with tears, she whispered, "Yes." He slipped the ring on her finger — one last time — then stood and wrapped his arms around her. With her head on his chest, he knew she was pressing against the tattoo with her name on it.

"I have one more question." She gave him a look, telling him she was suspicious, but then she nodded. "Will you let me kiss you forever?"

Instead of answering, she went up on tiptoes to bring her lips to his. She kissed him deeply then stopped to whisper, "Welcome home. I love you."

Dean and Bowie squeezed into their little circle, making it bigger. With his arm around the boy and the woman he loved, Cole knew that with them, he was finally going to have the life he'd always wanted.

Epilogue

♥

Janelle Novak

Janelle ran her hands over her hair, hoping the neat chignon would stay pinned in place, and making certain she hadn't accidentally left a pencil or two stuck in it. Looking in the rearview mirror, she put on a light coat of lip gloss and checked her makeup. Simple, neutral. Nothing too colorful or unprofessional. Even the outfit she'd chosen was in more muted tones than she usually wore. She could only hope the navy dress and black pumps would give her an air of confidence and mask the desperation she was feeling.

She got out of her car and shivered in the chilly late January air, pulling her wool coat closely around her. Normally she'd be in leggings and a sweater, but that wouldn't do for this meeting. Leaning into the car, she grabbed the folders with all of her financial information. As she brought them to her chest, she whispered,"Please, please, let this be enough. I have to get this loan." She took a fortifying breath hoping the cold would freeze out her fears and walked into the Bank of New Hampshire for her eleven o'clock appointment with a loan officer.

A receptionist, who couldn't have been more than twenty-two, pointed to an office and told Janelle Mr. Chandler would be with her shortly. She turned down an offer of coffee. Her stomach was a mess, and she didn't think she'd be able to hold the cup steady. She'd probably end up spilling it on herself, the loan officer, or the papers she's brought. And they wouldn't make it strong enough for her to enjoy anyway.

Looking around the intimidating office with its wood furniture and framed certificates, she realized this wasn't the first time in her life she was somewhere she didn't expect to be. She didn't expect to be accepted to Parson's School of Design, she didn't expect to not be able to find a job that allowed her to design clothes (and pay the rent), and she certainly didn't expect to move back to Fable Notch five years ago let alone love living here.

As she sat waited, Janelle thought about the last several years. Returning to her home town hadn't been an easy decision. When she graduated from high school, she'd told everyone she planned to take the New York fashion world by storm. The fact that only her best friend, Eden Barrett, and Bette Brown, the woman who'd been like a grandmother to her after the death of first her mother then her father, believed Janelle didn't matter. She was going to have the life she dreamed of, far away from people who didn't want her around — including her stepmother, Victoria — or who thought of her as that poor girl with the dead parents who always wore modified hand-me-downs she'd sewn herself. She'd show them all.

But it didn't take long after graduation to learn that the best jobs went to the people who knew the right people – or slept with the right people – and that wasn't her, on either count. Okay, it could have been her on the second count, but she'd been determined to make it on her own. For four years, she ignored every salacious suggestion of "advancement" hoping her talent would be enough to get her the job she wanted.

There had been one opportunity she'd considered. She'd attended a fancy event at the Metropolitan Museum of Art and met someone she'd been attracted to. They'd left together and went to his place where she discovered that his family owned one of the most successful labels in the industry. When he'd learned she wanted to be a designer — after they'd gone to bed — he offered her a job or at least a recommendation. It had been as tempting as he was. Especially since the offer was based on him appreciating the dress she'd worn, a design of her own, and her input on a drawing of his and not on anything sexual.

But Ash Royce wasn't just fashion royalty. He was a known player. And if she'd accepted, no one would believe she hadn't earned the job on her back. Instead, she'd snuck out while he was sleeping, and he remained a wonderful, one-night-stand who lived on in her fantasies.

But as time went on and the job she dreamed of never materialized, she made the decision to return to Fable Notch. It was only supposed to be a short-term change to regroup, save money, and make some decisions about her future. At first Janelle saw herself as a failure, something Victoria was all too happy to remind her of as she made yet another request for errands and hemming. But it wasn't long before she'd reconnected with Eden and found comfort and support from Bette. She'd even realized that the younger of her two stepsisters, Devon, had grown out of the bratty teenager she'd been and become a likeable young woman.

And then there had been the opening of her beloved store, Tailor Thrift.

Janelle had been home for barely a month before she'd run from the house where she'd grown up and straight to Bette and the spare bedroom she offered. Borrowing Bette's car, her days were spent doing temp jobs at some of the area businesses and several nights a week waiting tables at the upscale restaurant at the Castle on the Hill hotel. The money was as good as in New York and went much further. In her free time, she did what she always did – sketched dresses she would never get a chance to make and alter the occasional thrift finds she bought.

It was the day Bette asked for help clearing the attic that changed everything. Lured by the promise of being allowed to keep whatever she wanted, Janelle followed Bette up the narrow stairs and into a small piece of paradise. Like the way Beauty reacted when she saw the Beast's library, Janelle practically squealed at the sight of all the clothes Bette had hidden way. She'd seen the woman's overstuffed closets, but never imagined there was more – so much more. Bette clearly loved fashion as much as Janelle did, but was a shopper, not a designer.

They'd spent the next several hours organizing Bette's stash and when they were done, Janelle had a pile of clothes to modify and keep. There was also plenty remaining to would be donated.

"You've got a boutique's worth of clothes here," Janelle said as she continued to separate outfits into categories: casual wear, knits, cocktail dresses, blouses, pants, sweaters.

Bette looked around the room and sighed."I do. I didn't realize how much I'd bought and put away over the years. When Lawrence sees this, he's going to flip. Or laugh. I suppose he's not unaware of all I've accumulated. Maybe I should hide it in the old store. The building is completely empty at the moment, although that would only be a temporary solution, until we find a new tenant."

With her husband, Lawrence, Bette had run a hardware store on the main street of the town. It was in a good-size building which also had an apartment upstairs which the Brown's rented out for extra income. When they'd decided to retire two years before, they'd sold the inventory and a new business moved in but hadn't lasted.

In a flash, the two concepts came together. *A boutique's worth of clothes* and *completely empty at the moment*. As if someone had placed a picture into her brain, Janelle could see a store filled with a curated inventory of secondhand clothes for women and men and plenty extra for her to alter and redesign to her heart's content. She dropped to the floor, suddenly boneless. She didn't know what her expression was, but it must have been worrying because Bette rushed over and put a hand on her shoulder. "Are you okay?"

She was more than okay. She was excited for the first time in months. Months? Probably years.

"Bette, what if I didn't just want the clothes? What if I wanted the building too?"

It hadn't taken long for Janelle to get the store up and running. With help from Eden and Devon — and with Bette'sblessing — she'd repainted the space and decorated with as many mirrors and fashion prints as she could find. She drove all over New England going to thrift stores for more inventory, bought bulk lots online, found used clothing racks and even bought an L-shaped front desk from a salon that was going out of business.

By the time Tailor Thrift opened, Janelle was living above the store and bounding out of bed every morning with energy and excitement. The store was everything she'd envisioned and more. She spent her days helping customers and reaching out to estate sales for possible inventory. At night, she'd head to her apartment with its growing piles of clothes, some of which she repaired, others she restored, and a few were remade.

It took a little while for the store's reputation to grow, but once she added more altered clothes and started her YouTube channel, things took off. Bette accepted only a minimal monthly rent, which helped Janelle's early success, and last year, after Lawrence passed, she told Janelle she was planning to leave her the building when she died. Janelle was touched by the offer but said she would rather have Bette around. Still, it was good to know that the place would always be hers.

Then four months ago, things came crashing down.

Bette didn't like living alone and decided to move to the Crawford Senior Center. Janelle had seen the toll widowhood had taken on her friend and was in full support of the decision. Bette planned to use Lawrence's life insurance along with the proceeds from the sale of her house to provide the finances she needed. Unfortunately, when she went to put the home on the market, she learned her son, Gregory, had taken out a loan the year before which had used all of the existing equity in the house. Left with no other alternative, Bette needed to sell the building as soon as possible.

And that was why Janelle was sitting here waiting for Mr. Chandler, Loan Officer, to tell her whether they would grant her the loan she needed so that Bette could have the retirement she deserved.

"Ms. Novak," said a deep voice, startling Janelle out of her thoughts. "I'm Bert Chandler."

Janelle took the extended hand and shook it. "Thank you for meeting with me."

"Thank you for opening such a well-stocked thrift store," he said as he sat behind his desk. Even though he was smiling, Janelle felt as though she'd been sent to the principal's office. "You've saved me quite a bit of money since my daughter became a teenager."

Taking this as a positive sign, Janelle allowed herself to relax. "I'm so glad she likes the store. I've worked hard to create a special place. As well as a lucrative one."

He gave her a nod and held out a hand again. "Let's see your financials." She turned over the files to him and sat there trying hard not to fidget. It wasn't a big file and minutes later he said, "Is this everything?"

"Everything?" She couldn't imagine what she was missing.

"You haven't listed any appreciating assets." She must have given him a strange look. The only time she'd heard that expression it meant something very non-business like. "Items of value that increase over time. Property or stocks. Or how about art?"

As if that was an option. "My YouTube channel has been growing consistently for more than a year. Each month it earns more, and while the monthly gross at the store fluctuates, you can see that business is strong and getting stronger." Did he hear the fear in her voice?

"I do see that, and what you've built is impressive and shows a lot of potential, but that's not likely to be enough. For the bank to give you a loan of this size they need something substantial for collateral." Janelle's heart fell. She had nothing like that. She was her only asset. "Maybe there's someone with assets who can co-sign the loan, guaranteeing payment."

Janelle thought of the people who supported her. Eden would co-sign in a minute, but she'd recently opened her own business, and the bank probably wouldn't see her as a good risk. Bette was out of the question, even with her standing in the community. For a split-second Janelle considered her parents' home. But when her father died, it had been left to Victoria. There was no way she'd help, and the substantial life-insurance policy her father left her had been used for her college tuition. That gave Janelle an idea. "I don't have any debt, Mr. Chandler, and very few fixed expenses. I know I can make the payments. I will do whatever it takes." She'd survive on ramen noodles and coffee. She'd done it before.

"I respect your determination. I'm sure it has been a big part of what's made your store so successful. But without a down payment of at least...." He looked through the pages and at her total request. "...$100,000 or collateral of an equal or greater amount, I have to tell you that I think the chances of the bank approving your loan are very small."

He may as well have asked for a million dollars. If she had money like that, she'd hand it to Bette and pay for Crawford herself. But she wasn't giving up. "Does this mean you're not submitting my application?"

"Of course not, Ms. Novak. Your store is a unique part of our town. Unfortunately, that's not something the bank, as an institution, considers. I'd love to see you receive a loan, but I don't want you to get your hopes up. You may need a Plan B."

A few minutes later the meeting was over. Janelle drove to her store and walked around, looking at all she'd done, all she'd created. Everything in here made her proud and happy. She couldn't lose it. But $100,000? She couldn't think how it would be possible.

Going upstairs, she took off the suffocating outfit and changed into something comfortable. Then she fell on her bed and texted Eden. *That was probably a waste of time.*

How can I help? Exactly the response Janelle would have expected from her friend. If only she had an answer. She sent a shrugging emoji. Eden responded with, *How about company and chocolate?*

It was the best choice for the moment. *Can you come here? Don't think I should be out in public.*

Later that afternoon Eden arrived with a pan of macaroni and cheese as well as Dani Vaughn and Sheridan Behr, two of the other women Janelle had become friends with since moving back. Sheridan brought chocolate cookies from her place, the Just Right Café. Dani brought beers from the Seven Brothers Brewery and a virtual hug from Laurel Stewart who ran the place. "Laurel wishes she could come, but Thursdays are busy," Dani explained.

"I'll tell her thanks the next time I see her," Janelle said. She was grateful for the support, however it came.

For the next few hours the four women ate, drank, and searched for other financial opportunities but there weren't many options available. Janelle couldn't bear to try a Go Fund Me page. Not only would it humiliate her, but Bette as well. Eden suggested they ask her father, a real estate mogul in the area, to co-sign, but they agreed being tied to Patrick Barrett was a bad idea. Especially since he might want the building for himself.

"I'd suggest Nick as a co-signer," said Dani referencing her new fiancé, "but since he's trying to build a new business, he probably doesn't look good on paper either."

"Short of selling a body part or winning the lottery, I don't know what to do," Janelle said. For the second time that day, Ash Royce entered her head. He was a man with all the means and, from what he'd told her on their night together, none of the opportunity. She had an opportunity she loved and none of the means. It wasn't fair.

"There's always a chance they'll say yes," Eden offered, putting her arm around Janelle. She cherished her friend's optimism even if she didn't share it.

A week later she had her answer. She needed a Plan B.

He's fashion royalty. She's the queen of thrift.
Now their career hopes are pinned on one another!
Read Janelle and Ash's story
Can't Let You Go
And hear about all of Elena's new releases by joining her newsletter at
https://bit.ly/NewsFromElena

Acknowledgments

First, I need to thank family lawyer David M. Lipshutz for taking the time to talk to me about custody cases and what Mia would have had to do to keep Dean. David was patient, thoughtful, and answered all of my questions – something that not only helped me but I'm sure is one of the reasons he's so good at what he does. Our call helped me develop that plot line and gave me some important new ideas. Thank you, David! And thank you to Kerry Gans who put me in touch with David after my appeal for help on Facebook. Those who say social media friends aren't real haven't had the moments I have.

As always, I have to give a shout out to the writers who help me stay in my joy for this work – even on days when it's hard. Thank you to the Monday Mastermind group – Sara, Lisa, and Laura. Our weekly calls for sharing support and knowledge make a huge difference in my life, and I appreciate you all. The She-Nanigans, Paula, Misty, Win and Delia – almost three years together! Thank you for your support and allowing me to support you. And the Morning BFA Office writers – I am more consistent and more productive than I have ever been in large part because of you! Thank you for sharing your struggles and successes and giving me a place to share mine.

Many thanks to my editor, Kelly Helmick at DogStar Creative, who made this book stronger with her wise insight and helpful suggestions. I'm so lucky to be working with you. If my blurb made you curious about the book, then I have Jessie at Book Blurb Magic to thank. Thank you also to my proofreader Emma Thompson who not only fixed my typos but contributed her medical knowledge to make Cole's recovery more accurate.

I also need to acknowledge... that I put a covered bridge where there isn't a covered bridge in New Hampshire. Call it literary license. There *are* many covered bridges in the area, some for vehicles, some for pedestrians only, but I needed one in a specific area, so I put it there. Please don't go looking for it. The hairpin turn on the Kanc? That *is* there. Drive safely.

Love and gratitude to my husband and sons who know and accept that I can go from bouncy highs to stressy lows without warning and love me through my process, whatever it might look like. And thank you, dear reader, for completing the circle. John Cheever said, "I can't write without a reader. It's precisely like a kiss – you can't do it alone." I am grateful for your support!

About Author

Elena Markem writes emotionally rich contemporary romances about dreams, love, and taking a chance on both. Her stories reflect her belief that life is about the passions we pursue, the people who support us along the way, and never giving up on what we want.

She can't start work without coffee, fall asleep without reading, or listen to Broadway musicals without singing along (badly). She loves time spend with her husband and sons as well as weekends with girlfriends, rom-com and old movies, and anything that sparkles.

Feel free to join her on her ongoing quest for the perfect planner, the best diner breakfasts, and the gooiest chocolate chip cookie. In the meantime, she hopes you'll enjoy spending time in her sexy books where you'll find strong heroines, heroes who find them irresistible, and at least one scene involving comfort food. Stay in touch by signing up for her newsletter at www.elenamarkem.com to get sneak peaks and free stories or follow her on Facebook, Instagram and Tiktok!